Your
Drowning
Heart

AURORA STENULSON

This book is for my sisters and life-long best friends,
Sarah, Amie & Sandi.

We've been through a lot, haven't we?

CONTENTS

Chapter One   7

Chapter Two   29

Chapter Three   38

Chapter Four   54

Chapter Five   68

Chapter Six   88

Chapter Seven   101

Chapter Eight   120

Chapter Nine   130

Chapter Ten   149

Chapter Eleven   157

Chapter Twelve   179

Chapter Thirteen   184

Chapter Fourteen   198

Chapter Fifteen   213

Chapter Sixteen   225

Chapter Seventeen   232

Chapter Eighteen   242

Chapter Nineteen   248

Chapter Twenty   253

Chapter Twenty-One   264

Chapter Twenty-Two   275

Chapter Twenty-Three   286

Chapter Twenty-Four   292

Chapter Twenty-Five   309

Chapter Twenty-Six   318

Chapter Twenty-Seven   326

Chapter Twenty-Eight   330

CHAPTER

ONE

Paloma

"Get out." She throws my backpack at my chest. It's almost like she's looking through me. Like I'm not here. Or *she's* not here.

My bag fumbles in my arms before I catch it. "I don't have anywhere else to go."

This statement is obviously not resonating with her since she kicks my shoes at me. "That's not my problem, Paloma."

I quickly slip my feet into my tennis shoes, afraid if I don't, she will force me out into the rain barefoot. Before I open the front door, I give her a pleading look. "Can I at least have my phone?"

She has to give it to me.

She knows it's my lifeline.

I immediately regret my question when I see the change in her expression. My comment completely sets her off. The rage rises in her eyes before she hurls the closest thing in her reach at me. In this case, it's the TV remote.

"Get out!"

It hits the wall as I leap down the porch steps.

Thankfully the rain is letting up. I can walk to Levi's house before I'm completely soaked and before it's too late to ring the doorbell.

His parents are incredibly strict and religious. I don't think they would even answer the door if someone came by after 8:00 pm. And it's just my luck that it's getting close to that time now.

I decide to ditch the sidewalk and take the shortcut to Levi's. Which means I must run through my neighbors' backyards without being spotted. At least I have the perks of living in a small town on my side. No one has fenced yards and the ones that do won't hinder my shortcut trail.

I only set off two motion detector lights on my way to Levi's. One of which was his.

I hold my breath before ringing the doorbell. I have no idea what time it is or what to expect if his parents answer the door.

After a moment, the door swings open.

A rush of relief washes over me when I see it's Levi and not one of his parents.

He's wearing his headphones, that are only covering one ear, and holding his Xbox controller in his hand. He looks surprised when it registers that he is staring at me.

"Hey," he says this more as a question than a welcoming greeting.

I'm sure I look pitiful. My shoes are covered in mud and the rain was just heavy enough to soak my jeans and hoodie.

Levi opens the door wider for me to come in. "What are you doing here?"

"My mom kicked me out." I step past him and pull my hood off. I can only imagine what my hair looks like. But right now, I don't even care. I'm just happy to have a place to stay for the night.

"I hate when she gets like this," I say. "She must be off her meds again." Speaking of meds, I just realized I forgot mine.

Levi stops me from walking down the hall to the living room by standing in front of me. He speaks in a low voice, "You know my parents want you to call before coming over."

"Sorry, I know. But she took my phone."

Levi looks down the hall then back to me. He inhales deeply before saying, "Let me tell them you're here real quick."

I pull my shoes off. "Okay?" I'm a little annoyed he's not being more receptive to my situation.

He heads for the living room then doubles back to me. "You weren't going to want to stay, were you?"

"*Levi*," I'm either dating the world's biggest airhead or he's trying to get rid of me. "My mom kicked me out. I literally came here because I have nowhere else to go."

He nods for longer than he needs to, like he's trying to convince himself it's a good idea for me to stay. "I'll be right back." He pulls his headset down around his neck and disappears into the living room.

Since Levi's parents are religious, I'm sure they will see me as a charity case. I can see them opening their home to me just so they can brag to the church about rescuing me.

As I'm waiting for Levi, I notice that the huge cross hanging above their front door has tiny words carved into the wood. It says things like, *love, mercy, grace,* and *hope.*

"They said you can't stay."

I flip my head around to see Levi biting at his lip in anticipation.

My heart drops to the bottom of my stomach. How do they have decorations in their house encouraging love and mercy, but refuse to show love and mercy to me?

I don't even know what to say. I'm shocked. It's not like they haven't fostered before. Am I any worse than the foster kids they've brought into their home?

Levi clicks the triggers on his controller. Waiting for an answer. "Paloma?" He's saying my name in a way that makes me feel like he's trying to hurry me and get me to leave. He's my boyfriend, he should feel some sort of sympathy for my situation.

I push my hands through my hair. Panic is spreading through my veins. When I meet his gaze, I realize he's not even affected by how freaked out I am. At this point I'm desperate.

"What if I stay just for one night?"

"They aren't going to go for it," even his voice is lacking empathy, "Can't you stay with Candice?"

"She lives across town."

He moves around me and opens the door. "I'm sorry, it's not my problem."

That's the second time I've heard that in less than an hour. Am I that much trouble that I can't even stay for an hour? Or get a ride? Or use his phone? Actually, now that I think about it, I don't want to use his phone or get a ride from him.

I can hear my heart beating in my throat. I can't tell if I'm more hurt or angry that he doesn't care the slightest bit for me.

"You know what, Levi," I shove my muddy shoes back

on my feet before running my shoulder into him as I make my way out the door. "You're right. I'm not your problem. And I'm never going to be your problem again. Because we're done." I purposely stomp in a puddle that I intended to splatter mud onto his car, but it mostly splatters mud up my pants.

"Paloma, wait," Levi says, but it must have been more of a reaction that he calls for me than him *actually* wanting me to come back since he closes the door when I keep walking.

A part of me wonders what he would have done if I had stopped and turned around. I'm sure I would have been even more disappointed by his reaction than I am now if I stuck around to see.

Candice lives about three miles away. It's getting late and it's a school night so hopefully her grandma doesn't freak out when I show up at their doorstep. She is old, so she might not even hear me knock on the door.

I wish my mom had just given me my phone. This is one of the worst episodes she's had. It's embarrassing having a mom with bipolar disorder. When she takes her meds, she's fine. I would even go to the extent to say I enjoy her company. But when she's off them she doesn't eat or sleep. She's so unstable and finds the most minute things irritating. I can't even bring friends over because I never know what sort of mood she's going to be in when she gets home. Not that I have friends that I would invite over besides Candice.

I walk across the bridge that connects one side of town to the other. I feel exposed when I'm under the streetlights. What if my mom changes her mind and decides she wants me to come back? I'm not sure I want to go back. At least not tonight. She needs to cool off. And after the incident with Levi, so do I.

It's times like these I wish I could call my dad. He left when I was little. I don't blame him. I wouldn't want to stay with my mom either. I don't know if he's tried having contact with me since every time I bring him up my mom says, "He can have a relationship with you when I see some child support."

I like to imagine he's handsome and rich. Living in the corporate world of New York in an expensive apartment with a view of the city. I also imagine a giant box hidden in my mom's closet that's full of letters written to me from my dad. Like you see happen in the movies.

How convenient would it be if I could call my imaginary New York father right now and ask him to come and get me so I could live with him instead of my mom.

But that's not reality.

Maybe I don't want to know what reality is. For all I know, he's in prison somewhere. If that's the case, I would rather not know him and cling to the image of the imaginary father I made up in my mind.

The rain finally stops before I get to Candice's house. I notice her light on in her room. I decide to skip the front door and tap on her window until she sees me. Plus, I don't want to alert her grandma.

Candice is in her bed scrolling on her phone when she notices me at her window. She jerks as if I've startled her then she points at her bedroom door and exits the room. I walk back to the other side of her house where she is waiting for me at the front door.

She waves me inside. "What happened?" She says this as if she was expecting me. Unphased by my unannounced visit. I shouldn't be surprised she knows something is up. Why else would I be at her house this late?

When it's been raining.

On a school night.

I adjust my backpack. "My mom kicked me out."

"Surprise, surprise." Her tone is still unphased.

I follow her to her room. Her grandma must be in bed already. The house is quiet and still. "It felt real this time. Honestly, she scared me."

Candice pulls out a pair of pajamas and tosses them to me. "Yeah, how?"

I set my bag on the floor. "She threw a TV remote at me and kept my phone." I slip out of my jeans and pull on her pajama bottoms. "I barely had time to put my shoes on before she hurled it at me."

Candice shifts her weight onto one hip while she allows me to vent in her bedroom and change into her pajamas.

It almost feels like I'm not just changing out of my wet clothes into dry clothes, but it feels like my life is changing in a drastic way too. As if I'm stepping into a new world where I'm completely in charge of myself.

"At least she had the sense to throw my backpack with my homework at me before she kicked me out." I let a puff of laughter escape my throat, but quickly realize what's happened to me isn't really that funny.

Candice plops back down on her bed. "I'm sorry, Paloma, but your mom is psychotic. You should just leave."

"And go where?"

"You could stay here."

I lay on the bed beside her. "I don't want to be a mooch."

"You wouldn't be."

"I don't have a job. I don't have a car. I don't even have a phone right now. And I doubt anyone in this town wants to hire me with my reputation."

She tugs on my hair. "Give yourself some credit. And don't think like that. I would hire you, you're a good person. You just have a messed-up mom."

I can't help but think of myself as a burden in this town. I have nothing going for me. I'm a junior at a high school where I've known the same people my entire life. Which means everyone's parents know who my mom is and know she's crazy. Who wants anything to do with the town's crazy lady or her daughter? The only people that like my mom are the ones she's managed to manipulate into believing what she says is true. And she *always* twists the truth.

The only reason Candice and her grandma welcome me is because Candice is a little rough around the edges and most people are afraid of her. And her grandma is a recluse, so she never hears any of the gossip around town. There's no judgment in this house and I haven't set foot in a safer home in my entire life.

"I stopped by Levi's before I came here," I say, pulling my hair up on top of my head.

Candice raises one eyebrow. It makes me a little sad she's so confident in her smug expression. She doesn't have to say anything. We both know how selfish and spoiled Levi is. It just took me a while to realize I was more in love with the idea of a boyfriend than I was with Levi.

I flick at a piece of lint on her pillow, then inhale deeply before admitting what a piece of garbage Levi has been this entire time. I also don't want to admit that she was right about him.

But I do anyway.

"He basically acted ashamed of me and then told me to leave before I could even dry off."

She sits up. "I told you!"

"You don't have to say anything."

Why did I bother telling her the truth?

She laughs at herself. "I hate when I'm right about guys.

They're all selfish. That's why I don't even bother with them. Especially in this town."

I hate when she's right too. And I hate when I don't listen to her. I could have saved myself a lot of trouble with Levi if I had followed Candice's uncanny intuition about him.

She turns her light off and flings the covers over us. "We'll figure it out tomorrow. Let's get some sleep."

I'm not sure I'm going to be able to sleep. But I'm glad I have a place to stay.

For now.

...

"Your mom called." Candice finishes putting her mascara on her eyelashes before opening the voicemail and handing me her phone.

I catch a glimpse of my reflection in the bathroom mirror while Candice brushes her hair. I look exhausted, to say the least. I'm not sure I'm ready to hear my mom's voice right now, especially when I'm lacking all confidence in myself.

I play the voicemail on speaker. Maybe having Candice hear it with me will help dull the sting of whatever my mom says.

"Candice, it's April. I'm calling to see if you have heard from Paloma. She ran off last night and didn't come home." That's a lie. *"I'm getting worried. She was so agitated that she took off without her phone."* Another lie. *"If you see her, please have her call me."*

I place the phone on the bathroom counter. "Are you kidding me?" I lean on the wall and hit the back of my head against it.

"She's a psycho." Candice puts her phone in her back pocket and leans her shoulder into the wall so she's facing me. "She is convincing though."

I roll my head to face her. "Don't say that. You know she's lying."

"I know she's lying," she leaves the bathroom, "but I'm not so sure the school will think that."

I hadn't even considered that my mom would call the school.

She traps me when she does this sort of thing. She gives me no choices—like forcing me to leave the house. Then before I can tell anyone my side of the story, she's already convinced the entire town that I'm the bad guy.

Candice returns with a pair of black skinny jeans and a white fitted t-shirt. Her style is different than mine, but thankfully we're about the same size. I take them.

Before I turn the shower on, I poke my head out of the bathroom door and peer into her bedroom where she's gathering her things for school. "You don't think she called the school for real, do you?"

She lets out a laugh that sounds more like a scoff. "I'm certain she's already called the school." She walks past me, "I wouldn't be surprised if she's waiting at the school for you when we get there. Just to pretend like she cares."

"I hope not." I shut the bathroom door and head for the shower.

My throat feels tight and dry. Why can't I have a normal mom and a normal life? Why is everything a confusing game with her?

I quickly rinse off, I don't mind that the shower didn't have time to warm up. The cold water reminds me that I'm still alive and that this nightmare I'm living is real.

And since it is real, I'm going to take control of it. I have to make a decision. And I've decided, I'm not going back. This is the last time my mom does this to me.

I just need to figure out how to make sure of it.

After my shower, I run my hands through the tangles in

my hair, but I don't bother with makeup.

When I meet Candice in the kitchen, she's finishing a cup of coffee. "Want some?" I shake my head. She knows I don't drink coffee. I'm not sure sixteen-year-olds do, besides her. She digs through her cupboard. "How about cereal?"

"Honestly, I'm not hungry right now."

"Okay, no breakfast then," she closes the cabinet. "Would you rather be super early or super late to school?"

I tilt my head. "What about...*on time?*"

Her posture slumps like she's dissatisfied with my confused response. "I'm trying to help you avoid your mom."

Before I respond, the TV turns on in the master bedroom and her grandma begins to cough.

I look down the hall then back to Candice. "Probably super early then."

"Alright," she says. "We better go soon." Candice takes a bottle of her grandma's prescription pills and dumps them in her hand before passing me into the hall. "I'll meet you in the car. The key is on the hook."

I gather my damp clothes into my backpack and opt for holding my homework in my arms, so it doesn't get wet. I'm starting to wish I would have at least tossed my clothes into the dryer before I went to bed last night. But in my defense, I was emotionally drained by the time I got here.

I take the key and head outside with my shoes in one hand. The mud has mostly dried, so I whack them on the driveway cement a few times before slipping my feet into them.

There's still a sogginess inside my shoes. I feel bad for whoever gets close to me today since they probably smell gross too. I wasn't wearing socks last night and now Candice's car is going to reek of feet.

A moment later, Candice joins me. The radio turns on as she starts the car.

"Ready?" She avoids talking about what kept her with her grandma. From the handful of pills and the distant cough I heard down the hall, I'm assuming her grandma is sicker than Candice lets on about. Which means, Candice is in charge of taking care of her grandma and herself.

"I guess so." Thankfully she doesn't say anything about the odor my shoes and wet clothes are creating in her car.

She quickly pulls onto the road.

My palms clam up and my knee begins to bounce in anticipation. It takes about two minutes to get to school from her house, and I'm not excited about any potential encounter I might have with my mom when we get there.

I want to ask about Candice's grandma, but she gets weird when we get personal about her life. She's great when I need feedback or want to vent. Everything is so straightforward and honest. She's quick to tell me if I'm being stupid—*like with dating Levi*—and she doesn't judge me when I don't listen to her and keep acting stupid—*like with dating Levi.*

But when it comes to her, she's more closed off. It's just how she is. And I'm sure it's not easy taking care of her grandma and trying to finish high school at the same time. I would be worried about my future if I was her. After we graduate, I wouldn't be surprised if she stays in this abhorrent town fueled by gossip and rumors just to continue caring for her grandma.

Even though we are best friends, there's a lot I don't know about Candice.

When we pull up to the school, there's no sign of my mom. Hopefully showing up early pays off and I can get through this day.

"I'm going to walk around to the other side," I say,

unbuckling the seatbelt. "That way if you see her on your way in, you can let me know in class."

"Sounds good" She shuts her car off, then heads for the main entrance. "See you in World Lit. with an update."

I hurry to the lower doors on the other side of the building. I've never been more eager to get inside this school.

I feel a rush of adrenaline.

Not even running from the cops would get my heart racing this fast. Not that I've run from the cops before. I just imagine if I were to ever be in trouble and feel the need to run from the cops, I wouldn't be in this much of a panic.

Before I reach the doors, I run into something and stumble backwards. Or rather, *someone.*

"I'm sorry—" I begin to say, but when I realize who I've run into I stop talking.

"Walk much?"

It's Levi.

This day just started, and I can't wait for it to end.

"Can we not do this?" I adjust my notebook in my arms. The run-in must have jostled me into reality since I suddenly feel the clothes in my backpack dampen my back through my t-shirt—*Candice's* t-shirt.

He opens the door, barely keeping it open long enough for me to get through.

"Your mom called." *She didn't waste any time making her rounds, did she?* His voice is snarky, and I hate to admit how right Candice was about him.

He looks at me with the most disgusted expression I've ever seen on his face. He must think I'm even more pathetic than last night.

I don't bother asking what she said. I can tell he's about to tell me because he puts his arm out in front of me and almost pins me between the wall and his body.

"She told my parents that *you* ran away. And that you were out of control before you left."

I push his arm out of my way and walk to my locker. "She's a liar."

He ignores me, turning the other way. Then he yells down the empty hall at me. "Paloma Smith is crazy *and* a runaway!"

I clench my fist at my side. For a split second I imagine punching his stupid face. I know I would never punch anyone, but the fact that I'm entertaining such a thought makes me worry a little about myself. I don't want to end up like my mom.

I relax my hand and exhale out a puff of air through my nose trying to steady my pulse. Thankfully it's still early enough that most people haven't arrived at school yet, so no one heard Levi's stupid voice or his stupid comment.

"Paloma?"

My stomach jumps into my throat and my face goes hot. If someone heard Levi, that rumor is bound to spread through the entire school before lunch time. And what's worse is that it will spread throughout the entire town before school is over. Leaving me no chance to get the truth out. Or tell anyone that my mom was the one who forced me to leave.

"I hate this place."

"What was that?"

As I turn to face the voice, I release a breath I didn't realize I was holding in. "Sorry, Mr. Grandstill. I thought you were someone else."

Mr. Grandstill adjusts his glasses and then folds his arms over his chest. Really, his arms are resting at the top of his belly. "Your mom called."

I know I should be used to hearing that by now. I mean this is the third time in less than twenty minutes someone has told me that she called them. But it still sends a surge of anxiety through my spine.

"Let me guess. She said I was angry and ran away last night."

He makes a sound like he's sucking air through his teeth before he says, "What's your least favorite class?"

He completely ignores my comment. Which makes me think what I said wasn't far from what my mom told him.

But, what does my least favorite class have to do with my mom calling? Maybe she wants to come to the school and *rescue* me.

I can't wait to graduate and get out of this place.

"Second period, Team Sports," I say.

He nods then turns to walk up the stairs. "Come to my office second period. I'll let your teacher know you won't be in class today." His footsteps disappear with him.

I'm so confused.

When I get to my locker, the bell finally rings indicating school is starting. Normally in this situation I would feel some sort of relief knowing my classes are going to preoccupy me. But the whole thing with Mr. Grandstill has me feeling uneasy.

I sit next to Candice in class. We are the only ones in the back row. The genius kids are in the front and all the jocks and popular girls fill out the middle rows. I should probably thank them for leaving the back to us since our teacher doesn't pay attention to what we're doing—or saying.

"No sign of your mom on my way in," she says.

"I didn't see her either." I unzip my bag, but the wet clothes are starting to smell so I zip it closed again and slide it behind my chair with my foot so no one has to endure the odor. "Guess who I did see?"

Candice raises her eyebrow as an indication for me to

continue.

I decide to skip telling her what happened with Levi. She might say something to him in my defense, which would make everything worse. I would rather be under the radar than in the spotlight right now.

Is it too much to ask to finish high school unnoticed?

"Mr. Grandstill," I say.

"So?" She pulls out a pack of gum and hands me a piece before tossing one into her mouth.

"He told me that my mom called him." I bite half the stick of gum and fold the other piece in the wrapper then tuck it into my front pocket for later. "And he wants me to skip second period and go to his office."

Her expression doesn't change. "Well don't worry. He's been around since before Wi-Fi and knows your mom is a psycho. You're not going to get in trouble if that's what you're worried about."

"How do you know?" I say.

"I just do."

"What if he has some sort of guidance counselor obligation to call the police and report me as a runaway? Or send me to foster care? Or—"

"Stop."

I look down at my shoes. Despite knocking the mud off this morning, they are still pitifully dirty.

"I just hate not knowing what's going on," I say.

Candice shifts in her seat so she's facing me. It startles me a little because she was kind of aggressive with her movement.

"Listen," the bell rings again for the start of class. She looks around the room briefly then speaks under her breath, "Mr. Grandstill is cool. He's not like other teachers. Believe it or not, he's *actually* on your side. So, stop freaking out, okay?"

I nod. I'm sure my eyes are wide and my expression is covered in shock because Candice basically admitted she knows Mr. Grandstill. She didn't say it out right, but I know Candice enough to understand that the words she used to describe Mr. Grandstill alludes to her having some sort of personal connection with him.

But Candice doesn't have personal connections with anyone. Not with other students. Not with teachers. Not really with her grandma. Not even with me, and I'm her best friend.

I decide not to ask Candice to elaborate on the whole Mr. Grandstill thing. Not that she would if I did ask.

Instead, I pretend to focus on *The Scarlett Letter*. Which is already difficult to focus on without the added distractions from my personal life. My thoughts are bouncing around in my head at a pace I can't keep up with.

After class, Candice reassures me once more I can trust Mr. Grandstill before she disappears to her next class. It's weird she's pushing this so much. She doesn't care about anything this passionately.

When I get to Mr. Grandstill's office, he's helping someone switch their classes. So, I sit in one of the comfy chairs outside of his office and pick up a magazine for an art school in Georgia.

I kind of like photography class. Maybe I could create a portfolio and apply next year. Georgia sounds nice. Honestly, anywhere sounds better than here.

"How's it going, Paloma?" Mr. Grandstill approaches me. He sits in the chair next to me, his hands clasped between his knees.

My eyes shift from him back to the magazine as my palms instantly clam up. "It's going." I try to play it off like nothing is bothering me.

"Everything okay at school?"

I flip the page. "Yep."

"Things seemed a little tense between you and Levi this morning."

I blow a strand of hair out of my face. "I thought everything was fine."

He clears his throat. "And your mom?"

"She's *great*." My voice is way too happy for anyone to believe that statement. Especially after what I said to him about her this morning.

I half expect Mr. Grandstill to shift in his seat and demand me to tell him what's going on. But he doesn't. Instead, he picks up a magazine and begins to flip through the pages.

I wait several minutes until I feel so uncomfortable with the silence that I can feel my skin itching on my neck. I snap the magazine shut, trying to get a rise out of Mr. Grandstill, but he casually skims the pages over in his hand.

I stand as a last attempt to get him to talk.

He only looks up at me from the top of his magazine just enough to reveal his eyes over his glasses, and says, "Is there something you wanted to say, Miss Smith?"

I lean on one hip and fold my arms.

What kind of weird game is he playing? My mom plays games, but I can always tell what she wants me to say for the game to stop. The game Mr. Grandstill is playing is completely foreign to me.

Since he doesn't seem like much of a threat, I feel brave enough to say, "You're the one that called me to your office and then didn't have anything to say to me."

He nods. "Ah, that," he closes the magazine and tosses it on the table. "You see, I've already excused you from your entire class so there's no point in sending you back now. I thought you might want to talk about the phone conversation I had with your mom, or maybe about what happened with Levi this morning, or maybe why your shoes are covered in dirt and you smell so bad."

My mouth drops open.

What kind of high school employee has the audacity to speak to a student like that?

He continues in the same irritatingly comfortable manner. "But since things are *good* at school, and everything is *fine* with Levi, and your mom is *great*, I guess there's not much else for us to talk about. Is there?"

I feel sort of bad for not being more transparent with him—even though he is mocking me. Especially because he got me out of class for the entire second hour. Which is *team sports*. Which is like PE on steroids. I already survived freshman PE why do I need another gym class?

I sit back down and kick my bag away from us so neither of us has to endure its stench. "It's just my clothes from last night."

He sinks back into his chair and rests his chin in his palm. "What is?"

I keep my gaze on my bag. It's easier to say difficult things when I'm not looking directly into someone else's judging eyes. "The smell. My clothes got wet last night when I walked to Candice's house in the rain."

He nods. "You might try washing them instead of carrying them around in your backpack. That's what the rest of us do."

I let out a laugh. "You're not like regular teachers, are you?"

"I'm not a teacher at all."

I finally face him. "I lied about my mom."

He clasps his hands on his belly. With an unphased expression he says, "I know."

He seems so casual, and I'm completely perplexed by how this meeting is unfolding.

"Do you want to talk about it? I might be able to help," he says.

I fold my lips in. What if I tell him she's a psycho like Candice says? What if Candice is wrong about him and he sends me to foster care? What if no one believes me and takes my mom's side and I get in trouble for the things she's accused me of doing?

My stomach feels suddenly empty. I think it's been twenty-four hours since I've eaten. "Do you have any snacks?"

Mr. Grandstill rocks out of his chair and retrieves something from his office. He doesn't even seem to mind my communication skills are all over the place. He tosses a Nutri-grain bar into my lap on his way back to his seat.

He's holding one too and tears it open to take a bite. "You missed breakfast?"

I nearly devour the entire bar in one bite. "More like today's breakfast and yesterday's lunch and dinner."

His office phone rings. "Hold on," he rocks out of his chair again and heads for his office. I watch him in case it's my mom again.

He glances at me, then back down at his phone then speaks in a low voice when he answers. "Hello. Yes, she's here now," he shuffles some papers on his desk, "I really don't think that's necessary." Whoever is on the other line cuts him off, then he says, "She's fine."

I feel frozen to my chair. I can feel my veins pulsing through my body.

"If you just give me a second to—" He pulls the phone from his ear and looks at it for a moment before placing it on the receiver. They must have hung up on him.

This time when he comes out of his office, he takes one knee in front of me which makes me uneasy. His expression doesn't make me feel any better when he says,

"Okay, Paloma, I need to be straight with you."

All I can focus on is the small bit of spit gathering in the corner of his mouth. It doesn't seem like the right time to be worrying about that, but it keeps my mind from being plagued with whatever he's about to tell me.

"Normally, I wouldn't disclose information like this with a student." He looks behind himself before continuing. "Your mom has been calling the school all morning. I know she's lying, but I can't tell you how I know."

I hug my arms around myself. "It's okay, I have a feeling Candice told you." My voice is shaky when I speak, which floods me with more anxiety since I realize I can't even hide how scared I am right now.

"I can't say where I got the information. But I want you to know that I'm here to help you. I also want to make sure you understand how urgent your situation is."

My heart bounds up into my throat so hard I feel like I might cry. I swallow it down, so he doesn't think I'm bothered by any of this.

Mr. Grandstill stands up and reaches his hand out. "Let me see your phone and I'll give you a number I want you to call."

"She took my phone."

He drops his head back and places his hands on his hips. "She took your phone," he repeats. "That's alright. We can still make this work. It's just going to be a little trickier." He goes back into his office and pulls his phone to his ear. He's already punching numbers when he says, "Who's your best friend?"

"Candice." But I get a sense that he already knew that.

He tells the person on the other line to send Candice to his office then he hangs up.

He's scribbling something on a piece of paper before

approaching me again. "Keep this information safe," he says, folding the paper and handing it to me.

I can't take it anymore. The last ten minutes have been the longest and most anxiety ridden ten minutes of my life. "What's going on? Whose number is this? Why are you freaking out? It's freaking me out!"

"It's going to be fine. But you must listen to me if you want things to change." He faces me and without hesitation says, "You need to leave town and emancipate yourself, immediately."

CHAPTER

TWO

Jaxon

"Is it recording?" I pick up the sign and back up next to the wall before pulling my blindfold on.

"Yeah, but you're out of frame." Birdie guides me by holding my shoulders. "There. Now, don't move."

I kind of want to take the blindfold off to see the reactions of the people walking through the mall when they pass by.

I shift slightly to get more comfortable since I'm going to be standing here for a while.

"Jax!" Birdie's voice is slightly frazzled and irritated.

"What?" I'm starting to wish I hadn't worn a hoodie because I'm already starting to sweat.

Birdie's hands are on my shoulders again and he's adjusting my position. "I told you not to move." He fixes my microphone then I hear him shuffle quickly back to the camera.

He's a little intense when it comes to filming. I should be thankful he's a perfectionist. Without his creative eye behind the camera, I don't think our YouTube channel would be doing as well as it is. I can't take any credit for it. It's all been Birdie's ideas. I just show up and stand in position.

The latest production is a copy-cat idea from a Sick Puppies music video he found from 2007. And he's put his own creative-Birdie-twist to it.

I'm not sure how else to put it.

You see, Birdie is rich. And I don't mean rich in the terms of nice cars and a nice house. He does have those things, but it's more. It's an understatement to say his parents are loaded.

He's rich in the sense of, they don't wear the same underwear more than once, rich. Having one room of their house dedicated to racing kid-size electric Hummers, rich. Owning a massive movie theater in their mansion house with a hundred recliner seats, rich.

So, because of Birdie's loaded parents, he's able to do cool stuff. Like create YouTube videos where I'm doing embarrassing things like wearing a blindfold while holding a FREE HUGS sign and handing out cash to make people feel better. It's fun and all the money we make from the YouTube channel we give back to random charities.

Birdie is adjusting my position again. "I swear, Jax, if you can't stand still, I'm going to pinch you."

"I'm not even moving." I lift my blindfold up above one eye so I can look at him. "Seriously, pinching? Punch me if you want my attention."

"I would. But I don't want to ruin my manicure." He pinches my arm playfully. "Now, stay put!"

I pull my blindfold back down. This is the third time we've done this. And the third mall we've posted up at.

Suddenly, I'm nearly toppled over. Huge arms wrap around me. It must be a football player. This guy has got to be a giant since I'm 6'1 and he's lifting me so high up my feet are dangling under me.

"Hey, buddy," I manage to say through my compressed lungs.

He sniffles. *They always sniffle.*

I pat his back with one arm. "What's going on, man?"

He sets me down but continues to hug me. "It's just the pressure." His voice is deep and melodic. "I'm just dealing with a lot of pressure right now."

A part of me wants to peek and see if it's a Cowboy's football player. He feels and sounds like he could be one. But I've been sworn to secrecy. If Birdie doesn't get permission to post the video of them before the huggers go, he blurs out their faces in the videos.

He finally releases me. I hear him trying to gain his composure through deep breaths.

I pull out a wad of cash and hold out a couple hundred-dollar bills in his direction.

"It'll get better," maybe he doesn't see the money, "I want you to have this. It might help with whatever's going on."

He gently pushes my hand. "I don't want that. I just needed a hug."

"I get that." I extend the money again. "But if you don't want it, maybe you know someone who might need it? Maybe you could give it to a stranger that looks like they could use it?"

He pushes the money back again. "I like that," he pauses and sniffs briefly, "But I have enough money." Another sniffle. "You know what, you've inspired me. I'm going to use my own money to give to the next person I see that needs it."

Yep, definitely a football player.

"That's awesome. Pay it forward, man," I say waving blindly and hoping it's in his direction.

"Keep doing what you're doing. And thanks for the hug." His heavy footsteps quiet into the depth of the mall as he walks away.

Almost immediately after he's gone, a younger guy approaches me for a hug.

Then an older gentleman.

Then a few giggly kids.

Hours tick by and it seems as if I haven't gotten a second to sit down or hydrate. It's surprising how many guys have stopped for a hug today. The last two times we've done this, I would say the majority of the huggers are girls. Maybe it's the part of town we're in? Maybe guys are dealing with a lot more stress this week than the last couple of weeks? I don't know what it is, but the emotional side of guys is almost more draining than the girls.

"Excuse me?" A soft voice says near me.

I straighten my posture. "Hey, how's it going?" If I lift my head slightly, I can see a pair of dirty tennis shoes attached to whoever is standing in front of me.

Okay, this is the last hug and wad of cash I'm giving before I stop for a break. I don't care what Birdie has to say about it.

"Is this real?" She's speaking so quiet I can barely hear her.

I open my arms. "Yeah, it's re—"

Before I finish my response, she's flung herself into my arms. She feels so tense.

That's the thing about hugging so many people with a blindfold on. It's like taking away the sense of sight makes all my other senses heightened. I can almost feel a person's character. More than their character, I can feel their personality and emotions. It's the weirdest thing. And I can feel that this girl is carrying the world on her shoulders.

"It's going to be okay." I hug her back as if it's the last hug I'll ever give.

She feels like she needs it. As if she hasn't experienced a hug once in her entire life. She's so much smaller than me that my arms feel long enough to wrap around her twice.

"I know it feels like it's the end of the world," I say. "But it's not. There's an *other side* to whatever you're going through."

She gets stiff in my arms, but she doesn't let go of me.

I'm not sure what to do. I've never hugged someone that felt so broken. This feels out of my scope of practice.

Normally, the huggers tell me what's going on, then I tell them it will be okay and it will get better, hand them some cash, and they leave, happily.

I'm honestly considering offering this girl a ride to therapy or something.

I wait until I feel like she's never going to relax. Or let go. Or cry. Maybe if she cried, she would feel better? I don't want to make her cry, but I don't know what else to do.

I follow my weird-heightened-senses-intuition about her and say, "I know it seems like it's just been one thing after another, but if you let it out, you'll feel better."

She lets out a quiet whimper and holds me tighter.

I hold her head against my chest. I inhale slowly, hoping it will coax her to do the same. "It's better to let it out. I promise."

She chokes on a sob. "M-my…" another choking sob, "My mom kicked me out." She squeezes me tighter. "I broke up with my stupid boyfriend." She's bunching the back of my sweatshirt into her fists as she squeezes me even tighter. "And ever since I moved to Dallas, I can't seem to find a job anywhere."

I don't think she meant to, but she pushes me over as she tries one last attempt to hug me as tight as she can. Not that she could hug me any more intensely. But the surprise of the push sends me stumbling backward.

I try to catch myself on the wall but it's farther away than I anticipated so I fall to the ground. *I should have stayed in position where Birdie set me.* She falls against me. Somewhere in the mix of it all, my blindfold falls, covering my mouth.

Birdie is kneeling next to us before I can figure out what to do next. "Oh my goodness, are you okay?" he says.

My eyes are locked on the girl. I'm a little shook from the fall, but even more shook by how pretty she is. Even with her swollen eyes and red nose from crying.

I pull my blindfold down around my neck. "I'm good," I say to Birdie, then to her I say, "Are you okay?"

She looks at me blankly.

Birdie takes her arm, lifting her to her feet. "That was so dope. I got the entire thing on camera."

She jerks her arm from his hand. "You were recording that?"

I finally pull myself to my feet. "It's not what you think." I reach for the money in my pocket and extend the rest of the cash to her. "You didn't even make it to the best part."

"What is this?" Her eyes flash between the money, me, and Birdie. "Is this some sort of joke? Is that even real money?"

What's happened to this girl that's made her so untrustworthy? I take her hand and slap the money into it. "It's as real as that hug was."

34

Her mouth falls open, but nothing comes out.

Birdie rests his hand on her shoulder. "You sure you're okay?"

She continues to stand in disbelief.

"Come on," I say motioning Birdie to follow me. "I broke her fall. She's fine."

Birdie follows me and begins packing up the camera.

When I know she can't hear us I say, "Cut that part out, alright?"

Birdie shoots me a look. "Are you delusional? What happened back there was…." he flips his hands around as he gathers his words, "…you can't even script that!"

"Cut it."

"I'm not cutting it."

I fold my arms over my chest and harden my voice, "Cut it, Birdie."

"You're insane if you think I'm cutting it."

"If you don't cut it, I'm not doing this anymore."

He scoffs. "You're the worst. No one is going to care if you trip and fall." He tilts his head in thought. "Actually, people would love it. Imagine the views that would get."

I pull my mic out of my shirt and hand it to him. "It's not about the fall." I look back at the girl. She's counting the money in her hand, but she hasn't moved from where we left her. "What she's going through is different. It's like she's been living her entire life with a broken heart."

"You would know all about that, wouldn't you?"

I push his arm playfully, "Shut up."

Birdie smiles, but it quickly fades. "Oh no."

I pull my blindfold from my neck and stuff it into my pocket, then adjust the sign under my arm. "What?" I say, without looking at him.

He takes my hand in his and pats it with his other hand. "Oh, you poor thing. You're into that girl, aren't you?"

"Whatever." I pull my hand from his grip. "Let's go."

Birdie stays in stride next to me as we make our way to the exit. "What happened to your commitment? Hmm? What happened to, *I'm single until I die*. And, *There's no time for girls*."

"I don't sound like that."

He raises his brow.

It doesn't matter anyway. She's just another *hugger* on this YouTube journey we're on. I'm ready to bail on this *free hugs* idea and get back to doing something less intense.

I hate that a free hug and handful of money couldn't fix her. It's always fixed everyone else's problems. At least momentarily. I did this because it seemed to help people and make them feel better. But that girl made me feel lost.

"I just wish I could have helped her more," I say a little more defeated than I intended to.

Birdie tugs on my arm until I come to a stop. "Jax, in all seriousness, I don't think you will be able to live with yourself if you don't at least get her name."

I fold my lips together. I don't like getting attached to many people. Not because I'm worried that they are going to hurt me, or that they won't live up to my expectations, or anything like that.

I don't like getting too close because I'm afraid that *I* will hurt them. And I'm already close to all the people I need in my life.

I look past Birdie. The girl is walking away in the other direction.

I feel a tugging at my core, as if my conscience is telling me to run after her.

But I don't.

I watch her turn to the food court and disappear around a corner.

I didn't think that letting her go would make me feel

worse, but it does. Instead of peace, I'm left with a nagging conviction in my soul.

CHAPTER

THREE

Paloma

"You're still in bed?" Roma is leaning on my doorframe when I look up at her. "I thought you were job hunting today?"

My head feels like it was filled with rocks while I was sleeping. My hair is stuck to the sides of my face, probably from the tears I cried last night.

Roma makes a noise. Indicating she wants me to respond to her question, which I thought was rhetorical.

I exhale, as my mind prepares my mouth to open. "I can't do it anymore."

Roma's eyebrows draw together as her forehead creases. "No one said emancipation was going to be an easy task." Her Spanish accent is apparent when she says this. And so is her irritation with me. "I gave you a month to figure your crap out. You've almost reached your limit."

I had a feeling this might happen. That I would become a burden to her.

When Mr. Grandstill was set on emancipation as my only option to free myself from my mom, Candice asked her Aunt Roma if I could rent her spare bedroom. All I had to do was find a job.

Pretty easy, right?

Wrong.

Completely, wrong. Who would have thought it would be an impossible feat to get a job in Dallas?

I've been to every possible business within a three-mile radius. Even a hole-in-the-wall canine boarding facility wouldn't hire me. I don't even like dogs. They must be able to sense how pathetic I am and refused to give me an application. Or any chance at this impossible task of emancipation.

And now I've become the burden I feared I would be. My own self-fulfilling prophesy.

"I can't do it today." I roll back into bed, covering my head with my blanket.

"If you don't get up right now, you're done."

I don't understand why she cares today. She hasn't said but two words to me since I moved into her apartment. Granted she's usually at work at the hospital all night and sleeping during the day when I've been searching for some sort of employment.

I lift my head up to look at her.

I'm not sure how to take her expression. She looks more disappointed than angry. Not what I was expecting.

"Roma, please. You know I don't have any other option. I need to prove I'm an adult before I can file for emancipation." I adjust myself to face her better, I can feel my heart starting to race. "And I can't do that without you."

She narrows her eyes at me then drops them to the floor. She looks as if she's having a war within herself, her eyebrows keep shifting between worry and frustration.

The knot emerges in my throat. The one that keeps showing up when I'm alone. The one that tells me that this is hopeless—*pointless*. The one that makes me want to abandon this entire situation.

Why am I even pushing so hard? It's not like my mom ever really did anything to hurt me. Sure, she's held my arm a little too tight at times. And pushed me a little too hard when she's having an episode. But she's never physically hurt me to the point of what I would call abuse.

I could go back.

Maybe it would be better this time. Maybe if I go back she will realize how much she really cares about me and that we only have a year and half left together before I graduate; if the school will let me come back after weeks of being absent. Maybe she will make the most of the next eighteen months we have together.

"I'm sorry for being a burden and wasting your time," I say, covering my head with the comforter as I lay back down again.

All I hear is Roma approach my bed and say, "What are you saying? That you're done trying?" Her voice is still hard.

The tears are filling my eyes now. I'm afraid to go forward with this. I'm afraid to leave my mom. But I'm also afraid to go back to her. She might have changed, but she's probably the same. The worst part of this is that it almost feels better to be around my mom's insanity. At least it's normal and I know what to expect. Which is better than this whole fast-track to adulthood thing I'm failing at.

I sort of choke on my crying, trying not to let it out for Roma to hear.

"Paloma, answer me."

A chill goes up my back when I hear the hardened tone of her voice.

What if Roma is bipolar like my mom? Since I don't know the extent of Roma's bipolar disorder, I answer her because I'm afraid of what she's capable of.

I sniff back the mucous emerging in my nose before saying, "It's too hard."

Before I know what's happening, Roma has ripped my covers off my entire body and tossed them on the floor. "Get out of bed."

I cling to the mattress. I'm certain I look terrified. "I can't today. I just need a day to lay in my bed, then I'll be out of your apartment tomorrow. I promise."

"You're not giving up."

What?

"What?" I'm surprised she's sort of encouraging me in a strange intense way that is completely foreign to me.

Roma throws some clothes at me from the closet. "You're getting up and you're taking care of yourself."

Her supportive reaction doesn't seem bipolar. This is different. It's like she actually…wants me to succeed.

"You don't understand. I—" My throat tightens before I can finish my statement. Or am I just using what she doesn't understand as an excuse? I don't know. Either way, I can't tell her I left my medication at home. If I tell her she would ask why I was on it. And I'm not telling anyone about that. Ever.

She folds her arms over her large chest. "Try me."

My breathing intensifies. I want her to know. Maybe then she would understand me and my entire situation better. I'm sure she would let me stay after she knew. But my mouth won't open. I can't say it out loud. I physically can't utter the truth to her. And I don't know why.

She shifts to one side. "I'm a nurse. There's nothing I haven't seen or heard. It would be unheard of for you to shock me."

I want to believe that. I open my mouth, but nothing comes out. The tears stream down my face. The snot runs from my nose. The air comes in and out of my lungs. But for whatever reason, I cannot get these words out of my mouth.

What Roma does next, surprises me. She takes my pillow and holds it to her face and screams for longer than necessary to get her point across.

I can't tell if she's being so strange because that's who she is, or maybe she's just severely sleep deprived from working the night shift for who knows how long.

Suddenly, the knot shrinks in my throat and my heavy breathing steadies.

She tosses the pillow at my lap. "Try it," she says, like we are all the sudden best friends sharing a fun new game together.

It's weird.

But just weird enough that I want to try it. I press the pillow to my face and let out a squawk.

Roma laughs at this and for the first time I notice she's missing a tooth far back in her mouth. "That was pathetic. Try again."

I do as she says, but this time I inhale deeply before letting out a scream that's been buried inside me since I can remember. It lasts so long that when I run out of air and pull the pillow from my mouth it feels as if my head is floating.

Who knew screaming into a pillow really worked?

Apparently, Roma.

"Now," she says with a smug grin. "Tell me."

I bite at the inside of my cheek. The knot is gone from

my throat, but my heart still feels heavy. If I tell her about my medication, she might think I'm crazy, and I don't want her to kick me out because she thinks she has a crazy teenager living in her apartment.

But maybe it will help my situation. I push at my cuticles and look down at my bare feet pressed against the bed.

"If I tell you," I bite at the inside of my cheek again as I look up at her briefly; just long enough to catch her eyes gleaming down at me. "Will you please give me today to just take a little break from everything?"

She gives me a small smile and says, "Yes. I can do that." Her finger shoots up in my direction as a warning. "But just this one day."

I nod.

"And as I said before, you won't shock me with anything," she says.

"Okay," I draw in a deep inhale. "Last year, my mom thought it would be a good idea to put me on some antidepressants."

"What kind?" She sounds so normal when she asks this. As if I'm just another patient she's seeing at the end of her shift.

"Lexapro."

"And you ran out and feel down?"

"No."

"Need a refill?"

"No."

"I'm not following." She sits on the edge of the bed near my feet. "You thought I would be upset you were on antidepressants?"

"I thought you would think I was crazy."

She squeezes my leg. "In this day and age, everyone is taking some sort of medication for something."

"But I'm not taking it anymore."

She tilts her head in confusion. "Why not?"

"I never thought I needed it, honestly. I just took it because my mom and my doctor thought I should. But when my mom kicked me out, I didn't have a chance to grab my pills."

She presses her mouth together in a line and draws in a deep breath through her nose before releasing it slowly, as if she's trying to gain her composure before speaking.

I don't blame her for being frustrated with me. I probably sound stupid. And she's probably incredibly irritated by the end of her shift after listening to stupid people like me all night. Now I'm here, invading her life with more stupidity.

"You realize you've been detoxing the last three weeks, right?"

I guess I hadn't thought about that.

"No."

She tosses her hands up. "No wonder you don't want to get out of bed. Your body is trying to adjust to all this stress without any medication. You need to be taking extra care of yourself right now. The chemicals in your body are out of balance."

How am I supposed to do that when I can't even get out of bed?

She pulls out her phone. "Okay, first things first." She leaves my bedside for the kitchen. When she returns, she hands me a glass of water and a pop tart while her phone is pressed to her ear. "Drink this. You don't want to get dehydrated."

I take a sip. "Why would I get dehydrated?"

"Hello," she's talking to whoever is on the other end of her phone call now. "I would like to schedule a massage as early as possible."

· · ·

I'm face down on a massage table and have never felt more exposed in my life.

Apparently, Roma has a massage punch card that she was able to use for my appointment. She said a massage would help with the detox process.

The building that the massage therapist works at is just kitty-corner to Roma's apartment building. So, Roma didn't even have to drive me anywhere since I was able to walk here in two minutes. She seemed overly pleased about that. I'm sure she was excited to get rid of me and get some sleep.

The door opens and someone turns on soothing ambient music.

"Would you like hot stones before your massage?"

I knew the massage therapist was a guy. But this guy sounds my age. Even with the sheet covering my body, I feel so much more exposed that a young guy is the massage therapist.

"That's fine." I say in the most mature sounding voice I can manifest.

He begins placing warm stones on my back. The heat relaxes me. Roma was right, this really is an amazing way to detox.

I feel a stone start to slip by my neck. I shift, trying to keep it in its place but it continues to slide off. Before I can reach for it, it falls to the floor. I lift my face from the massage table and reach down to grab the stone.

But before I can, the guy is kneeling next to my face. And it's just my luck, it happens to be the same guy with the *Free Hugs* sign at the mall.

By the expression on his face, he recognizes me too.

I pretend like I don't know him. "Sorry, I tried to catch it before it slipped off."

"You're the sad girl from the mall."

Wow, he's not even going to try and pretend like he forgot about that embarrassing experience.

I fold my arms over the table and rest my chin on them. "No, I don't think you have the right girl."

He sits on a large exercise ball in the corner of the small room and tosses the rock in his hand. "You're the sad girl, I would recognize your face anywhere."

I guess I should stop the act. "Oh, right. You're the guy that tripped with the *Free Hugs* sign."

He laughs. Then fixing his eyes on me, he says, "Actually, you knocked me over."

"I don't think I did." I slip my arms next to my sides and nestle my face back into the massage table. I'm ready to get this over with and get back to my bed. "You seem a little young to be a massage therapist."

He places the rock further down my back, probably to ensure it won't slip off again. "I'm not. My dad is the massage therapist. I just help with the rocks."

"It's Tuesday. At ten o'clock in the morning."

If it weren't for the ambient music, the room would have gone silent for several seconds before he finally says, "Yes, you're right, it is ten o'clock on a Tuesday morning." He's mocking me. Then diming the lights, he says, "Also, that was super random."

"No, I didn't mean-," I scoff, "I mean, why aren't you in school? How old are you?"

He pokes his head under the table where my face is squished in the small hole of the massage table. He's so close I can smell his strawberry gum and whatever sort of guy-soap he used to shower with. "I could ask you the same question." Then he returns to whatever he was doing.

I close my eyes tight. Just in case he does that again, he won't know that I know he can see my smashed face.

Before I can say anything, he leaves the room. Closing the door.

The door opens again.

For some reason, the depression I was sulking in at Roma's apartment has been replaced by snarky-ness since I've encountered *Free Hugs Guy* for the second time.

"Did you decide to stop being so rude and come back to answer my questions?" I say.

"Excuse me?"

My eyes nearly shoot out of my head at the floor.

That's definitely not *Free Hugs Guy's* voice. That's a *man's* voice.

I pull my face from the table and look back at the door to see what looks to be *Free Hugs Guy* in twenty years. When my racing heart of shock steadies, I realize it's *Free Hugs Guy's* dad.

"I'm so sorry. I thought you were Free Hu—" I stop myself from finishing that statement so as not to embarrass myself any further. I have got to stop calling him *Free Hugs Guy*.

"It's alright." *Free Hugs Guy's* dad rubs his hands together with some oil. "I'm Pat, your massage therapist. It's nice to meet you, Paloma."

I didn't tell him my name. I also didn't tell his son my name, so how does he know that?

"How did you know my name was Paloma?"

He removes the rocks from my back, "I saw it written down on my appointment planner. It's a very unique name."

I really am pathetic.

"Was there anything specific bothering you today?"

I exhale. If I'm going to take this detox thing seriously I better start being honest about it. "Well, Pat," I face him briefly, "It's okay if I call you Pat, right? I'm trying to be an adult and I'm not sure if I'm old enough to be calling someone as old as you Pat."

He begins working on my feet. "That's why I told you my name is Pat. But in the future, I wouldn't call any more adults *old*, just to be on the safe side."

"Right." I clear my throat, hoping it will clear out all my worries piling up over how he might react to what I'm about to say. "So, I recently stopped taking some medication. Like three weeks ago. And my best friend's aunt thinks a massage will help with the detoxing process."

He stops massaging and drops my foot against the table. "What sort of medication?"

Great. Just when I thought I was making progress with honesty and adulting. "I've just started talking about it, like an hour ago. So, I still feel some shame over the fact that I was ever taking them."

He approaches me and leans his face under the table. This sort of gesture must run in *Free Hugs Guy's* family. "Paloma, you were supposed to give all your medication information when you filled out the intake form. If you're on any type of heart medication I need to know that."

I scrunch my face in confusion as best I can while it's smashed in the face holder. "Isn't heart medication for old people?"

He keeps his face next to mine under the table. "Yes, usually. But it is one of the red flag medications for massage therapists." He starts talking faster, "What I'm saying is, if you take certain types of medication, you shouldn't get a massage. And if you do get a massage, you should make your massage therapist aware of your medications, so he doesn't accidentally dislodge a blood clot into your heart."

This makes me see how serious he is. "It was an antidepressant." I blurt out to get him to stop freaking me out with all his medical talk.

He drops his head and exhales. "Okay." He stands and moves back to working on my feet. "That's fine. It should be out of your system by now, but the massage will exacerbate any of the withdrawal symptoms you have been experiencing. Just so you're aware."

Great. Thanks, Pat, for making me aware of how much more my life is about to suck.

He continues, "So, I suggest you stay hydrated." *Roma's got me covered there.* "Eat healthy anti-inflammatory foods." *Does a pop tart count?* "And make sure you're sleeping well and taking it easy for the next day or two." *Well, I have today covered at least.*

"I don't understand why people like getting massages with all these rules."

He laughs, and it sounds just like *Free Hugs Guy*'s laugh, only older. "The massage itself is worth the detox symptoms later," he says through his laughter.

And, of course, Pat was right.

The massage made me feel like I was having a mild out of body experience. It took me half the time to finally relax, but once I did, the massage was amazing. I didn't realize I had muscles in some places until they were massaged.

I don't realize the massage has ended until the ambient music shuts off.

I'm on my back now, and when I open my eyes *Free Hugs Guy* is standing above me.

I quickly throw my arms over my body to make sure the sheet is still there. I just had a brief out of body experience and now *Free Hugs Guy* is here to bring me back to reality.

"Don't do that," I say still holding myself.

He's upside-down standing above me. "You fell asleep."

"No, I had an out of body experience," I argue. I'm not

sure why I'm arguing with him. He did give me a free hug, let me fall on top of him, and then gave me a handful of money.

"Most people have out of body experiences when they're asleep."

He's got a point. But I don't want to give him any credit, so I change the subject. "You never told me how old you are."

"Seventeen."

I feel a little less exposed now that I've been laying here for... How long have I been laying here for?

I pull myself up on my elbows. "Okay. That's one answer to one question."

He narrows his eyes in thought. "What were the other questions?"

"Why aren't you in school on a random Tuesday at ten o'clock. And why did you come in here without knocking?"

"I knocked." He places the rocks that were on my back into a basket and unloads new ones into the rock heater. "You didn't answer, so I came in to make sure you didn't die."

I nod, accepting his behavior as normal.

He continues, "It's four o'clock now. I go to online public school. And, there's another client coming in so I need to clean this room."

I look around the room and wonder how many more rooms there are like this in the building. "Oh. That's embarrassing."

"So, it would be super cool if you could—," he breaks eye contact and looks at my clothes resting in the chair, "get dressed in like 30 seconds so I can switch the sheets before the next client checks in."

"Oh my—I'm so sorry." I don't hesitate another second. I jump from the table with the sheet around me and grab my clothes in one handful. "I can't believe I fell asleep that long. Please tell your dad, next time he can wake me up."

"I didn't mean right now."

"What?"

He points to my body. "You could wait to put your clothes on until I leave."

I freeze. Realizing I've been throwing my clothes on with him standing right in front of me. Granted I've been mostly covered by the sheet. He probably didn't see anything. *I hope he didn't see anything.*

"Wow," I say. "Could you just—" I motion to the door.

He flips around. "Yep." Then he exits the room, quickly closing the door behind himself.

I finish tossing my clothes on, hoping it will keep me from feeling how mortified I am.

It doesn't.

I feel just as mortified when I walk out of the room. And even more embarrassed when I see *Free Hugs Guy* behind the front desk.

"Remind me never to show my face here again," I say trying to sound confident in the last ever few words I plan to utter to this guy.

"Too late," he says with a smirk. "I've marked you down in two weeks."

I stop and turn around to face him. "You can't just mark me down without asking me if I want to come back."

"Roma's orders." He half shrugs. "Sorry, I just take down the appointments."

I approach the counter and lean on my forearms. "I thought you just did the hot rocks?"

"I do rocks too. And the sheets." He grins. "And sometimes I even mop." He's trying to be funny.

I lift my chin and examine him with narrowed eyes. He's

smiling a stupid smug smile. But I can't help but notice how attractive he is when he's not talking, or tripping, or seeing me in my most mortifying moments.

"You know," I say, "I don't know your name."

He holds his hand out. "I'm Jax."

Of course, he has a name like *Jax* that perfectly fits his tallness, and attractiveness, and coolness, and all the other words that end in *ness* that describe him.

"I'm Paloma," I say shaking his hand. Which seems like a weird thing to do after we spent several minutes hugging at the mall. Not to mention the fact that he just saw me half naked moments ago.

"I know."

"You do?" I smile.

He points down at the appointment book.

I quickly wipe the ridiculous grin from my face. "Oh, right."

I don't even say goodbye. My body's chemical imbalance is so out of whack right now I can't even figure out what I'm feeling.

As I make my way to the exit, *Free Hugs Guy*, I mean, *Jax*, says, "See you at ten o'clock in two weeks, Paloma."

I don't argue. Even though I'm not coming back. Instead, I wave to him without turning around.

I hate that detoxing is affecting my brain, my body, and my emotions so much. Why can't I be around a hot guy without feeling like I need all his attention? Why did I have to watch him in the mall for so long before approaching him? Why did I even bother hugging him?

If I had just kept on with my job hunt, I would never have had the opportunity to confess so much stupid stuff about myself to him. He probably thinks I'm pathetic now that he knows my mom kicked me out and I'm jobless.

I didn't even thank him for the money he gave me that

I used for groceries and a portion of the rent I owe Roma.

Which reminds me, I have about fifteen hours before I have to find some sort of employment.

CHAPTER

FOUR

Jaxon

Birdie hands me a basket of towels.

I begin to fold them as he sits on a chair in the corner of the room and props his feet up on the massage table.

He sips at his frappe, eyeing me intently. "Okay, something is up with you. You're never this quiet."

"Nothing is up." I place the folded towel in a cubby under the table.

Birdie nudges my leg with his glittery shoe. Knowing him, it's probably designer. "Spill the tea," he says.

I finish folding the last towel, place it under the table, and flick the light off as I exit the room. Purposely avoiding Birdie the entire time.

"Come on," Birdie says. "You've been so weird all morning. What happened?" He gasps and stops in front of me. His eyes are wide and worried. "It's not…"

I move past him. "No, everything is fine with that."

He exhales in relief. "Then what is it?"

He's not going to let this go.

"Remember *sad girl?*" I sort of gave her that nickname when we watched the video of her this weekend during Birdie's video editing session. He was unimpressed with me when I stood my ground and made him cut the parts out with Paloma. There was something too raw and authentic about her. It would have been wrong to publish probably one of the most sincere and private moments she's had since she was kicked out of her house. I couldn't take that moment from her. It would be cruel to display it on the internet for the public to see.

Birdie nods. With the frappe straw in his mouth, he says, "*Sad girl,* the one that tackled you?"

"Yeah, her." I know he remembers who she is, he's just trying to get under my skin.

He leans against the wall, and I switch the laundry over. I can feel him about to burst from anticipation. "Spill. The. Tea!"

I press start on the washer. "She was here yesterday."

He nearly drops his drink. "What? She was here? How did she know you worked here? Is she a stalker? Should we be concerned?" He gets in front of me again and blocks my way. "Jax, who is she?"

"Her name is Paloma."

Tilting his head, he says, "That's about as odd as naming your son, *Birdie.*"

"Despite her *odd* name," not that I think her name is odd at all, "she is completely normal."

He raises his eyebrows and walks in step with me to the front of the building. "I totally thought you were going to say she was a crazy stalker."

I make my way around the front desk and look through the appointments for the day. The receptionist is out on maternity leave so I've been doing more at the office. "Nope, she's just a regular girl with a case of bad luck. She's coming back for a massage in two weeks, so I'll let you know if anything changes between now and then."

"Or you could let me know what you think of her right now."

I drop my head back and roll my eyes. "I just did."

When I glance up, Birdie is peering out the front window. I walk over to stand next to him. He tilts his head at me and smiles when I see what he's talking about.

"She's a stalker," he says, proud of himself and what I know is his *false* discovery.

"She's not a stalker." We both stare out the window. She's walking on the other side of the street. Before right now, I had thought maybe she was one of Roma's patients from the hospital. And she felt so sorry for Paloma that she gave her one of her massages. But now I'm wondering if maybe Roma made the massage appointments for Paloma because Paloma is living with Roma.

Birdie taps his foot on the floor. "Then why is she hanging around here again?"

I shrug and walk back behind the counter. "I don't know. It doesn't matter."

"I think it does."

I ignore him. As I flip through the appointments, I realize it's going to be a slow day. Which means I need to find something else to keep my mind preoccupied and away from any thoughts of Paloma.

"Just say hi to her," Birdie says, pleading me.

I shake my head, keeping my eyes on the appointment book. "Not a chance."

I don't know why he's pushing this. He knows I don't

have anything to do with girls and especially relationships.

Without warning, Birdie leaves the building.

It takes me a minute to realize what he's doing. But when I do, I can't help but feel a little angry at him. And betrayed.

I watch helplessly as he runs to the streetlight across from where Paloma is standing. He calls out to her above the traffic and waves her over. She waves back when she notices him. When the light changes, she crosses the street and talks with Birdie for what seems like an eternity. But I'm sure it's only a few seconds. It just feels like everything is in slow motion. And I'm in some sort of paralyzing trance. Helplessly watching possible destruction unfold before me.

Birdie must have said something about me since he motions in my direction and then they both look over at me through the windows. Why is this building covered in windows?

It's too late to avoid them now. Birdie holds the door open for Paloma as she enters the building. When she looks at me, it sends a flutter through my chest. I pull my hand up to steady my heartbeat.

"I wasn't expecting to see you again so soon," she says. Her hair is fixed and she's wearing a little bit of makeup. She looks…happy.

"Were you headed somewhere?" I ask. She might make my heart flutter, but it's just another reason to make this conversation short and politely get her to leave.

She pushes on her cuticles nervously, but she hides it well with the genuine smile on her face. "I'm getting a job today."

Birdie leans against the counter. "Where?"

"Leave her alone," I say to Birdie. "She would tell us if she wanted us to know."

She adjusts the small purse strap on her shoulder. "It's fine."

"We don't need to know where you work," I say this mostly because I want as little information about her as possible. All I need to know is if she wants hot stones before her massage or not. Other than that, she can keep her personal life to herself.

She's looking at me with a confused expression. Almost hurt. I don't know why. I'm not being rude, just honest. And in my defense, my honesty is coming out very politely in my opinion.

Birdie ignores my comment and smiles at her. "You were saying…"

She picks her face up and smiles back at him halfheartedly. "Well, I don't exactly have a job yet. But I'm determined to find one today. I have a good feeling about it."

"Sweetie, I can get you a job in two seconds," Birdie says. "Just say the word."

At this point, I'm not even sure why Birdie is my friend. Can he not keep his mouth shut? Not even for his best friend. He knows I don't want to be around her. It's like the guy has no filter sometimes. Or consideration for his best friend's requests. Just to reiterate, his best friend is *me*. So, he has no consideration for *me* and *my* requests.

Paloma turns her attention completely to Birdie. With widened eyes full of hope she says, "Are you serious? You would do that for me?"

He nods. With the same proud smirk he had when he labeled her a stalker five minutes ago. I wonder how she would feel if she knew what he really thought of her.

He drops his wrist, holding his palm out in front of her. "Phone?" We barely know her and he's already using one-word sentences to communicate.

"No," she says gently. I guess, these two have a lot more in common than I would have ever guessed since they're both using one-word sentences.

"Why?" Birdie says.

Her cheeks begin to redden after he asks her this.

I don't have to ask; I can tell by her expression she doesn't have one. Which is embarrassing for any teenager. And it makes me feel sorry for her in a way that tugs at my soul just like I felt at the mall. And in the same way I ignored that tugging feeling at the mall, I'm ignoring it again right now.

Birdie must also realize she doesn't have a phone, since he gives her another one-word sentence, and says, "Oh." Then he takes her hand in his.

Why doesn't he just let her leave already?

"Nonetheless, I can get you a job."

Her eyes light up with hope again. "Really?"

"I like you, P." Now he's already given her a nickname. "It's okay if I call you P., right?"

She nods with a dumbfounded expression coating her grin.

"Do you want to hang out with us today?" He says this to her but flashes his eyes at me, knowing good and well that I'm doing everything in my power to keep my composure right now.

She scrunches her shoulders. "I actually really need to find a job," she says.

"Good," Birdie says, pulling her out the door. "We were just heading to see one of the best headhunters I know."

I pull my phone out and text my dad, letting him know it's a slow day and I'll be with Birdie.

I purposely leave out the fact that Paloma is with us. I don't need my dad getting involved like Birdie is.

* * *

Birdie insisted Paloma sit in the front seat. So, I was stuck in the back of his Audie, where my knees were bent up to my chest and my legs fell asleep during the forty-five-minute drive to his mansion. It feels as if I'm walking on marshmallows when I emerge from the car.

Paloma doesn't waste any time scaling the stairs to Birdie's mansion entrance.

"Why are you walking like that?" Birdie says quietly.

So now he's trying to save me from humiliation?

"Someone thought it was a good idea to cram me in the backseat of your car," I say.

He walks ahead of me. Not before saying, "You're a baby," and rushing to meet Paloma.

When I finally meet them inside, Paloma is drinking in the double marble staircase. I'm sure I looked just as wide eyed the first time I saw it too.

"Is your dad Jeff Bezos or something?" Paloma says, her eyes still locked on the enchanting staircases.

That makes both Birdie and I laugh. The girl has humor. I'll take it. But nothing more.

"No," Birdie's dad says as he emerges from the living room, followed by Birdie's mom. He takes Paloma's hand in his. "Aatmay, Birdie's father. And this is my wife, Dipti."

Birdie approaches the threesome. He places his hands on Paloma's shoulders. "This is Paloma. She's my new best friend." Birdie sings the last part.

I scoff. Which makes them all flip their heads around to me. I know he's joking, but it's still obnoxious. I don't want Paloma thinking she's going to be hanging out with us all the time.

"I thought Jax was your best friend," Dipti says playfully.

Birdie waves his mother's remark away. "Jax is old

news." He flutters his eyes. "Paloma gets me in a way Jax doesn't."

"Is that so," Dipti says.

They are talking about me like I'm not here, which would bother me if it was anyone else, but since it's Birdie's family it sort of feels like it's my family too.

"Well, it is nice to meet you," Dipti says, facing Paloma again.

"Wait," Birdie says, "Since, Paloma is my new best friend, and she desperately needs a job." Birdie pouts his lip a little when he says this.

Dipti lifts her hand. "Say no more." Without hesitation, she takes Paloma's hand, and they walk back to where Dipti's office is.

Before they disappear behind the wall, Paloma gives us an unsure expression. I'm sure she's overwhelmed by the generosity Dipti pours out to literally everyone she encounters.

I've never asked, but I wonder how much money Birdie's family makes every second. Yeah, I said, every *second*. Not day, not month, not year, but every *second*. I'm sure it's outrageous.

Aatmay is standing between Birdie and me, his hands clasped behind his back as he inspects us.

"You boys are staying out of trouble?" It's less of a question and more of a statement that he expects from us.

"Of course, Sir," I say. I like to use very official terms for Aatmay since I feel a little intimidated by him. Even if he wasn't rich, his presence is dominating—a little frightening too. But I respect him and want him to know I do. So I will continue to call him *Sir* for the rest of my life.

"Where did you meet your new *best friend*?" he says mocking Birdie.

Birdie stretches his arms out above his head, he's

obviously a lot more comfortable with his dad's dominating presence than I am. Through a yawn, Birdie says, "She tackled Jax at the mall."

Aatmay flashes his gaze at me in surprise. I'm just as surprised a girl as small as Paloma was able to knock over a guy my size too.

What I want to say to him is, *It sounds worse when Birdie says it like that, but what really happened was that a broken girl physically tried to crush me as intensely as her heart had been crushed before she got to me—physically knocking me over in the process. She didn't actually tackle me...I really only lost my footing.*

Aatmay looks back to Birdie before I can defend myself.

"We clicked instantly," Birdie says, snapping his fingers.

Aatmay's expression grows firm. "You've known her for a few days." He nods, like he's thrusting a dart at Birdie with his face. "Next time, make sure you get to know your friends more before you bring them to our house."

Birdie gives Aatmay a *what's-your-problem* expression before saying, "Pot called the kettle black." Then he nods at me, indicating he wants me to follow him.

I give Aatmay an awkward smile before we part ways.

I feel a little uncomfortable at their passive aggressive behavior. I know Aatmay means well. He only said that to Birdie because during one of their recent celebration parties they had a client steal several rare (and expensive) decorations. But the experience has made Aatmay hyperaware of opening the doors of his home to anyone he doesn't know well.

I sprawl across the couch on the back patio. "You don't think Paloma would do anything sketchy, do you?"

Birdie plops next to the pool and takes his shoes off. "Not at all. She seems super chill." He flicks his feet in the water. "Do you?"

I shake my head. "No, I don't get that sort of vibe from

her. She's cool."

"Glad you guys don't think I'm some psycho killer," Paloma's voice echoes.

I lift myself up onto my elbows. "Not cool," I say pulling my eyebrows together. I feel a little violated she was listening to us talk about her.

She shrugs. "You literally just said I was cool. I heard you."

"That's what I'm saying." I sit up to face her as she takes a seat next to me.

Her eyes narrow. "Okay...?"

"You were eavesdropping." I lock eyes with her, which I immediately regret since it sends my heart crashing around in my chest like a hurricane.

If her intense hug revealed her brokenness, then her eyes are the tunnels to her lost soul. *I hate my emotional sixth sense right now.*

I drop my gaze, afraid I might choke on my words if I continue to look into her eyes. "Eavesdropping is not cool," I say.

She runs her hands through the bottom of her chopped hair. "Wow. Okay, sorry for approaching your conversation unannounced. I'll make sure to send a messenger next time."

Birdie splashes water at me, but to her he says, "He's just worried you're going to hear something he's hiding from you."

If looks could kill, Birdie would be dead right now.

His comment lightens the mood for Paloma though. She perks up and nudges me with her shoulder. "What sort of things are you hiding?"

"Nothing," I say. She's eyeing me. She's touching me.

Stop.

Stop.

Stop.

Birdie rolls his eyes.

"You know," Paloma says. "Since me and Birdie are best friends now, that sort of inadvertently makes you and me best friends too."

I chuckle to myself. My laughter is more of a reaction to the disbelief I feel from her comment than actual amusement. "Is that right?"

She nods and shifts her posture, closing the distance between us.

Birdie joins us on the patio. "She's right, Jax. We all just became the three amigos. So, no secrets, right?"

I give him a look of warning.

Thankfully, he takes the hint, and faces Paloma. "Did mama-bear find you a new career, P.?"

She forces air through her clenched teeth, then says, "Your mom is amazing."

Birdie crosses his legs and leans over to tap her knee. "What'd she find for you?" He draws back slightly. "Tell me it's something you're going to love and not a fast-food place you settled for."

She folds her mouth together, holding in her laughter at his enthusiasm, then says, "She found me a nanny position for a pregnant lady."

"Girl, I hope you like kids or we can march back in there and get you a different job." Birdie stands up as if he's about to have a word with his mother.

Paloma pulls him back to his chair playfully. "I love kids," she says through a laugh. "And this is just temporary until the little girl starts school in the fall. Maybe I can get my GED and apply for college or something. That way I have something to look forward to after I'm finished with this job."

Just then Aatmay appears on the far side of the patio

near their home. He doesn't say anything and since I'm the only one that notices him, I fling my leg at Birdie to get his attention.

He flips around. When he sees his father, he looks back at us with a frown and says, "I'll be right back."

The two disappear into the mansion house.

I realize I haven't been alone with Paloma once today. Birdie has been the best buffer. It was hard enough being in the same room as her after her massage when she was dressing in front of me.

Since I'm actively avoiding her because of all the tugging and pulling she causes inside of me, I decide to continue avoiding her by scrolling through my phone.

It doesn't last long.

Before I can leave to walk around the garden, or dip my feet in the pool, or move literally anywhere but here where I'm sitting next to her, she says, "So, how long have you and Birdie been friends?"

I shift on the patio couch so that I'm as far away from her as possible without making it apparent that I'm trying to avoid her. "Since eighth grade."

She pulls her eyebrows together and scrunches her nose. "I thought you said you did online public school?"

"I do." I glance at her just long enough to see that she's looking at all parts of me. My face, my feet, my torso, my hair, and she's not being shy about it. This whole avoiding an attractive girl thing is starting to seem like an impossible task.

I say, "Birdie goes to the same online school. We met at one of the middle school dances."

"That's crazy." She says this as if she wants me to know she's not listening to me at all.

I decide the best way to keep avoidance while still being in close contact with her is to continue talking.

"I didn't know anyone at the dance. It gets wild when you put hundreds of hormone-crazed and socially awkward thirteen-year-olds in a gymnasium with pop music on full blast."

Her eyes are flashing between mine.

I decide to continue with my slightly overexaggerated version of the story. "None of the girls had the guts to ask me to dance. And I wasn't interested in any of them enough to brave the possibility of rejection. Then, out of nowhere, Birdie asked me to dance. And I said yes. We've been best friends ever since."

She doesn't even bother saying anything in response to my story.

Birdie didn't actually ask me to dance. But we did become friends that night after we realized we were the only two guys avoiding the dance floor. I thought my exaggerated story might get her attention.

It doesn't.

It's almost like she's in a trance.

I can't help myself and wave my hand in front of her face. "Are you okay?" I say.

Now she's giving me *the look*.

The sort of look a girl gives right before she kisses you.

Before I know what's happening, our lips are pressed together.

I don't know why I turn against myself, but I give in to her kiss.

I run my hands through her hair. And she clasps her hands around my wrists.

My heartbeat rises up into my throat and even though we are sitting on the patio, my breathing feels like I've just sprinted an entire marathon.

My mouth wants to keep kissing her. Even my hands want to continue touching her. But my mind screams at me to stop.

Instead of stopping myself, "Oh, doll," Birdie's voice forces us apart.

When we face him, we're both out of breath.

Paloma flashes her eyes between me and Birdie, holding her fingers over her lips.

Birdie pets the top of Paloma's head, looking at her endearingly, and says, "I hope you're ready to get your heart torn out of your ribcage."

CHAPTER

FIVE

Paloma

I'm sitting in the back of the nicest car I've ever ridden in. Which says a lot since I was just in Birdie's car the other day.

This car is black on the outside with black interior. There's not a speck of dust or the slightest evidence anyone has ever been inside of it.

Unlike Birdie's car that had Red Bull cans rolling all over the floorboard. This car is a lot bigger than Birdie's too.

I felt sorry for Jax sitting in the back when we went to Birdie's and again when they dropped me off at Roma's.

"How much longer?" I say to the driver.

He points to the GPS. "Seven minutes."

My nerves ball up into my throat. The same way they did when I thought it would be a good idea to kiss Jax.

I have no idea what came over me. He was talking about the first time he met Birdie and I couldn't focus on anything except for the deep melodic sound of his voice.

Dipti had just set me up with a job. Making my emancipation progress forward one step further. And then it was just me and Jax sitting out on the patio. My euphoria took over and I couldn't keep myself from wanting to stop his mouth from talking and feel his lips against mine.

I couldn't focus on anything except his mouth.

And the way he uses his hands to explain what he's saying.

And his piercing crystal blue eyes.

And his confidence.

And his hair. Oh my gosh, his hair is perfect.

"For you, Miss Smith," the driver says lifting his arm around to reach me in the backseat. He releases a brand-new iPhone into my grip.

"What's this for?"

He adjusts his suit sleeve that scrunched up after he reached back to me. "From Dipti. It's so the Laurent's can contact you. The code is one, two, three, one, two, three."

I hold the phone in my hands. Wondering what the Laurent family is going to think of me.

Today is a sort of trial run to make sure I'm a good fit for them. Dipti arranged for the driver to transport me even though I insisted I could figure out transportation. But when I found out the Laurent's live in Highland Park, I took her up on the offer.

But just until I can figure out my own means of transportation.

The driver comes to a stop. "A driver will meet you back here at five."

"Thank you." I force a smile and exit the vehicle with my new phone in hand.

I wish he was coming back to get me. He kept the radio at a decent volume and didn't bother me with any small talk. Hopefully the next driver is trained in the same manner.

I feel incredibly alone and out of place once he drives away.

The house is huge. Not like Birdie's mansion house, but still, I can tell the Laurent's are well off.

Just as I'm about to gather the confidence to approach the house, one side of the large double doors flings open, revealing the cutest little girl.

"Nanny! Nanny!"

Great, she's already named me. I know that's my position, but it feels odd being called *Nanny.*

She rushes to me, her blond curls bouncing with each stride.

I open my arms to welcome her. As if she's known me her entire life, she glues herself to my waist.

"Nanny, I have so much to show you." She replaces her grip on my waist with a grip around my arm. "We only have five hours to get everything done. Come on, Nanny, why are you walking so slow?"

I let her pull me inside where a man is rattling off an intense conversation on his phone. I can't make out what he's saying because the language is foreign to me.

I'm intrigued by the sights and sounds as we venture farther into the home. There's artwork all over the walls but not a family photo in sight.

The man catches me staring at a sculpture in the corner.

Instead of a welcoming expression, he looks at me with a wide-eyed stare.

I smile, trying to lighten the awkwardness I'm feeling.

He says something to whoever is on the other end of the phone, then ends the call. He doesn't take his eyes off me the whole time, which is making me feel less awkward and more concerned.

The girl pulls at my arm. "Let's go upstairs, Nanny, that's where my room is."

"Lissy, release her please," he says to the little girl. His foreign accent is thick. I'm guessing it's Italian or French, I can't quite figure it out yet.

The girl slumps forward. "But Daddy, she's so slow if I don't hold her hand."

I laugh. I can tell she's going to keep me busy.

The man lifts his gaze to mine. "I'm so sorry, I didn't realize you had arrived during the call. I don't usually—" He wipes the air with his hand, waving away the rest of his statement. "Welcome to our home, this is, Elise. We call her Lissy." He holds Lissy's chin in his grip for a brief moment as he smiles at her. Then he holds his hand out to mine. "My name is Claude Laurent."

When I grasp his hand, he places his other hand around mine.

"I'm Paloma," I say smiling through the strange feeling rising in me as he continues to hold my hand in his grip for longer than necessary.

"What is your last name?"

That's an odd question. Or maybe I just think it's odd because he's *still* holding my hand in his.

"Smith."

He cocks his head like he's confused by my last name, then he finally releases my hand with a smile. "Enchanté, Paloma Smith."

"Can we go now, Daddy?" Lissy says.

He picks her up and pecks her cheek. "Make sure you are polite to Miss Paloma, yeah? She is our guest today."

She laughs as he tickles her gently. "I will!"

Claude sets her down and she takes my hand again as

we head for the stairs.

I turn back to see Claude still standing at the bottom of the staircase, his arms crossed over his chest, and that peculiar look on his face as he watches us disappear around the corner.

Lissy quickly has me take a seat in a tiny chair at her tiny table with the tiniest tea set decorating the tablecloth. I love her room, it's everything pink and yellow and turquoise, and everything I would have loved as a little girl.

She hands me a lamb. "Nanny, this is Lamby." She shoves the little lamb leg into my hand and pinches her voice pretending to be Lamby, "*Enchanté, Nanny.*"

She is so full of excitement and energy.

"How old are you, Lissy?" I say, making sure she knows I'm talking to her and not Lamby.

She places Lamby gently back on her pillow. "I'm five. I get to start kindergarten this year and learn the Pledge of Allegiants."

That's interesting since her dad is obviously French with his lack of personal space and *Enchanté*s. Maybe she's already learned the French Pledge of Allegiants and the American one seems intriguing to her. Do the French have a Pledge of Allegiants?

"Well, I can teach you that," I say pretending to pour tea into one of the miniature cups.

Lissy's eyes light up and her mouth falls agape. "You can?"

I nod. "Sure, then you'll be ahead of the curve when you get to kindergarten." I wink at her as a smile spreads across her face causing the cutest dimples to emerge at the points of her mouth.

"I like you, Nanny," she says pulling a trunk down from one of the shelves in her closet. "I think mommy is going to like you too."

"Where is your mommy?" I should probably introduce myself and finish the tour of the house before I continue playing with Lissy.

Lissy is pulling a pirate costume on over her frilly dress. "She's at the baby doctor today." The dress is bunching up in the back of her pirate coat making her look like she's hiding a boulder underneath it. The sight forces a laugh out from my throat.

"Do you know when your mommy is going to have the baby?" I say.

She pulls a pirate hat onto her head. It's slightly big for her, so it comes down below her eyebrows. She tips her head back to look at me and says, "When I go to kindergarten."

"Are you excited to have a new baby brother or sister?"

The brim of the hat flaps up and down as she nods.

"You're lucky to have someone to play with." I push at my cuticles. "I didn't have any brothers or sisters when I was growing up."

"Who did you play with?"

I tilt my head in thought. I didn't really play with anyone. But I don't want to tell Lissy that, she's too young to understand. And I can tell she's curious enough to ask me *why* over and over until she gets an answer she's satisfied with. I want her to be satisfied before she gets curious enough to ask *why*, so I say, "I had my mom and my friends to play with."

"Nanny?" She says this while she's inspecting a missing button on her pirate costume.

"Yes?" She really is a little doll.

"Do you know how the baby got in my mommy's tummy?"

My eyes widen as I bite my bottom lip, hoping I can hold it there long enough to figure out an appropriate response.

Thankfully, I don't have to.

"Ma chérie." Claude enters the bedroom and sweeps Lissy from her feet into his arms. "Why don't we show Paloma your tree house, okay?"

Her face brightens at his suggestion as she wriggles out of his arms and rushes out the door.

Claude spreads his hand out in front of us, indicating he wants me to leave before him. "After you," he says with a grin.

I smile politely but really, I'm not sure how to feel. I'm going to continue telling myself it's his cultural background that makes him so friendly. I can't imagine I would allow myself to be in a similar situation with a married man if he were an American.

Lissy doubles back when she realizes she left me behind. She takes my hand again and continuously calls me *Nanny* as she tours me around her home. We are followed closely behind by Claude the entire time.

When we make our way outside, Lissy lets go of my hand and skips to her Pinterest worthy treehouse. She rushes up the ladder with her dress bouncing under her pirate coat. It's an equally hilarious and adorable sight.

I turn around to share a laugh with Claude, but when I do, he's inspecting *me*.

He missed the entire scene of his daughter; wasted the moment to stare at me. To him, I'm just a random nanny. He should be enthralled by his child, not staring at me in wonder.

I don't know much about French people, but this seems sort of bizarre—for any culture.

"Will your wife be home soon?" I say, immediately wishing I had noted my tone before allowing it to leave my mouth.

He gives me a side grin as he steps forward, closer to me. "She had several appointments today. I don't expect her home until dinner."

I swallow hard. The hairs on my arms straighten and I feel suddenly airy. Like gravity has left me. But not in a good way. I look at my feet to make sure they're still connected to the ground.

"You're welcome to stay for dinner," he says looking intently at my face for a response.

"I—" My phone buzzes in my back pocket.

Weird.

I haven't given my number to anyone. *I don't even know what my number is.*

I pull the phone from my pocket. I have a text from a random number.

How's the interview?

Shortly after I read the text, I receive another one.

This is Dipti 😋

A sense of relief washes over me.

"I can't stay," I blurt out as I quickly reply to Dipti.

Me: Good. Could you send a car to pick me up now, please?
Dipti: Everything okay?

Claude shifts his weight to one side as he glances up at Lissy in the treehouse. "Some other time then, yes?"

Me: Yep. Something unexpected came up.
Dipti: I will send a car now. Call me when you can

talk.

I release a puff of air as I return my phone to my pocket. "Actually, I have to leave soon. Something came up."

Claude's face falls into a frown. "But you have not been here for more than an hour. We still have the schedule to go over."

I shake my head and plaster a remorseful expression on my face. "I'm so sorry. I don't know what to say."

Claude holds his chin for a moment, then says, "I will give you my contact. Then you can let me know a better time that works for you."

I reluctantly place my phone into his hand. I can always block his number if he becomes a problem, I guess.

"A car will be here to pick me up soon."

He nods, punching his information into my phone.

Then I hear a ding. But it's not my phone dinging.

It's *his*.

"Now, I have your contact as well," he says with a grin as he hands my phone back to me.

"Nanny-*yy*, the ship is leaving without you!" Lissy's voice calling to me is a relief from this strange encounter with Claude I'm having. I more than welcome her invitation, anything to get me away from her father.

I shrug at Claude as a way of letting him know duty calls.

As I scale the ladder, I call up to Lissy, "Hurry, Lissy, I think I see a kraken swimming towards us!"

"What's a kraken?" she says, poking her head down to face me as I emerge into her immaculate treehouse.

I'm struck with awe at the sight of her life. It's better than a fairytale. "It's like a giant squid that crushes pirate ships with its huge tentacles."

"Eww!"

I laugh at her response and pull my attention from her

awesome treehouse back to our game. "I know, so we better hurry and steer this ship away from here."

I feel the rush as if I'm actually escaping the wrath of a giant kraken. But in reality, I'm escaping from the weird vibes I'm getting from Mr. Laurent. Maybe if I call him *Mr. Laurent* to his face he will remember that he's a married man, with a pregnant wife, and I'm a misfit teenager babysitting his daughter.

After Lissy changes the theme of our imaginary game three times, Claude waves from the backdoor and says, "Paloma, I think your car has arrived."

I face Lissy with a smile, but she doesn't seem happy to see my face. She's pouting her bottom lip and her big brown eyes are piercing my heart. *Why is she so cute?*

I reach my arms out to hug her. "I'll be back," I lie.

"Promise?"

It feels so wrong to lie to a five-year-old. But she's probably going to forget about me once she falls for a new nanny. I have to tell myself she'll be fine. It's the only way I can walk away from this.

"I promise," I say through a gut-wrenching fake smile.

We scale back down the ladder and Lissy walks me inside. She notices cookies on the kitchen counter and distracts herself with them.

"Bye, Lissy," I say waving to her. "Thanks for saving us from the kraken."

"Bye, Nanny," she says with a cookie in her cheek. "Don't forget to come back and play with me again."

I smile wistfully. I hate that we bonded so quickly. It would be easier to leave if she had been a brat.

Before I open the door to leave, Claude blocks my way. When I look at him, he seems almost like he's in pain.

"Please come back, we will pay you very well." He must be on to me and my decision to never come back here.

His eyes are darting between mine for a response. "She really likes you. It is difficult to find a good nanny that can keep up with her. You saw yourself how much energy she has."

I open my mouth to speak but nothing comes out.

He steps out of my way and holds his temples with one hand. "Terra will be so disappointed if you do not come back." He says this more to himself than to me.

I look back at Lissy in the kitchen. She's abandoned the cookies, now coloring a picture at the table.

I can't deny the instant connection I felt with her. I've babysat a handful of times and none of those experiences compares to how easy it was for me to hang out with Lissy.

"Okay," I say quietly. And against all my instincts.

Claude's expression is full of eagerness and hope when he looks up at me. The color seems to have returned to his face as well. "Okay," he mimics.

I nod. "I'll come back when your wife is home so we can talk about the schedule or whatever."

He gives me a look of gratitude and clasps both his hands around mine. Again.

I pull my hand away. "I'll text you."

"Thank you, Paloma," he says.

His appreciation for my change of heart sounds sincere. But I'm not buying it. And I've also decided that if I'm going to be working for them, I'm going to be in charge of our outings. Which means, whenever Claude is home, I'm taking Lissy to the park.

I pull the door the rest of the way open and scoot out quickly. "For sure," I say as confidently as possible. I don't want him to think I'm some sort of weak girl that can't hold her own.

I hear the door close behind me. I decide not to turn around and look back since I don't want to know if Claude is staring at me again.

When I reach the car, I'm still deep in thought about whether I should come back for Lissy or cut my losses with Claude and never look back.

"Not a good fit?" the driver says.

Only, when this driver talks, I recognize his voice. And when I recognize that it's Jax's voice, I realize I'm not in a brand-new Mercedes or Lexus or whatever the first car I was transported in was. I wouldn't even consider this car Uber worthy.

My stomach flutters but I try to hide it with my attitude. "Why are you here?" Is all I manage to say.

I suck in a breath when I catch a glimpse of his crystal blue eyes in the rearview mirror.

"I wanted to talk to you," he says.

He couldn't have waited for a normal time? He had to show up unannounced at my possible new place of work? When I'm in the middle of an internal crisis.

"About what?" I say, knowing he's going to bring up the kiss.

The intense, amazingly wonderful kiss that was interrupted by Birdie.

The kiss that was forgotten about by everyone but me and left in the very forefront of my mind for the last few days.

"Why don't you come sit up here?" he says, flipping around to sink his blue gaze into me. "It's weird you're sitting in the backseat."

I try not to allow his eyes to affect me. "Don't drivers normally chauffeur their passengers around in the backseat?" I open the backdoor and climb into the front.

"I'm not a chauffeur," he says putting his car into gear.

I quickly realize his car leaves little room for personal space and our shoulders are inches apart. I clasp my hands between my legs to keep from seeming like I'm trying to get any closer to him. I can't tell if he's into me like I'm into him. Maybe I'm the only one feeling these feelings between us. Maybe he thinks the kiss was a mistake and that's why he's picking me up to talk about it. Why did I compulsively kiss him?

"I take it the kid wasn't a good fit," he says again, pulling forward and finally away from the Laurent's residence.

I let myself look back at the house once more to see if Claude is there. When I don't see any sign of him at the windows, I let out a breath of relief. "The little girl, Lissy, she was great."

"What was the problem then?"

"Why does there have to be a problem?"

He shoots me a look of confusion. "Why else would you want to leave four hours early?"

I sift both of my hands through my hair, trying to gather my thoughts into words.

He flashes his eyes between the road and me, searching my face for an answer. "What? Was the dad a perv or something?" He says this half-jokingly, but when he sees the serious look on my face his demeanor changes.

With my hands still in my hair, I look at him in regret. *Why didn't I just lie and say the kid was a brat?*

Jax grips the steering wheel and turns down a side street.

"What are you doing?" I say, slightly panicked.

He veers into a neighborhood and swiftly pulls over next to the curb. He shifts in his seat to face me, one arm on the steering wheel with the other bent over his headrest. "Listen, Paloma, if some guy made you uncomfortable or did something to you—"

"No," I say, realizing how quickly this could ruin Claude if I don't stop it from escalating. "It was nothing like that." I mean it sort of was, but not really. That's why this is so difficult to explain.

He drops his head. "Okay," when he looks up at me, his expression doesn't change. It's still just as concerned as it was before. "So, what happened?"

I press at my cuticles but stop when I notice he looks at my hands. I clear my throat. "Best friends?"

He draws his head back in confusion. "What?"

If I'm going to open up, I need to trust him. Birdie already told me I was setting myself up for heartbreak. So, if Jax doesn't like me the way I like him, I'll settle for best friends. Which I know we obviously aren't there yet, but I wouldn't mind working towards that status. Especially since Candice is two hundred miles away.

"Best friends? Three amigos? Tackle buddies? Whatever you want to call us," I say playfully.

A smile spreads across his face. "Okay, okay, I get it. What about that?"

"If I'm going to talk to you about best friend stuff, then we have to be on the same page."

"Alright, I think I know how to be a best friend." He smirks. "Not so sure about the tackle buddies thing though. I don't remember anyone calling us that."

"Just erase that part," I say.

He shifts in his seat again, this time in a more relaxed position facing forward but with his eyes still on mine. "No way, I'm going to make sure Birdie calls us tackle buddies from now on."

"Oh my gosh." I cover my face with my hands.

He holds my arm gently which sends a reverberation through my arm and down my spine. I drop my hands to look at him for some sort of indication about what that means when he touches me.

"For real though, if you don't want to tell me what happened, you should probably talk to Dipti about it. She's really cool and won't judge you for anything."

I nod. "Sometimes it's hard to say things out loud."

He pulls his bottom lip in his mouth, then says, "I get that. Sometimes, you just can't think about it and you just have to say it."

I nod again. I also realize I'm looking too much into his touching. With a deep inhale, I don't think and I just speak. "So, Lissy is a great kid," I say. "I've never connected so well with a kid like that before."

Jax grins from the side of his mouth.

"Even her imagination was fun. And nothing about her was annoying. I could actually have a conversation with her that made sense, and she's only five." I fix my gaze at a garbage can up ahead before getting into the rest of what I have to say. "But there was something odd about her dad."

"Odd how?" His voice is stiff. I'm not trying to alarm him, but I get a sense that his protective primal male defenses are emerging.

I keep my eyes forward, afraid he might read too much into my expression. "He didn't really have any personal space. Like he shook my hand too long when we met. And he seemed to always be around and watching everything I was doing."

I glance at Jax. He's taking in all the information before responding.

"And, he's from France," I add quickly. "Paris. Europe somewhere, I don't know exactly where he's from, but he has a French accent."

This causes Jax to exhale deeply, as if the emotions broiling inside of him steam out in one breath.

I wait for his response. But he sits forward and puts the car in gear, pulling onto the road again.

"Where are we going?" I say, confused by his behavior.

He flashes me a smile. "Where do you want to go?"

"I don't know. Roma's I guess." I pop my knuckles, then say, "What did you think about what I told you about Lissy's dad?"

He taps the steering wheel. "Sounds like a normal dad that's paying close attention to his daughter's potential nanny."

When he puts it like that, it makes me seem stupid for worrying about Claude at all.

"Oh, okay. Well, that's good." I pull out my phone to preoccupy myself. Now that we've talked about my concerns about my new job, all that's left to talk about is the inevitable. And I don't know how to have a conversation about something I don't know an answer to.

His music plays quietly under the silence between us. Then I have a thought to avoid the inevitable kiss conversation.

"Why did you pick me up instead of one of Dipti's drivers?"

He clicks his blinker on and turns with his eyes fixed on the traffic. "I told her I would."

"How did you know I needed a ride?"

"I told her I wanted to pick you up after work." A strand of hair falls against his brow when he looks back before merging into the lane next to us. "She told me five o'clock. Then an hour later she told me there was a change of plans and you needed a ride immediately."

"She just lets you pick people up without consulting with them first?"

He brushes the loose strand back onto the top of his head with the rest of his styled hair. "No, but since we're *tackle buddies*, she was fine with it."

Right, I forgot she has no clue that we are more like strange acquaintances than friends.

"Any other questions or confessions?" he says with a

quick flash of an entertained look.

I shake my head. "No."

He nods once, then folds his mouth in like he's keeping himself from talking about the kiss too.

When he pulls up to Roma's apartment building, I give him a brisk *thank you* then exit the car as quickly as possible.

It's obvious he doesn't want to talk about the kiss because he never wanted it to happen in the first place. Or maybe he kisses girls like that all the time and it's completely normal for him to act this way afterward. That's probably why Birdie thought I was going to get my heart broken. He knows what kind of guy Jax is and knows he will play around with my heart.

I don't want any part of that.

But at the same time, I can't stop thinking about him.

Before I reach the entrance, Jax calls out to me.

I turn around to face him. His driver's door is open and he's standing next to his car. "I was thinking, since we're tackle buddies," he says this as he's leans onto his arms against the roof of his car. "And you don't have a car. And I do. I should probably get your number so you can let me know when to pick you up."

"That's okay, I can get Dipti to send a driver for me."

I cannot figure him out. His conversations seem so short with me, then he kisses me. Or he's the opposite and completely friendly like today when he picked me up and looked at me in a way I've never seen him look at me in the handful of encounters we've had. But if he was interested in me he would have talked about the inevitable, but he didn't mention the kiss at all. So he's not interested.

I have no idea what's going on inside this guy's head.

He deserts his car and meets me near the building.

"What are you doing?" I say unsure of his gesture while my heart is bouncing around between my lungs.

He hands his phone to me. "I need your number."

His blatant remark sends me into a rush of emotions. And to top it off, he balances himself by placing his arm up against the building and I get a quick whiff of his scent.

"Do you need some help putting your number into my phone?" he says, apparently aware of my sudden onset paralysis.

It takes me a moment to realize I'm holding his phone in my hands like an idiot, dazed by how good he smells. *And looks.*

"I don't know my number," I manage to say over my pounding pulse. It's like I'm entranced by his presence. I can't help but stare at him like he's a perfectly sculpted Greek statue.

"That's okay." He takes the phone from my hands, placing it into his pocket. "Here." He reaches his hand out to me. "I'll give you mine."

I hand him my phone without thinking—and without taking my eyes off him. While I watch as he puts his information in, I feel that feeling I had with him on Birdie's patio. The one that makes me want to drink him in.

He places my phone back into my hand and motions back to his car in a sort-of-jogging manner.

"See you later, tackle buddy," he calls out from his window before merging back into traffic.

I give him a half smile and a stiff wave.

I don't even have a second to steady all the gushing emotions inside of me before he disappears. I rush up to my room, quietly closing my bedroom door so as not to disturb Roma sleeping.

I flop onto my bed in exhaustion. It's mental exhaustion, but it's turning into physical exhaustion. Detoxing from my medication makes almost everything I do feel like a big deal. And since today I was accomplishing my goal of obtaining a job, my mind and my body feel like they've just defeated Mount Everest.

My phone vibrates.

When I pull it out, I have four texts.

One from Dipti,

Did your ride arrive? 😊

I quickly respond to keep her from worrying about today.

Yes, Jax took me home. Thank you for everything. I love my new job and can't wait to officially start.

One from Claude,

Thank you for your time today. Lissy enjoyed your company, and my wife is looking forward to meeting you soon. Let me know a time that works best for you.

After my conversation with Jax, I decided I've been looking too much into everything today and will give Claude another chance. Hopefully his wife doesn't double-book herself when I stop by again.

I reply,

Lissy is great. How does your schedule look for tomorrow afternoon?

He almost immediately responds,

See you tomorrow afternoon.

The last two messages are from Jax.

Hey tackle buddy.

And then,

Also, I wanted you to know, I don't normally kiss girls I'm not dating. Since I don't date, I don't kiss. I hope you don't think I'm lame. It's a lot easier to text about this than to say it out loud in person.

I knew he wanted to talk about it.
I smile and text back,

Me too. I've never done that before. It was sort of out of character for me. Hope it doesn't make our friendship weird.

He responds,

You made this friendship weird when you called us tackle buddies.

I hold my phone against my chest and let out quiet giddy laughter to myself.

Me: Want to chauffeur me back to my job tomorrow?
Jax: Come by my dad's work when you're ready.

I flip around and collapse against my pillow.
This day could not have turned out any better.

CHAPTER

SIX

Jaxon

Being friends with Paloma has been a lot easier than I imagined.

Once we got over the whole incident when she kissed me, it's been fun hanging out with her the last several weeks.

Speaking of Paloma.

I look at the time. I'm supposed to give her a ride to work today but she's late.

She hasn't been late since we started doing this. I send her a quick text.

"Hey, Jaxon," my dad says as he meets me at the front desk. "Could you make sure when my two o'clock arrives you put my grapeseed oil with eucalyptus on the stand?"

I nod, reaching for the eucalyptus oil under the counter.

"I'll get it ready now, I might not be back before they get here."

"Are you taking Paloma to work again?"

"Yeah," I say, rolling my sleeves up before I mix the oils together.

"How's she doing?" I can hear the concern in his voice.

I twist the lid onto the oil bottle and give it a quick shake before handing it to my dad. "She seems to be adjusting to her nannying job. I know she likes the little girl she's caring for."

My dad takes the bottle. "How is everything else going?"

I can tell there's more to this than I'm aware of. It seems my dad is not just a massage therapist for his clients. He's also a listening ear. Maybe even an unofficial therapist for a few clients. And I'm getting the sense that Paloma might be one of those clients.

"What are you getting at, Dad?"

Averting his eyes to the floor, he scratches at his chin with his thumb. This is the number one indication that he's trying to buy time before delivering some sort of bad news.

I move around the counter. "I already told you when I met her at the mall, she confessed some heavy stuff. And that she's living at Roma's because her mom kicked her out." I plop myself into one of the waiting chairs. "If you're going to ask me what her political stance is or if she believes in God or something, I don't know the answers." I say this half-joking.

He keeps his eyes on me without saying anything.

I relax my neck on the back of the chair, rolling my head to face him. "I have a feeling you're trying not to break some sort of confidentiality code right now."

He lets out an exhale before saying, "Jaxon, you know I would tell you if I could."

I shrug. "It's fine. Maybe next time you might try to do a better job at pretending like you don't know what's going on with her." I twist my face. "You know?"

"Just be a good friend and be patient with her."

I throw up a salute to him. "Besides Birdie, I'm the closest thing she has to a best friend." I shift my eyes to my phone and send Paloma another text.

"Alright, good." He points the grapeseed oil at me and says, "I better leave this in my two o'clock's room before I forget."

I lift myself from the chair. "I'll be back later."

"Don't forget you're still a teenager with homework."

"It's already done," I say, pushing through the entrance doors. "Aside from literature, because it's boring."

My dad gives me a wave and makes sure I hear him say, "School, then work, then friends. In that order," before I'm completely out of the building.

I've already sent two texts to Paloma without a reply. Since I'm on my way to get her now, I figure a phone call is necessary.

It goes straight to voicemail.

So, her phone died and she's either sleeping in or she lost track of time.

I'm not certain which apartment is Roma's. I've dropped off a pressure point ball and a heat pad on two different occasions for Roma, so I've been to her apartment. And I know what floor she's on. But now that I'm inside the building and looking at the doors, I can't remember which door belongs to her.

I don't want to bother my dad with asking what her apartment number is. He's working anyway and won't get the message in time.

I decide to walk down the hallway in hopes it will jog my memory.

One door sounds like it's running a daycare on the other side. I don't remember hearing that the last couple of times, so I have a good feeling Roma was farther down the hall.

The elevator dings and an older gentleman emerges as the doors spread open. Hopefully this guy can help me find Roma's apartment.

I look at my phone to check the time. If I don't get Paloma on the road soon, she's going to be late for work.

The man is between me and the daycare door when I wave and approach him.

"Excuse me?" I say.

He fumbles with his lock. "Stay away," he says as his eyes flash between me closing in on him and his rattling doorknob.

"No, it's not like that," I hold my hands up in surrender, "I was hoping you could help me find a woman named—"

Before I can finish, he rushes into his apartment, slamming the door behind him. So much for asking him for help. I don't think that I'm that unapproachable, but apparently I'm intimidating enough to scare that man.

To my amazement, Roma walks out of her apartment just as I was ready to start banging on doors one by one until I found hers.

"Hey, Roma," I approach her quickly before she sees me. There's literally no time to waste now.

When she turns to face me, the stern expression on her face quickly lifts into a smile when she sees it's me. "Jax, hi," she searches me as if she's expecting me to bring her another relaxing aide from my dad.

I point to her apartment. "Paloma isn't home, is she?"

Roma frowns, her eyes search her door in thought. "You know, I'm not sure. I got off work at seven this morning and went straight to bed. I barely had a second to make coffee. I was just heading out to my appointment with your father." She pushes the door open for me. "I haven't seen her, but that doesn't mean she's not in her room."

"You don't mind if I—" I let my words linger in hopes she invites me in.

She moves aside. "Not at all. I'm in a hurry though, so I'm going to go. Just make sure you lock the door when you leave."

I smile politely. "Will do. Thanks, Roma."

She closes the door behind me. I stand in the living room, scanning what I can see of the apartment. I've never been passed the entrance, so I'm not certain where the bedrooms are located.

I find an open door on the far side of the living room. "Paloma?" The room is pitch black, but when I turn the light on, I quickly realize it's Roma's room. She must have black out curtains over the windows to help her sleep during the day.

I close the door and make my way to the other side of the apartment. There's a small hallway with an open bathroom door and a closed bedroom door.

I'm confident this must be Paloma's room and it makes me feel nervous that I might surprise her. Or scare her. I don't want her to think an intruder is in the house.

I gently knock.

No answer.

I knock a little louder. "Paloma? It's Jax. Are you in there?"

Nothing.

If she's not home, where is she?

I inhale deeply before deciding I'm going to brave whatever is on the other side of the door. I push out a breath of air and swing the door open. But what I find is even more distressing than standing on the other side of the door was.

The curtains are drawn. They don't have the same blackout affect that the curtains do in Roma's room. There's enough light beaming through the window that I can see Paloma across her bed on her side with her knees pulled into her chest.

And she's not asleep.

She's crying.

I make my way to her bedside, squatting down so our faces are level.

At first, I don't say anything. I take in the disheartening sight of her. I can see her pillow is dampened with tears and her face seems so hallow, expressionless. I'm not sure she's even mentally connected to her body right now.

"Paloma?" I whisper.

Her eyes stay fixed on nothing in particular. But at the same time, they are fixed on something deep in her thoughts.

I stand up and open the curtains, allowing the light to fill the cold parts of her room, and her mind.

"You're going to be late for work," I say, sitting on the edge of her bed.

She doesn't move.

She doesn't speak.

If it wasn't for the minor rise and fall of her body, I might not know she was breathing.

This sort of thing would probably alarm most people. But I'm more familiar with it than Paloma will ever understand.

"I tried to call before I came over," I say, smoothing the sheet with my hand. "But since it went straight to voicemail, I decided to check on you."

I want her to say something snarky.

I want her to hit my arm with the back of her hand and say how dare I come into her room uninvited.

I want her to be okay.

But, she's not.

I know *this* is what my dad couldn't tell me.

I understand now that he was trying to warn me of *this*.

I don't know exactly what has happened to push Paloma into this daunting state, but I know she's in no condition to be in charge of Lissy or herself today.

I text Dipti,

Paloma is sick today and can't find her phone. She wanted to make sure the Laurent family knew she wouldn't be able to make it to work. Could you relay that information for her?

It's not a real lie. Paloma is sick. Maybe not in the physically ill way most people, and probably Dipti, would think. But she is sick. She's suffering and mentally sick from something. What has her here, I don't know. But I'm going to find out.

She's become a friend to me. I can't deny that I care about her. And because I feel more than qualified for this situation, I'm going to help her.

I lay across the bed near Paloma without touching her. For several minutes I watch her breathing as her back gently rises with each inhale.

I get a text.

It's from Dipti,

Not a problem. I've let the family know. I hope she feels better soon. Let me know if she needs anything!

I don't know how Dipti became like a second-mom to me, but I'm grateful for her. And now that I've known her for so many years I can't imagine life without her genuine kindness and generosity. I really don't deserve her. And right now, I feel guilty that I'm not being completely honest with her about Paloma's situation.

Because I know what's going on with Paloma.

I know that vacant look in her eyes.

I know the uncontrollable draining of tears.

I know the inability to speak.

I also know, there is hope. And there's another side to this numbness she's feeling.

And I want her to know that there's more. That's why I lift my head up onto my arm and scoot a little closer to her.

"You're not alone, Paloma." I pull the strands of hair plastered to her dampened cheeks out of her face. "I'm right here with you."

She's still; motionless.

"Paloma," I swallow hard, knowing what I'm about to do could either make our friendship stronger or force us apart. "I'm going to hug you, so if you don't want me to hug you, you should tell me right now."

She doesn't move or speak.

"My arms are wrapping around you." I tuck one hand under her head and the other around her arm and torso.

She lays limp in her same position.

"I'm getting closer to you and I'm going to apply moderate hugging pressure." I pull her closer to me and hug her. Her head is tucked under my chin, but her matted hair sticks up into my face. It smells like purple, if purple were a scent.

Her body feels as vacant as her eyes. I don't even think she cares that I'm holding her in my arms—or notices me at all for that matter.

I speak quietly against her temple. "If you get it out of your head, you'll feel better." I feel her tense in my arms when I say this, pulling her knees a little bit closer to her chest. "It's a matter of choice. You have to *want* to get out of this."

She sucks in a deep shuddered breath.

I hope that's an indication of some progress.

I keep my voice low. "I know it feels like you can't. But you can." I'm feeling the familiar sixth sense I had about her when I first hugged her at the mall.

Her voice is nasally from crying when she says, "I'm not strong enough."

I can't help but smile. Even though she thinks she can't, at least she's talking. If I can keep her coming up from this, she'll get out of the pit sooner than she thinks.

"What's on your mind?" I say, my voice steady.

"I can't do this, Jax."

"You can."

"You don't understand."

"I think I understand better than you think."

This sends her flying from her resting spot under my arms to a standing position on the floor.

It surprises me, but also gives me some hope.

"You think you understand what I'm going through?"

There it is. The reaction I was looking for. Even though she's still crying, at least she's feeling emotions other than numb.

"Paloma, I understand what you're dealing with a lot more than you think." I scoot across the bed. Standing with her. My eyes fixed on hers. "I know you can't let yourself feel numb like that. I know it's unhealthy to lay in bed and skip work because you're physically incapable of moving, or speaking, or even turning your phone on and asking for help."

Her eyes narrow.

Honestly, I'm glad I'm getting a reaction out of her. Even if it is a heated one.

"You don't know anything about me," she says.

I tip my chin. "I know you never learned to ride a bike. I know you own three pairs of jeans. I know you hate pizza."

She crosses her arms and shifts her weight to one hip. "That's nothing."

So, she wants to do this the hard way.

"Alright, I'm not going to hold back."

I watch her eyes flutter when I say this, as if she regrets pressing me.

I give her a moment to change her mind. When she doesn't, I say, "You feel alone. You feel like a burden to everyone you meet. You don't want to get too close because you're afraid people will leave. Somedays you wake up feeling like the world would be better without you. Today is one of those days. You just want it to be over. You want it to end. You feel nothing and everything. And you think it's too much. You think you couldn't possibly matter to anyone enough to live another day."

The tears well into her eyes as she clenches her jaw, trying to keep the tears from escaping.

I hate that I'm right about how she feels.

I take a step, closing the space between us. "But the world would suck without you."

When she blinks, the tears drop down her face and hit the floor.

She hits my chest with her hand, but it's so weak and broken that I don't feel anything. She covers her face with her hands. And sobs.

I watch her helplessly. My heart is drowning in the

broken cracks of her heart.

I quickly remind myself I can't feel this way about her. We agreed to be friends. We're tackle buddies. Our conversations are light and sarcastic.

But this moment is returning all those feelings I felt for her at the mall, and when she kissed me on Birdie's patio, and when she told me she was worried about how friendly Lissy's dad was.

I feel hurt for her.

I feel jealousy.

I feel protection.

I feel responsibility.

I feel the stupid tugging at my soul again.

It's like I'm fighting with myself. Half of me wants to let her in. The other half wants to let her go. And another part of me wants to try and make this friendship work because she is really cool, and I like hanging out with her. But how do I tell her that if I let her in, she's going to get hurt? How do I fall for her, knowing it's going to end in disaster?

She drops her head to my chest.

Without hesitation, I close my arms around her. "I'm sorry, you're feeling so crappy today."

She backs away, I release my grip, and she sits on her bed. "I should probably text Claude," she says with a sniff, then picks up her phone from the nightstand and turns it on.

I sit next to her. Not sure if I'm going to regret being so compassionate towards her later. "I took care of it."

She shoots me a look. "How?"

"I talked to Dipti."

She sets her phone back on the nightstand. "Oh," she clasps her hands between her knees. "You didn't have to do that."

I smile. "That's what tackle buddies are for," I say, nudging her with my shoulder.

Before I can decide if her expression is welcoming or hostile, she's closed the space between us. I can't look away from her. It's as if she has a hold over my ability to control my own movements. And despite my inability to move away from her, I cave to her yearning gaze when she kisses me. *Again.*

Why do I keep letting this happen? I know what's happening. I know she feels that same connection I do. But why can't she deny it like I'm trying to do? Why is she making it impossible to be around her?

Maybe she misinterpreted my hug. I only hugged her because I knew how much she needed it.

I thought I was clear that we are just friends. Tackle buddies. Nothing more. And friends are allowed to hug, aren't they?

Apparently, we are the type of friends that shouldn't be left in a room alone since we can't keep ourselves away from each other.

I use every ounce of strength to pull away from her.

"Why are you kissing me again?"

She's inches from my face when she says, "I don't know. I don't know what's wrong with me."

The light flicks on and Paloma jumps away from me.

"I know." Roma is standing in the bedroom doorway. I completely forgot she said she was coming back after her massage.

I rise from the bed, waving my hands in front of me. "Roma, this is not what it looks like."

"Oh, but it is," she says. She doesn't seem upset, but she doesn't seem happy either.

I clasp my hands around the back of my neck. "I'm so sorry. I honestly came here to give her a ride, but she was just so sad and—"

"And you two thought a good old fashion make-out session would cure the blues?"

Who even calls it that anymore?

I'm speechless.

Paloma is speechless.

Roma is completely unimpressed.

She flicks the light off. And before exiting the room she says, "Next time, take your hormones somewhere else."

"Yes, Ma'am," I say.

Yep, Roma just made it to the official respect list. It's the same list that Aatmay is on. And since I'm now afraid of Roma in the same way I'm afraid of Aatmay, I'm probably going to refer to her as *Ma'am* until I die.

After Roma retreats to her room, I turn to Paloma who looks equally mortified and stunned.

"Want to get out of here?" I trace her arm with my finger. "Some fresh air might help."

She cocks her head at me. "Fresh air? In the city?"

I smile. "I know a place with some real fresh air."

CHAPTER

SEVEN

Paloma

I hang my hand out the window as Jax pulls down a dirt road lined with trees.

"Are you ever going to tell me where you're taking me?"

He taps his steering wheel with his thumbs as he grins from the side of his mouth. "Didn't anyone ever tell you how a surprise works?"

"Nope." I peel my eyes from his grinning face, and look out my open window. "I've been surprised by you randomly showing up in my life more than I ever was surprised as a kid."

"That's super sad." His tone lets me know he's being serious.

"It's fine."

He stops the car and faces me. I've noticed this is

becoming a normal occurrence for him when he wants my undivided attention while we're in the car.

"Why do you always say that about everything?" he says.

I scan the empty dirt road ahead of us as I gather my thoughts. "Because it is fine. I didn't experience surprises. It's not a big deal."

"That's not why you're saying it." His crystal eyes are piercing into mine when he says this. It's making my guard go up.

I slap my hands on my thighs. "Okay, why am I saying it then?" How was I just kissing him an hour ago and now I'm so irritated by him?

He drops his head and inhales deeply.

I'm about to jump out of the car and walk back to Dallas. I'm not sure if it's because Jax is acting superior when he made it very apparent that he understood my vulnerable state this morning. Or maybe I want to flee because I have a slight headache from crying for the last twenty-four hours. Or maybe it's because I don't want to be in this conversation and the only way I know how to end it is to leave.

"You minimize," he says gently with his head still down.

I don't know where he gets off telling me the reasons why I do things.

He shows up, uninvited, unannounced, in my room when I'm feeling low in the same way he showed up at my work to pick me up. I'm the normal one in this friendship—relationship—whatever it is.

Normally when I'm down, I just take a day off to feel sorry for myself and once I crash from exhaustion, I wake up feeling like myself again. It's just a part of my life. It's normal. But, Jax has the audacity to force me out of my dark place and decides to take me out of the city and on a backroad just so he can tell me I don't mean I'm fine when I say I'm fine.

"I do not minimize," I say.

He looks up at me, but I keep my eyes forward. I know if I look at him, I'm going to have a war within myself on whether I should exit the vehicle or devour him again.

"Listen, Paloma." He puts the car back into gear and pulls down the road again. "I'm not trying to offend you."

"Well, try harder."

He laughs. But I wasn't trying to be funny, so I cross my arms to let him know he's irritating me.

"Can I ask you something without you getting all heated and weird?"

I purse my lips and raise my eyebrows when he looks at me as an indication for him to continue.

"Why didn't you learn to ride a bike?"

That's not what I was expecting.

I was preparing to discuss the minimizing he thinks I do. And any uncomfortable conversation I imagined having, was somewhere between the subjects of my dark breakdown or the second time I kissed him without warning. But asking me about my childhood is something I am not prepared to talk about.

"Well?" he says.

I force my embarrassment down, and pretend I'm not bothered. "No reason. I just wasn't taught."

"Minimizing."

I scoff. "I am not."

He lifts his eyebrow and glances at me briefly. "You are. It's not normal for a kid to not learn to ride a bike."

"It's normal for me."

"Why?" He traces my arm with his finger in the same way he did in my bedroom. "Do you have vertigo?"

"I don't even know what that is." I unfold my arms and

let him trace his finger down my forearm and into my hand.

There's something so calming about his touch. His presence, on the other hand, has the ability to infuriate me in a split second. But his touch is steady and reassuring.

He clasps his hand around mine when he says, "It's a balance issue. If you have vertigo, it makes it hard to ride a bike."

"It wasn't because of vertigo," I lose my voice on the last word because all my emotions are stuck in my throat.

I look at Jax to see what sort of emotions are plaguing his ability to communicate, but he's fine. More than fine. He's completely okay with the fact that we're holding hands and having a conversation.

Why didn't I ever feel this way when I was with Levi? Levi never once made me feel like my brain had escaped me, or that my heart grew so big it was about to burst through my sternum.

"Then what was it?" He gives my hand a gentle shake when he says this, which makes me smile.

I'm not sure I'm ready to answer him. So, I decide to flip the interrogation onto him. "How did you learn to ride a bike?"

He tilts his head in suspicion. "My dad taught me." He says this like it's an obvious answer. Which it is for most people. Just not for me.

"There you go." I shrug. "I didn't have a dad, so I didn't learn to ride a bike."

"Your mom didn't teach you?"

"Nope. She didn't have much time for things like that since she was working to support us."

"Where was your dad?"

I pull my mouth to the side and shrug. "No clue."

He gives me a pained look. "Sorry."

"It's fine." As soon as I let the words leave my mouth,

I regret it. Because I know what's coming.

"See!" he says. "Now you're minimizing something as tragic as growing up without learning to ride a bike because your mom was too busy and your dad wasn't around."

"It's just the cards life dished out to me."

He shakes his head. "That's not an excuse to minimize." He looks at me. "You were dealt a crappy hand, but it doesn't mean it's *fine*."

"Well, there's nothing I can do about it now." Which he can't argue with. "So, it is fine."

"Paloma," he says through a laugh full of disbelief at my incessancy. "You can be *fine*, without actually being fine." He pierces me with his eyes again. "Today was a prime example of that."

It feels as if his eyes didn't just pierce mine, but they shot straight to my heart.

I can't even defend myself because he's right. My less-than-ideal childhood still affects me. I'm fine most days, but some days it gets heavy and catches up with me; then, I'm not fine.

Like today.

"So, you don't eat pizza?" He pulls around a bend and suddenly we're in the smallest town I've ever seen. Which says a lot since I grew up in a town of 8,000 people. "Anything else you don't eat?"

I shake my head. "Nope, pizza is my only aversion."

"Perfect," he says, releasing my hand and pulling up next to what looks like a 1940's post war house that hasn't been renovated in decades.

"I hope this isn't the surprise," I say.

He puts the car in park and quickly jumps out to run to my side and open the door for me.

"It is," he says, then his expression falls. "Have some faith, huh?"

I lift my hands in surrender. "Fine, can I at least know where we are."

"You'll see," he says, holding my hand again as he guides me to the entrance.

It's as if he doesn't want to do anything without holding my hand, and it forces me to catch my breath.

I'm trying to ignore the creaking steps that feel as if the wood is going to collapse under my feet, when I notice something.

"There's a porch swing," I point out.

He stops in his tracks and turns to face the swing. "There it is, in all its glory." He says this like it's an inside joke I'm supposed to understand.

"I love porch swings," I say. "I mean, I love the idea of porch swings. I've never actually sat on one."

His face twists into disbelief. "That is astounding."

He guides me to the swing.

"Sit," he says.

I do as he instructs.

He kicks back and I lift my feet from the wooden porch-deck.

We swing back and forth for a moment, then he says, "Well? How does it feel?"

"It's everything I dreamed of." I give him a look of gratitude, but I'm surprised to see his expression. It's full of want and desire.

"Glad I could make one of your dreams come true," he says leaning into my personal space.

I'm about to give in to his yearning expression when the screen-door opens, and slaps closed.

Jax leaves the porch swing so abruptly that it nearly catapults me off.

"Mamaw," Jax says as he wraps his arms around a frail white-haired lady with a cane.

She lets out a gentle raspy laugh. "Oh, Jaxon, you should have called. I would have made you a pecan pie."

"That's alright, Mamaw." He motions in my direction. "This is Paloma. We came to get some fresh air."

She smiles at me, and says, "There's no fresher air in Texas than where you're sittin' right now."

I smile politely and stand to meet them on the other side of the porch.

"This is my mamaw, Mildred Ferrington," Jax says, with his arm around her shoulders, which are barely level with his torso.

"It's nice to meet you, Mrs. Ferrington." I'm not sure if I should have called her Mildred or Mamaw instead.

She grins a bright denture grin, and as if she can read my mind, she says, "You can call me Mamaw, honey."

I nod. Folding my mouth together because I'm trying not to laugh at Jax's stunned expression. He seems genuinely surprised Mamaw invited me to call her that. Maybe Mamaw isn't normally this welcoming.

Mamaw turns back to the screen-door, holding it open for us. "Well, ya'll come in and keep me company. You can get some fresh air when I take my nap."

I follow Jax into the vintage house. It's decorated in everything I would imagine a southern grandma in a tiny town to own.

I quickly notice a painting of an old guy praying that's hanging above the dining room table. I won't hold it against Mamaw that she might be religious since most people her age are.

In the kitchen, Jax begins rummaging around in the cupboards and refrigerator.

"Mamaw, where's all your food?"

Mamaw grunts as she sits down in one of the wooden dining room chairs. "I don't have any."

Jax let's out perplexed laughter, followed by a scoff when she doesn't elaborate. He looks at her blankly, then says, "Mamaw, you have to eat."

She raises her index finger. "I didn't say I wasn't eating, now, did I?"

Jax takes Mamaw's hands in his and squats down in front of her. His gesture and gentle concern for his grandma has me on the edge of swooning.

"Do you think it's time to let this place go and move in with us?" he says gently.

She shakes her head and slaps his hand. "I'm eighty-one years old. I can take care of myself."

"I'm not sure that's true. Your fridge is empty."

She glares at him, but I smile because her narrowed eyes and angry face are the cutest combination I've ever seen.

"I'm old," she says, "not senile."

Jax takes her hand in his again. "Then what are you eating?"

She relaxes her expression. "You're not giving this up, are you?"

"Nope," he says.

She lets out a sigh, before saying, "Mandy brings me breakfast and lunch, and I have supper at the senior citizen center."

Jax lets out a breath of relief.

She pats his arm. "Like I said, if I knew you were comin' I would have baked you a pecan pie so you had something to eat."

"I get it, Mamaw. I'll call next time."

She grins at him. "Good." She turns her posture toward me, and says, "Now, tell me about yourself, honey. I hope you're not hanging around my grandson because you're one of those groupies obsessed with his YouTube channel."

I nearly choke on my laughter.

Jax shakes his head with a smile. "Mamaw…" he says with warning.

"Well, I don't know," she says. "You've never brought anyone around for a visit. Besides that scrawny boy with an attitude."

"Birdie?" I say with interest. "You've brought Birdie here?" I say to Jax.

He finally takes a seat in the chair next to me. "Yeah, countless times and for some reason Mamaw still can't remember his name."

Mamaw leans her cane against the table. "He talks too much about the YouTube channel and all the groupies."

I cover my laughter with my hand.

Jax gives me a smile, then to Mamaw he says, "We don't have any groupies. I told you *followers* and *groupies* are very different things. And to be clear, Paloma is neither of them."

Mamaw gives me a bright denture smile again. I'm starting to think she only smiles like this when she's genuinely pleased about something. And in this case, it's because she must really like me.

"What do you think of his YouTube?" she says to me.

"I don't know," I shrug. "I've never seen any of his videos."

"You should," she says. "They're inspiring. And I would still think that even if it weren't my grandson in the videos."

I tilt my chin, and smile at Jax. "Well, I know what I'm doing later."

"You don't have to," he says.

The doorbell rings, pulling Mamaw from her chair.

"I can get it," Jax says as he makes his way in front of Mamaw.

"Alright, honey," she says, but continues to follow him to the entrance.

I keep seated and trace the lines on the table to keep myself from nervously pressing on my cuticles.

I hear happy chatter coming from the living room, but when Jax comes back to the table his face is flushed and he gives me an apologetic look.

Mamaw strolls in, followed closely behind by a gorgeous, long-legged girl carrying a tinfoil covered plate.

"I would have brought extra if I had known you had company," the long-legged person says.

Mamaw faces her. "I would have baked a pie if I had known they were comin'."

Long-legs places the meal on the table and reaches her hand out to me when she catches my eyes. "I'm Mandy."

"Paloma." I shake her hand.

I glance at Jax who looks more out of place than me right now.

Mandy flips her blond hair over her shoulder. "I can bring a couple more plates if ya'll are hungry."

I start to accept her offer but Jax cuts me off, and says, "We're not hungry."

I look between Mandy and Jax. Mandy's expression is hurt and Jax's expression is full of anguish.

I'm starting to get the feeling something happened between them and that's why he's acting so weird.

"Okay," Mandy says. She flashes me a smile, and says, "It was nice meeting you, Paloma."

I give her a somber grin.

Mamaw pulls the foil off her plate and says, "Thanks for lunch, honey. Tell your mama to come visit me sometime."

"I will," she says. She waves before exiting. "Bye, ya'll."

Mamaw and I wave back.

Just as Jax's posture starts to relax, Mandy reappears in the dining room. "That reminds me," she says to Jax. "How's your mom doing?"

When I face Jax, the color drains from his face and his eyes are boring into Mandy.

From what I've gathered, Jax doesn't seem like an angry or violent person. But the way he thrusts himself from the table has me rethinking that.

"Come on," he says, placing his hand on Mandy's back and coaxing her out of the house.

My throat goes dry. I feel like Jax inserted me into his life too quickly and now he's regretting it. Maybe this has something to do with what Birdie was warning me about. Maybe this encounter with Mandy is showing the real side of Jax, and he's really not the kind, free-hugs-giving guy I thought he was.

I'm tempted to go ask Mandy what sort of guy I'm really hanging out with. It seems like she would be a better source of information than any.

Mamaw takes a bite of her green beans, and says, "Are you sure you're not hungry?"

I hear the muffled conversation between Jax and Mandy outside and wish I hadn't allowed myself to witness the history in this family. I'm obviously an outsider and don't belong here.

"I'm good," I say, pressing my cuticles under the table.

The familiar feeling of being a burden is entering my core. It's inevitable. No matter where I go, or who I become friends with, I always turn out to be more baggage than they want to carry around. Even my own mother got tired of me.

"He hasn't told you, has he?" Mamaw says.

I lift my gaze to meet her concerned expression.

I shake my head. "About what?"

Mamaw's eyes crinkle in the corners when she smiles. "I like you, honey, and I think Jaxon does too. You seem like a nice girl," she plucks another green bean with her fork, "but I can see you're also a little skittish."

I suck in a sharp breath. Shocked she can read me better than I can read myself.

She adjusts her glasses, then leans across the table closer to me. "I don't know what your intentions are, but I know my grandson and I know his intentions. Jaxon never brings girls around. Let that speak for itself."

I have a feeling she's trying to tell me to bail now and save Jax the heartache, or commit.

"What about her?" I say, averting my eyes, and immediately regretting sounding like a jealous girlfriend.

She points her fork behind herself. "Mandy?" She laughs, "She lives down the street. Jaxon and Dillon used to spend their summers here. Mandy was the only kid their age in town, so they played together."

I smile at her reassurance, then say, "Is Dillon his cousin?"

She creases her forehead. "Dillon was Jaxon's brother."

"Was?"

The screen door slaps closed and Jax appears. "Ready?" he says to me.

I'm not sure I want to go anywhere with him now.

He has a brother he's never mentioned.

He seemed outraged by Mandy's presence for no apparent reason.

He refused lunch for us; when I was hungry and I'm sure he knew it.

Mamaw takes a last bite and hands her plate to Jax. "You haven't told Paloma about Dillon?"

Jax rinses the plate in the sink for her. "Not yet, it hasn't come up."

Okay, so he intended to tell me. I guess I have been hoarding the attention and controlling our conversations to ensure they don't get too deep.

Mamaw gets up. "I'll show you," she says, waving me to follow her.

She takes me to her bedroom and pulls a photo from her nightstand. The only people I recognize are Jax and Pat. Granted they are the only family members I've met in Jax's family, until now. The photo looks fairly recent since Jax and Pat look the same as they do now. I'm guessing the woman is their mom, and the other guy must be Jax's brother.

"That's Dillon," she says rubbing her finger across his face. "He was nine months younger than Jaxon. You know what they call that when siblings are born nine months apart?"

I shake my head.

"Irish twins." She gleams down at the photo.

"What happened?" I say gently, knowing that there's a sad story behind the reason she said that Dillon *was* Jax's brother.

She inhales deeply, before she says, "Dillon was different than Jaxon. He stayed in public school after Jaxon switched to online school. He loved sports and was always happy. Just a bright star, so full of life and energy." Her face falls. "But he got mixed up with the wrong crowd."

I don't know how she's keeping it together telling me this, because I'm holding back tears and I didn't even know him.

"His friends got him into doing things like drinking and experimenting with drugs. I know Pat and Bethany did what they thought was best, but in the end, it killed him. It's unfortunate they have to live with that reality every day of the rest of their lives."

I hold my hand against my chest. I can tell it's still difficult for her to talk about. I'm not exactly sure how he died, but I don't want to press her.

She sets the photo down. "Bethany didn't take it too well. But I don't think anyone ever gets over losing their child."

I have no words for her.

When we turn to exit her bedroom, Jax is leaning against the doorway with his arms folded over his chest in a relaxed manner.

So, maybe I misjudged him. Again. I'm not sure why I keep looking for reasons not to like him, and leave. It's like he was saying this morning, how I try to leave before anyone can leave me or hurt me. I think there's a lot of truth behind that.

And the fact that he noticed that about me makes me want to let him in. But only a little bit.

Mamaw pats his shoulder. "I better get my nap in soon."

Jax hugs one arm around her. "We will probably be gone before you wake up."

"That's alright. I'm glad you stopped by." She hugs him. "Come back soon. Both of you."

"We will," he says to her while he glances at me with a smile.

I follow them outside, where Mamaw hugs Jax once more and says goodbye to us.

Before we reach the car, Jax takes my hand and pulls me in the opposite direction down, what's left of, a cracked and misshapen sidewalk. "We didn't come all this way without getting some fresh air."

I follow in stride with him, careful not to roll my ankle on the crumbling sidewalk.

"How many people live here?" I say.

He shrugs. "Probably, three-hundred."

"Three-hundred?" I say with surprise.

"Yep, and that's an exaggeration." He kicks a broken clump of cement out of our way. "It takes about thirteen minutes to circle the entire town on foot."

I smile. "We're going to have to circle around at least twenty times if I'm going to get my steps in."

He gives me a concerned look before realizing I'm joking and nudges my arm with his elbow playfully.

We listen to the birds in the trees and our footsteps for a minute. I wish I had brought my phone. Right now would be a perfect time to check it, not that there's any cell service out here.

I quickly notice the houses are all outdated, and I remember that Mandy lives in one of them. I can't help myself, and say, "So, where does Mandy live?"

"Mandy?" He lifts his eyebrow at me, then points back toward Mamaw's house. "The blue one two houses down from Mamaw."

"What happened with you guys today?"

He pulls his mouth to the side, then says, "She was nosing around about things that have nothing to do with her. She doesn't get to ask me about my family."

I'm not sure why it made him so upset when she asked about his mom.

"Were you guys—"

"No." He says with a laugh. "She wanted to be more than friends, but me and Dillon always thought of her more as an annoying sister." He looks down at me. "Plus, she's not my type."

That surprises me since Mandy basically looks like a life-size barbie doll.

"Dillon was better at tolerating her." He lowers his gaze as his body stiffens.

"I'm sorry about your brother by the way." I feel his hand tense in mine.

"You know," he exhales deeply, "Mamaw blames Dillon's friends and our parents." He shakes his head like he disagrees with her. "But it wasn't their fault. Dillon liked to party. He also liked to play football. Which caused a lot of injuries that needed pain management. So, with his coach's insistence, and the doctor's okay, my parents let him take pain killers."

I can't imagine how he's feeling. I've never met anyone that personally lost someone. Besides Candice, but her parents died when she was a baby. She doesn't even remember them. The wound Jax and his family experienced is more recent, and still healing.

I don't know what to say to him, so I keep walking and wait for him to continue.

His jaw tightens, and he clears his throat. "He, uh..." His voice cracks.

I can tell it might be too much for him to say, so I stop walking. Standing in front of him, I take his other hand in mine. Holding both of his hands in an attempt to comfort him.

"You don't have to tell me," I say.

His glistening eyes meet mine and I feel my heart crack for him.

He clears his throat again and says, "I'm okay." He releases his grip and runs his hand through his hair. "I haven't talked about it with anyone besides my parents. I never had to talk to Birdie because he knew. And you know Birdie, he's not much for serious stuff like talking about death."

I smile even though I know it probably reveals how sad I am for him more than it gives him any reassurance or comfort.

"I'm glad you're the one I'm talking to about him." He motions for us to continue walking.

"Me too," I say.

He smiles.

I follow him off the path and down a ridge.

"Dillon loved it down here." He points to the emerging pond in front of us. "We would swim here all day until Mamaw came down and got us for dinner. He was the one that liked to have fun. Sometimes it would get us into trouble, but most of the time it was simple, innocent, fun."

He stops walking and stares out at the pond.

I stand in the stillness of Dillon's memory while Jax takes his time to remember his brother.

"One night," he says after a moment passes. "He took the pain killers before a football game, and again after the game. Then he went out to a party. He didn't bother inviting me. Not because he didn't want me there, but because by that point, he knew I wouldn't go. I never got into the party scene like he did.

"But that night, I felt like something was off. I felt like I should have gone with him or tried to get him to stay in with me. But I ignored the feeling and let him go.

"The chronic use of pain killers mixed with the alcohol was lethal. He knew that could happen. We all knew it could happen. But you just don't think it will ever happen. You don't think bad things happen to you, until they do.

"The next morning, we got a call that he had…" He covers his mouth. He swallows hard and his voice is quiet when he says, "that he had died."

He presses his palms to his eyes and lets out a breath of air.

I'm not sure what to do. What if I try to comfort him and he rejects it? Maybe he just needs to be alone. I could walk back and wait at the car. I don't know him well enough to know what sort of solace he needs.

Then I remember this morning.

I touch his shoulder and say, "I'm going to hug you, so if you don't want me to, you need to tell me right now."

He lets out a laugh mixed with a cry.

"I'm putting my arms around you," I say.

He laughs harder, wrapping his arms around me.

He's already squeezing me harder than I am squeezing him, when I say, "Now I'm applying firm hugging pressure."

We're both laughing now.

After a moment passes, he releases me but keeps his hands on my waist. "Thanks."

"For what?"

I lock my eyes on his. Even though he just released his emotions, he looks happier more than sad or grieving.

"For being you," he says.

I bite the inside of my cheek because I don't know how to respond to him. I also don't know what I did that is so great. I don't even know who I really am, or what it is about me he's so grateful for.

"Are you hungry?" he says.

I nod, relieved he's finally ready to eat something.

He takes my hand for the fourth time today, and my heart darts around in my chest.

"We have two options." He holds up his hand and lifts one finger. "Wait for Mamaw to wake up and sneak into the senior citizen center with her for some free dinner, which I can't promise is going to be any good."

I laugh. "Or?"

He lifts a second finger. "Or, we meet my dad at my house for some tex-mex."

"Tex-mex sounds like it's worth waiting for," I say.

Part of me is nervous to eat with his parents. The last

time I had a meal with a guy's parents, I quickly learned that mom's do not like me.

I wish I could say I am curious to see how Jax's mom is going to react to me, but I'm not looking forward to the meeting at all.

CHAPTER

EIGHT

Jaxon

As I pull into the driveway, Paloma is asleep in the passenger's seat of my car. I twist the ring on my finger as I try to decide if I should wake her or let her continue sleeping after this long, intense day.

I get a text,

Birdie: I was just inspired by a baseball game for our next video.

Me: What were you doing at a baseball game?

Birdie: Don't worry, this idea is going to blow minds.

I snap a photo of Paloma sleeping and send it to Birdie.

Birdie: Spill the tea!

Me: Just got home from Mamaw's. We're having tex-mex if you want to come over.

Birdie: On my way.

Me: You can convince me how anything related to baseball is going to be a good idea for a video.

Paloma shifts in her seat, fluttering her eyes open.

"Hey," I say.

She stretches her arms over her head. "How long have we been sitting here?"

"Not long."

She flips around to check out my house. "This is where you live?"

I turn the car off and get out. "Yep." She follows me inside.

"Well, are you going to give me the grand tour?" she says, kicking her shoes off.

"Sure." I flick the lights on. "This is the living room."

"Nice." She continues to follow me.

"Kitchen," I spin around, "the dining room, bathroom down that way." I point above my head. "And the bedrooms are upstairs."

She bites her lip, holding back a smile. "Can I see your room?" Color rushes to her cheeks when she says this.

When she finally releases her smile, I reach out for her hand. "Sure." There's something reassuring about the way I make her nervous. Not that I want her to be nervous around me, but the fact that she cares enough about what I think of her to feel nervous makes me like her more.

I open my bedroom door, she's quick to mess with the things on my desk.

She points to my dresser. "You have a TV in your room."

"I do."

She plucks the string on my guitar. "You play?"

"No, it's just for decoration." I watch her to see if she notices I'm joking.

She fake laughs. "You're funny, I like you."

I know when she says she likes me, she doesn't mean it in a serious way, but it feels good to hear her say it nonetheless. Especially because I think I'm ready to admit to myself that I like her too.

The door shuts in the hallway. When I flip around, I see the physical therapist leaving my mom's bedroom.

I meet him in the hall. "How'd it go?"

He looks a bit exasperated. "Not great." He adjusts his bag. "She wasn't very cooperative today."

I tuck my hands into my pockets. "Is she still awake?"

He shakes his head. "I don't think so, and if she is I don't think she wants to see anyone."

"Alright." I nod. "See you next week."

He tells me goodbye as he rushes down the stairs and out the door. I don't blame him for getting out of here as quickly as possible; my mom can be a lot sometimes. Honestly, I'm surprised he hasn't quit yet.

"Your mom is here?" Paloma says with curiosity in her voice as she peeks around me in search of her. "Should I meet her?"

I give her a cheerless smile.

"Or not." Her face falls downcast.

I take her hands in mine. "I didn't mean it like that." I look back at my mom's closed door. "I want you to meet her, but not just yet."

"Why not?"

I release her hands and clasp mine behind my neck. "It's complicated."

She moves past me and walks down the stairs.

"Paloma, wait a second."

She stops before she gets to the bottom of the stairs. "I don't get you."

"I don't get you," I say.

She's so hot and cold I can't keep up with her emotions. I know she has some issues. But I thought we really connected today. I thought we both shared a lot of vulnerability that dropped her walls down. If she's just going to run away when something happens that makes her slightly uncomfortable, I'm not sure she's ready to meet my mom.

"Seriously?" she says.

I make my way down the stairs. "Yeah." I stand on the step above her. "You're constantly shutting off. Which is bizarre, since you're the one kissing me all the time."

Her jaw drops. "Are you kidding? How am I supposed to be serious about you when I can't trust you?"

That hits hard. I don't want her to feel like I haven't been transparent with her.

I gentle my voice. "You can trust me."

Her face twists in confusion. "You didn't tell me about your brother."

"It hadn't come up."

"You won't let me meet your mom."

"I will. I just need to make sure you're serious."

"Serious about what?"

I swallow hard. Knowing if I let her into my messed-up life, it might break her.

"Me," I say.

She looks down, which seems like she's second guessing all of this.

Her eyes flash up to mine. She presses at her fingers, before saying, "I don't want to get hurt."

I pull her to my chest. "I don't want you to either." She

looks up at me. "But things like trusting each other take time. I need to earn your trust, that doesn't happen in one day."

She nods.

I quickly add. "And I need to trust you're not going to run off every time something happens that you don't like."

She blows raspberries and pulls herself from my grip. "I don't run off *every time*," she says playfully.

The door opens, and my dad comes in with several bags hanging from his arm.

"Hey, you guys are already here. Good," he says. "I hope you're hungry, I bought way too much food."

"I'm starving," Paloma says, as she follows my dad to the kitchen.

"I can't stay long," Dad says. "I have a client this evening. But I didn't want to miss out on dinner with you two."

"That was really thoughtful," Paloma says. "You didn't have to do that."

"I'm still a dad. I had to make sure everyone was fed," he says.

I hand Paloma four plates to set the table, then help my dad unload the food.

The doorbell rings just as we take our seats.

"I'll get it," I say.

When I open the door, Birdie walks straight to the kitchen, ignoring me.

"Hello, to you too," I say with sarcasm.

He wraps his arms behind Paloma's shoulders, who is sitting at the table. "Heyyy, P., I've missed you," he says to her.

"Birdie, oh my gosh." She pats his arm. "Should I get you a plate?"

I take my seat, and point to the empty plate next to her.

"That's Birdie's plate."

She looks over at me as Birdie slips into his place.

"I thought your mom was joining us?" she says.

My dad and Birdie both share glances, then look at me. I can tell they're going to blurt out something I haven't prepared Paloma for yet. So, I quickly come up with an excuse.

"Physical therapy was tough today," I say. "Maybe another time."

I give my dad a begging look.

He must take the hint, since he raises his hands out to us and says, "Let's say grace."

I lock my hands with my dad's on one side, but Paloma is reluctant to reach for my hand.

When I look at her, she has an expression of betrayal covering her face. It's mixed with shock and disappointment. She's probably upset I don't want her to meet my mom yet.

Pushing my hand closer to her, I say quietly, "You can meet her another time, okay?"

I smile, letting her know she can trust me when I say that. But she doesn't smile back.

She finally takes my hand.

After my dad says grace, Paloma rips her hand from mine.

And my dad and Birdie must have noticed the aggression behind her action, since my dad opens his mouth to say something but Birdie interrupts with, "So, P., how was your visit with Mildred?"

"Who?" she says, tilting her head.

"Didn't you see Jax's grandmother today?" he says, then takes a bite of his taco.

She stirs her food with a fork. Keeping her eyes down, she says, "Oh I forgot her name was Mildred. She told me to call her Mamaw."

The table goes silent. Dad and Birdie both stop chewing and stare at her.

"Are you serious?" Birdie says.

She nods, finally taking a bite of her food.

"You must have made a real impression on her," my dad says. "She doesn't let anyone call her that." He points his fork at me briefly. "Besides her grandkids."

She shrugs. Still avoiding eye contact with us.

If she's going to be upset, she doesn't have to be rude to my dad and Birdie. They didn't do anything. I was the one that didn't want her to meet my mom yet. But it's not forever, just until I can trust she's not going to bolt when things get tough.

She may not be bolting right now, but she sure is acting like she wants to.

Dad finishes the last bite and takes his plate to rinse in the sink. "Well, I better get going. I don't want to be late for my client."

Paloma scoots her chair back and stands up like she's finished eating, but her plate is still covered with food.

"Where are you going?" I say before realizing how intrusive I sound.

She shoots me a flustered look. "Can I get a ride?" She's still looking at me when she says this but talking to my dad.

"Of course," my dad says. "Don't worry about cleaning your plate, we need to get going right now."

He takes her plate and sets it next to the sink, then motions for the door. Followed by Paloma. Who I realize is very upset with me.

Birdie huffs, then says, "You can't leave. I haven't told you guys about my new video idea yet."

"I'll get a recap later," she says with a forced smile.

I leave the table and stop her from following my dad

out the door. "What happened?" I say.

She tries to move past me. "Nothing."

I stand in front of her, blocking her in. "Can you look at me?"

She pushes out a puff of air from her nose, then lifts her gaze reluctantly.

"You're going to meet my mom some time, I promise."

She shifts her weight to one side. As if I said something wrong.

My dad calls from outside. "Hey, you two. We need to go."

I look back at him. "One second."

"Do you want to give her a ride?" he says.

Paloma pushes her way through me and out the door.

She must have her mind set on leaving. And not with me. Maybe she's overwhelmed by the entire day. It's understandable. I also hurt her ego by not introducing her to my mom. Plus, she's probably sleep deprived. She did look like she had been crying all night when I found her at Roma's.

Since it's been a long day, and she's already in the car. I decide to let her go.

I close the door then drag my hands down my face when I meet Birdie back at the table.

"What was that?" he says.

"I didn't want her to meet mom."

He nods. "Yeah, that will upset a girl for sure. Why didn't you?"

I dig my elbows into the table, running my hands through my hair. "I don't know. She's all over the place. When she's in a good mood, she's fun to be around. But it's like she looks for the smallest things to get upset about."

"Yeah, girls are moody like that." He takes his plate to

the sink. "But you're the one that swore off girls and then got wrapped up with one of the most complicated girls in the world."

"I thought you liked her?"

He leans against the counter. "I do. P. is my friend, don't get me wrong, but I'm not going to pretend like she's got her stuff together. Even you can see that."

I drop my head back. "What am I going to do?"

He taps the counter before pushing himself off and sitting in the chair next to me. "I know you don't want to hear this, but maybe you could go back to being friends before whatever this is between you guys gets any more complicated."

"I tried to be her friend." I roll my head over to look at him. "But there's something that draws me to her." I shake my head. "I can't be her friend, man. I just can't."

He lets a small laugh escape his mouth. "Then it sounds like you're going to have to talk to her." He pats my shoulder, "And give her a second to be mad at you before you do that."

I smile, then scoot my chair out to clean my plate at the sink.

Birdie is giving me a look when I turn around.

"What?" I say.

He holds his fingers at his temples before saying, "I get that you didn't want her to meet your mom yet. But have you told her about, *you know*?"

"No."

I know he's trying to be a good friend. I know he cares about Paloma the same way he cares about me. But if I'm not ready to let her meet my mom, I'm definitely not ready to tell her about that.

"Jax," he says this with disappointment. "You have to tell her. She deserves to know."

"I'm not ready. I don't trust her yet." I leave the kitchen for my bedroom.

He meets me at the stairs. "You better tell her before you get serious."

When I get to my bedroom, I flop onto my bed. "I know." I thrust my arms over my head, frustrated. "I know I need to tell her. I will. But I don't even know if she wants to be my girlfriend."

"Maybe it will help her decide if she wants to be your girlfriend."

I lift myself up onto my elbows. "I don't think she will want to."

"You have to let her make that decision for herself." He sits in front of my computer. "There's nothing to do about it now. So, come check this out."

He pulls up an animation he created. He usually makes an animation of his ideas before we put it into reality.

"You know," I say. "You could save yourself a lot of time if you just told me what it is, instead of showing me."

He narrows his eyes at me. "Remember how the video turned out when we didn't have an animation before we shot the college idea?"

I laugh. "Oh yeah, that was bad."

"Yeah, it was horrendous." He plays the animation. "So, we're sticking to what works. And this works."

I watch as a cartoon pirate sits in the audience of a baseball game.

But my mind is still on Paloma.

CHAPTER

NINE

Paloma

I'm not sure why I didn't try to get a ride from one of Dipti's drivers.

If I had, I could have completely avoided the situation I'm in right now. Which is sitting in the passenger's seat of Jax's car awkwardly avoiding a conversation about last night.

"What time do you get off work today?" he says.

I keep my eyes forward. "Late."

"If you tell me what time, I can pick you up."

I want him to pick me up, but I also don't. I want to like him, but I also don't. And I want to talk about the fact that his family is religious, religious as in praying-before-they-eat religious, but I also don't want to talk about it.

"Eight-thirty." I brush a few tangles out of the back of

my hair with my fingers. I don't have time to care much about my appearance when my mind is plagued by things that make my stomach twist and turn. Like falling for a kind, thoughtful, gorgeous guy that's *religious*.

I'm not going to make the same mistake again, like I did with Levi. I wish Candice was here to interpret this whole situation with Jax.

"I'll pick you up at eight-thirty, then," he says.

He doesn't have the radio on today, which usually helps drown out any awkward silences. But today, he seems content with the screaming silence between us.

After a moment, he says, "Do you want a piece of gum?"

"No."

He tosses a piece of gum into his mouth and the aroma of strawberries fills the car.

"Are you still mad I didn't introduce you to my mom?"

I flip my head around to look at him. I can feel my forehead crease as I pull my eyebrows together. "That's what you thought I was upset about?"

I was more relieved I didn't have to meet her last night. I'm not the type of girl that moms want their sons to hang out with. It's as if moms have the ability to see my messed-up life and all my issues before I can introduce myself. Moms want better than what I have to offer for their sons.

"Isn't it?" he says.

I shake my head. "No. I get that you want to wait. She must be important to you since you want to trust me before I meet her." I force a smile. "She must be really great too."

Or really depressed.

Who stays in their bedroom for a religious family dinner, unless they're depressed? I know all about hiding in my bed until the hopelessness passes. I can't think of any other reason she wouldn't come out of her room last night.

He glances at me. "Then what is it? You're obviously still upset since you've barely said two words to me since you got in the car."

I press at my cuticles, trying to decide if I should tell him the truth or not.

He gently brushes my hair out of my face and waits for me to look at him.

When I do, he says, "Whatever it is, it seems like it's probably a misunderstanding."

I press my mouth together, then say, "I don't know how to talk about it."

Which is true. I'm afraid if I say the truth, it will offend him. And I don't want to hurt his feelings. But at the same time, he's not who I thought he was. He hides details about his life, like the whole thing with his brother, and whatever is going on with his mom. He also treats me like I'm his girlfriend, but he doesn't seem to want to put any labels on us, since he hasn't brought up anything about being in a relationship at all. Which also seems to relate to what Birdie said about Jax breaking my heart.

I wish this was easier. I wish I was better at talking, and I wish I was better at choosing guys to be with.

"Well?" he says.

"I'm serious, I don't know how to say it."

He takes my hand in his, and I don't stop him. "Just say it," he says with a smile.

I guess I'll start at the beginning where religion first put me off. "Okay," *here we go*, "Before I came here, I was with this guy."

His hand tenses subtly in mine, and his expression falls firm.

"He was a jerk," I say. "My friend, Candice, warned me about him. But I wanted to be his girlfriend so bad, I didn't see it."

Jax nods in anticipation.

I shrug. "I think I just really wanted a boyfriend, and I knew he liked me, so it made it easy to date him. There was never a spark or real connection between us. His parents were really strict and basically kicked me to the curb when I reached out for help after everything with my mom."

I tuck my hair around my ears and quickly glance at him to see if what I'm about to say affects him. "But the thing I'm trying to tell you is, his family was religious. They were super judgey and they never liked me because I'm not religious."

I brace myself. Half expecting him to turn down a side street and come to a stop so he can give me an earful.

"So, you're worried that we're religious?"

Not the response I was expecting at all.

I turn in my seat so I can face him completely. "Aren't you?"

He smiles. "Paloma, you realize you could have told me this last night, right?"

"I didn't know how to say it."

He laughs.

"It's not funny. I'm still not sure I said it how I wanted to," I say, twisting my knuckle until it pops. "Your family is religious, and I can't go through that again."

He parts his mouth for a moment before saying, "I've never liked that word."

"What? Religious?"

He narrows his eyes at me. "Yeah, it sounds so formal and there's this negative connotation that society has connected to it."

"Well, that doesn't change the fact that your mamaw has religious stuff in her house and that your dad prayed before we had dinner last night."

He can't deny it. No matter what he feels about the word.

He shrugs with a laugh. "My family believes in God. That doesn't mean they are going to judge you or shame you or refuse to help you when you need help, like your ex's family. It's not up to my dad, or Mamaw, or me or anyone else to make you believe in God." He looks at me. "That's your decision. Not anyone else's."

My stomach drops. But not because I'm afraid or upset. It drops, because I can't believe he said that. I thought all religious people set themselves on a pedestal. Not allowing anyone else's views into their forefront. I thought they all judged and condemned everyone else, but Jax is making me rethink it all.

And I hope what he's saying is real.

"I don't know what happened with you and that guy," he says. "But I promise, I'm not going to do anything to hurt you. And I know my family won't either."

My breath is shuddered when I say, "Then why did Birdie say I was going to get my heart broken after I kissed you?"

He flashes me a concerned look.

"He said that to me on his patio when he saw us kiss." I remind him.

He pulls his hand from my grip and runs it through his hair. "I remember."

Suddenly, my phone vibrates in my lap. I flip it over to see who it is. "It's my attorney."

He nods.

I answer. "Hello?"

"Miss Smith?"

"Yes?"

I've sent in my petition for emancipation, so I've been waiting for a phone call so that I can get a court date. I'm hoping the attorney has good news, but the tone in his voice says otherwise.

He clears his throat. "It seems we're experiencing a slight dilemma with your petition."

"What does that mean?" When Mr. Grandstill gave me this attorney's phone number, he reassured me that he was the best. But I'm beginning to rethink that.

"You see, everything comes down to paperwork. And we seem to be having trouble locating any identification for you to prove you're sixteen."

"Almost, seventeen," I say, glancing at Jax and wondering if he can hear the other side of this conversation.

"Since you don't have any form of ID, we need your birth certificate."

I switch my phone to my other ear. "But I told you that's at my mom's house."

"I remember you saying that." He waits a moment before continuing, "Is there anyone that might be able to get it for you?"

"No," I say, wishing I was born a year earlier so I didn't have to deal with any of this. "Isn't there another way?"

"There is," he says. "You can order a new birth certificate online. But it takes a few months to process and mail."

I slump down in my seat. Feeling defeated for the millionth time with this impossible process.

"But we probably don't want to go that route with the time crunch we're on," he says. "Especially if you can get it from your mom's house and send it to me asap."

I let out a puff of air.

"Miss Smith?"

I don't say anything.

"I know this is difficult," he says. "Take some time to

think about it and get back to me when you make a decision."

"Okay," I say.

"The sooner the better. I'll talk to you soon." Then he hangs up before I can make any more frustrated noises.

"Everything okay?" Jax says.

I shake my head. "No." Then I push out a breath of air again, trying to keep myself from crying in defeat before I have to go to work.

He glances at me then back to the road. "What'd he say?"

"He said they need my birth certificate." I look at him. "But that's at my mom's house and there's no way she's going to give it to me."

"Sorry," he says, dropping his grip to the bottom of his steering wheel. "What happened with all that anyway?"

"I told you, she kicked me out." I'm not in the mood to elaborate on my mom's instability.

"Is there any other way to get it?"

I nod. "Yeah, I can order one online, but it takes a long time to get it in the mail. I could obtain emancipation if my mom would sign my petition, but there's no way that she'd go for that."

"Why not?" He turns down the street where the Laurent's live.

"She just wouldn't."

Before we come to a complete stop, Jax rests his hand on my leg.

"Hey," he says. "For whatever it's worth, I'm here if you need anything."

I smile. "Thanks, *tackle buddy*."

"We've got to come up with a better name to call ourselves," he says, pulling into the driveway. "Especially if you're going to be my girlfriend."

I suck in a rush of air. Stunned by what he just said. Does he realize what he just said?

He smiles at my instant reaction to his comment.

He totally knows what he just said.

"What? You don't want to by my girlfriend?"

I hold back my smile. "I mean, I do. But I thought you swore off girlfriends?"

He adjusts himself in his seat to face me better. "I've had a recent change of heart."

"Okay?" I'm in such shock I don't even know how to respond to him.

"So, just so we're clear," his eyes are darting between my eyes and my mouth, "If I asked you to be my girlfriend, you would say yes?"

I tilt my head in confusion. "Y-yes?" I thought this was him asking me to be his girlfriend.

"Perfect." He nods. "And just so we're clear, I haven't asked you to be my girlfriend yet."

I let a nervous laugh escape my throat. "Do you just need reassurance or something?"

"No, I think it's better if you sit with the idea for a while before committing."

I open the door but stay seated. I have to get going before I'm late to work. "It's not like we're getting married. I don't think I need a lot of time to think about it."

He flashes me a side grin that makes my stomach flutter. "I know big decisions can be scary for you, so I want you to feel comfortable and confident and, most of all, trust me before you make a decision to say yes." The fact that he cares more about my heart in all this has me swooning.

He takes my hand and kisses the back of it. Which is normally a corny gesture that would make me cringe. But for some reason, when Jax does it, it makes me feel good.

"I really need to go," I say with a waning to my voice.

He puts his car into gear as I exit. "I'll pick you up later, *soon-to-be-girlfriend*."

"That's dumber than *tackle buddy*," I say closing the door before he pulls away with a smile spread across his entire face.

If my heart wasn't racing so frantically in my chest, I might fall dead to the ground.

...

"Come out, come out, wherever you are," I call up the stairs to Lissy.

She loves to hide until I can find her. She's very good at it too.

Sometimes she hides for thirty minutes. Which is astonishing for a kid her age to sit still in one spot for that long.

"Marco!" I say.

I hear a rustling sound in the closet, then a muffled, "Polo," behind the door.

I make my footsteps heavy, then say, "I wonder where Lissy could be hiding?"

She quietly giggles on the other side of the closet door.

"Maybe she's hiding in the closet." I open the door and pretend not to see her behind a fur coat. "I swear I heard something in here."

She jumps into my arms, giggling. "I'm right here, Nanny!"

I hold her in my arms for a moment. "There you are, I thought I lost you."

When I set her down, she folds her arms and pouts her lip.

I tuck a loose curl behind her ear. "What is it?"

She taps her foot.

I place my hands on my hips. "Lissy, you know I'm not

a fairy godmother. I'm just a nanny." I drop my arms and kneel in front of her. "So I can't read your mind. You're going to have to tell me what's wrong."

She furrows her brow. "You swore, Nanny. It's not lady-like to swear."

I scrunch my face and tilt my head trying to remember swearing.

"I did?"

She nods.

"I didn't mean to," I tap my chin, "I honestly don't remember."

She flops her arms to her sides and lets out a sigh. "You said that you *swore* you heard something in the closet."

I smile. "Oh that," I reach for her hand, "I'm sorry, can you forgive me? I promise I won't swear ever again."

She mirrors my grin and says, "I forgive you."

After Lissy's bath, I read her *A Midsummer Night's Dream*, the children's addition, four times before she's ready to turn the light off.

She always asks me stay and hold her hand until she falls asleep. So I continue our agreement and hold her hand until her breathing grows heavy and I'm certain she's asleep.

I slip my hand out from hers and leave the door cracked open as I exit her bedroom.

I sit on the couch downstairs and scan the paintings decorating the walls. I'm sure they are from the artists at Claude's gallery.

He and Terra are there now for an art show he's putting on. I'm not sure how fun it is for Terra being in her second trimester of pregnancy. Although, an art show of any kind doesn't sound fun for anyone, pregnant or not. But I wouldn't know what sort of things Terra enjoys, since I still haven't met her yet.

My phone vibrates.

Jax: How's Lissy?
Me: Sleeping. How's it going with Birdie?
Jax: We're working on the next YouTube video idea.
Me: Sounds fun.
Jax: I think it's his best idea yet.

The front door unlocks, and I hear a woman's voice along with Claude's accented voice.

Me: The Laurent's are home early. Can you still pick me up?
Jax: Yeah, Birdie's ready for a coffee run anyway.
Me: Coffee at eight-thirty at night?
Jax: It's Birdie.

I laugh quietly at his text and leave my spot at the couch. I straighten my shirt and hope I look presentable. I'm assuming the woman with Claude is his wife. And despite my requests for Claude to schedule a meeting with both of them, this will be the first time I've met her since I've started working here.

"The contrast of Steph's work is too dull," the woman says to Claude as she kicks off her heels. Her accent is American, which for some reason fills me with relief. "I told her not to change her style after the last show. But what do I know, I'm just her agent. She must have—"

She stops talking once she sees I'm standing in the entryway.

"Hello," I say with a hopeful smile. If she doesn't like me, I'm out of a job. And from the snippets of her personality I've just overheard, she seems pretty difficult to please.

Claude rushes to my side, placing his hands on my shoulders in the no-awareness-of-personal-space way he does things, and says, "Paloma, this is my wife, Terra."

She smiles. Her grin is beautiful, just like everything else about her. Even her perfectly shaped pregnant belly, that seems more like an accessory to the skin-tight dress she's wearing than a place where an actual tiny human is growing, is beautiful. But, although her smile is perfect, I can tell she's not exactly thrilled to see me.

"And this," Claude says to Terra, "is Lissy's nanny, Paloma."

I hold out my hand and she takes it.

"Nice to finally meet you," I say.

She faces Claude and says, "Wow, Claude, I didn't realize you hired someone so young."

The feeling of being an unwanted burden starts to rise inside of my core.

Claude finally drops his hands from my shoulders and approaches Terra.

He lowers his voice and says, "She is the only one that has been able to keep up with Lissy."

Terra is still eyeing me. And they must think because I'm young I can't hear their *adult* conversation, since Terra says, "Was there really no one else?"

Claude shakes his head. "No one willing to come back."

I'm not sure why they had such a hard time finding a nanny, it's not like hanging out with Lissy is that hard. She literally follows a schedule that includes playtime for half the day. Who wouldn't want this job? It's cake.

Terra inhales deeply and places her hand on her stomach. "And Lissy likes her?"

I stand awkwardly pretending not to hear them as I inspect the wall mantel and the perfectly healthy plants decorating it.

To my relief, Claude says, "Lissy adores her."

Terra approaches me. "Well, whatever Lissy wants, Lissy gets. And I guess that includes a pretty, young nanny."

Then she makes her way up the stairs.

I've never been called pretty by another woman. Or had my youth held against me like being young is a violation of my nanny position.

Once she's out of eyesight, Claude lets out a breath of relief.

He faces me and says, "How was Lissy this evening?"

"She was great," I say. "She's always great." I add, making sure he knows how happy I make Lissy. Hopefully he will relay that information later to Terra during pillow talk.

"Good," he says. "She looks forward to seeing you." He locks his eyes on mine which automatically makes me take a step towards the door.

"Well, I'm going to wait for my ride outside. I'm sure you're both tired and ready for bed," I say, hovering my hand over the door handle. "And since I'm not working until midnight, don't worry about paying me for the evening." I might be sucking up a little, but I want to make sure Terra likes me.

I need her to like me. I need this job. I need the money, but I won't make any money if I don't have a job. And I genuinely like this one. So, I'll keep sucking up until I'm certain Terra likes me.

Claude clasps his hand around my arm briefly, before saying, "Thank you, Paloma, but that won't be necessary. We will pay you for the entire time we asked you to be here. In full."

"Okay, thanks." I quickly open the door to exit. I'm so

ready to get out of here.

"Paloma," he says before I can leave, "Do not worry about, Terra."

I smile politely. "I'm not worried." Which is the farthest thing from the truth. He must be aware of my random onset of sucking up tonight.

He pats my shoulder. I'm not sure I'll ever get used to the fact that he feels the need to constantly touch me when we're having a conversation.

"She will warm up to you once she sees how much Lissy enjoys your company," he says.

I open the door and step outside. "Good to know."

He takes the door, closing it slowly as he eyes me. "I will text you the days we will need you next week."

I nod. "See you later."

I wait on the porch for a while but feel weird that I'm outside while the Laurent's are in their house. So, I move to the curb at the edge of the street to wait for Jax and Birdie.

• • •

Even though Birdie insisted that I sit in the front seat, I sat in the back of Jax's car. I'm not in the mood to sit close to Jax, with our shoulders inches apart in front of Birdie, until I know what me and Jax are.

"So, when will you start filming?" I say.

Birdie shrugs, gulping down the last bit of his coffee. "There's a baseball game tomorrow," he says chewing at the straw from his drink.

Jax pulls into his driveway. "I hate sports," he mumbles to himself.

Birdie exits the car, and we follow. "You're going to have a blast and you know it."

Jax lifts his shoulders. "It's a good idea, but I hate my

part."

We kick our shoes off inside. I notice the door to Jax's mom's bedroom at the top of the stairs. It's closed, but there is a thin line of blue light beaming under the door. Maybe she will emerge when she hears us, and I'll finally get to meet her before Jax asks me to be his girlfriend.

I'm not sure why he wants to wait. He already knows I would say, *yes*.

"Let's show P. the costume you're going to wear," Birdie says heading for the stairs.

"Yeah, I want to see it."

"No way," Jax says he reaches for Birdie's shirt but misses while he tries to stop him from running up the stairs.

I laugh, watching as they scuffle before Birdie runs the rest of the way up the stairs. Jax is skipping stairs as he follows behind him.

I begin to climb the stairs before I realize Jax is tumbling down them.

It's as if his legs gave out as soon as he reached the top.

He gains enough momentum to knock me off my feet mid-stair climb. I'm not even sure what's happened when Birdie hurries to meet us at the bottom of the stairs.

"Jax," Birdie says, pulling his arm and dragging him off me. "Come on, Jax."

I sit up.

"Are you okay, P.?" Birdie says with panic in his voice.

I nod. I nod because I'm not hurt. If Birdie re-worded his question, I might have answered differently since I'm unsure of what is happening right now.

"Good." He turns his frantic attention to Jax again, slapping at his cheeks rapidly. "Come on, Jax. Wake up."

"Should we call Pat?" I pull my phone out of my pocket, "Or an ambulance?"

"No, he'll be fine," Birdie says, he's pinching Jax's arm now.

My pulse begins to accelerate. I'm starting to feel scared. "What if he has a concussion or something?"

"That's not it."

"I think we should call his dad."

I feel Jax's hand wrap around my wrist. I look at his hand, then to his eyes. They are slightly opened and he's smirking.

"You don't need to call my dad, I'm fine."

Birdie slumps back. When he lets out a breath of relief it comes out as a laugh. "You suck, you know that?"

I'm so confused right now.

"Don't tell me that was a joke." I gently push his arm away and stand. "Because if it was, you're pretty messed up."

Jax sits up on his elbows. "It wasn't a joke. I just got lightheaded when I ran up the stairs."

"So lightheaded that you passed out and fell down the stairs?" The concern and anger in my voice surprises me.

Jax and Birdie share a look.

"What?" I say.

They both flip their heads around and then give me a look, like they're caught doing something they shouldn't be.

"It's nothing," Jax says. "Sometimes I get lightheaded if I run."

I look at Birdie.

"It's true," Birdie says. The caught look on his face shifts into a grin. "It's probably why he hates sports so much."

Jax lets out a noticeably nervous laugh. "Yeah, probably."

It's apparent they are hiding something. I'm not certain

what it is or why they are pretending like it's nothing. But all I know is that my defenses are rising. The familiar feeling to flee is beginning to seem like a better option than sticking around for whatever secrets Jax is keeping from me.

"I think I should go," I say.

Maybe it's a good thing he hasn't asked me to be his girlfriend. Now I have an easy way out of whatever this is. He didn't tell me about his brother. He kept his religion a secret. He doesn't want me to meet his mom. Maybe there are more secrets I haven't learned yet.

Birdie warned me Jax would rip my heart out. I should have listened. I shouldn't have let myself get so close to Jax. Because whatever secret he's keeping now seems like something he doesn't want me involved with at all.

Jax meets me on his feet. "No, please stay. I'll even put the pirate costume on for you."

He's giving me a pleading look. I search his face, then turn to Birdie—who looks just as puppy-eyed as Jax.

I force a puff of air out of my nose.

"Fine," I say.

Birdie claps his hands and makes his way up the stairs. "No racing this time," he says with a smirk.

As we walk by his mom's bedroom door, I can't help but wonder what's happening on the other side. Does she work? Does she leave? Does she care that her son can't even run up a flight of stairs without passing out?

"I'll meet you in there," I say. "I just need to use the bathroom."

"Okay," Jax says.

Birdie cocks his head to the side and places his hands on his hips. "Hurry up, we have a lot of work to do before the game tomorrow."

I smile and head for the bathroom. Not before looking

at the mysterious door of Mrs. Ferrington and wondering what has caused her agoraphobia to be so bad that she won't even eat dinner with her family.

In the bathroom I quickly pull out my phone to text Candice.

Me: Hey.
Candice: Hey, how's Tia's house?
Me: Roma is good. I think… I don't see her much since she works the night shift. How's finals?
Candice: Finals are there. How's divorcing your mom going?
Me: I need my birth certificate…which is at my mom's.
Candice: That sucks.
Me: I wish you were here.
Candice: Me too.

"P.? You're missing it!" Birdie calls down the hall to me.
"I'll be right there," I say.

Me: What are you doing tomorrow?
Candice: I had big plans to eat milk duds and popcorn in my bed while binge watching Riverdale.
Me: Or you could bring your milk duds and popcorn and come to a baseball game with me?
Candice: Who are you and what have you done with Paloma?
Me: It's for a YouTube video my friends are doing.
Candice: Sounds interesting. I'll see you at Tia's tomorrow.

I leave the bathroom and find Jax and Birdie in Jax's room.

Jax has an entire pirate ensemble complete with a wig and eyepatch.

"Arg," he says with a complete lack of enthusiasm.

I let out deep laughter that comes from my belly. I didn't realize how good it feels to laugh like that. I also can't remember the last time I laughed so hard.

His arms flop to his sides. "Okay, if you're going to make fun of me, I'm definitely not wearing this." He uncovers his eye, lifting the eyepatch. "What is it? The eyepatch too much?"

I can't wait to hear what Candice has to say about my new friends.

CHAPTER

TEN

Jaxon

"Here," Birdie says, tucking the familiar wad of cash into my pocket. Who knew pirate pants had pockets?

"Where's my…" I search around the trunk of my car.

Birdie gathers his camera equipment and bag. "Where is what?"

"The swords! I can't find the swords."

"You mean these?" Paloma says. "You handed them to me for safe keeping."

I take the swords. "Thanks."

After last night's incident on the staircase, I've been careful not to get too excited. I could tell Paloma was freaked out, and the fleeting look in her eyes when I came to made me realize she's not ready for the truth.

"You sure you've done this before?" Candice says.

"You seem pretty scatter brained for a pro-YouTuber."

Her sarcasm was funny when we first met an hour ago, but now it's become a little irritating.

Birdie lets out a laugh. "It's because Paloma is here."

Candice raises her eyebrow and pops her jaw.

When my gaze meets Paloma's, she looks more than satisfied by Birdie's comment. I'm relieved to see her smile.

Paloma and Candice find a place to sit in the stands while Birdie sets up his camera.

Once people start filing in, I cover my eye with the eyepatch, adjust my wig under my hat, and pull one sword from my belt.

"Him," Birdie says, nodding to a kid. "Ask him."

I motion toward the kid, when Birdie waves at me. "In the pirate voice," he says, as if I had forgotten that he's reminded me to use the pirate voice a hundred times since we left my house.

I nod. "Got it." Then to the kid I say, "Ahoy, there, lad." He gives me a confused look, so I continue, "I challenge you to a dual. Winner takes this." I pull out a couple of bills from my pocket and flash them in front of his face.

His eyes light up, then he looks to his dad, who smiles and nods, giving him the okay to engage in a plastic sword fight with a weirdo dressed in a pirate suit.

I continue challenging kids. After a while, a line forms with elementary aged children waiting their turn to have a sword fight and get some cash in the process.

Although the turnout is great, Birdie is not impressed by the footage. So much so, he stops recording. "Okay, kids, this is the last pirate fight," he says after he realizes everyone must think I'm the mascot since the game is between the Pirates and Stars.

After the sword fighting, the baseball game starts. I

approach Birdie for a new plan since I can tell he's irritated that his idea has been a flop so far.

"Why don't you sit in the stands for a while," he says, his arms crossed over his chest—an indication he's being serious.

I look at the stands at Paloma and Candice. Paloma notices me and waves with a smile. I wave back. "And then what, watch the game while I overheat in this suit?"

Birdie claps his hands. "I've got it! You can stand up in the middle of the game, and challenge..." he scans the audience, then points at a group of guys our age, "one of those guys to a dual."

"Okay," I say, giving my attention to Paloma who continues to shift her smiling gaze from me to the game, then back to me again.

"Okay," Birdie says. Then after a moment he pushes me and says, "Then go! And don't forget your pirate voice."

"Argh," I say with a less than willing tone, pointing my sword at him.

"*Go,*" he mouths at me.

I find my place in the stands and wait for Birdie to set his camera up in a new position for a better angle. I look back to Paloma but unintentionally make eye contact with Candice instead.

She abruptly says, "What?"

I twist a little more so I can see her better. "Where'd Paloma go?"

She tilts her head to the side and back again. "Concessions." She says this with annoyance in her voice. I wonder if the row of people between us notices her irritation.

"Thanks?" She's Paloma's friend, so I am trying to get on her good side. Maybe she's just overly protective of Paloma. Understandable.

151

The baseball game just started the bottom of the first inning, and it feels like we've already been here for an eternity.

Did I mention I hate sports?

When I catch Birdie with his eye behind the camera, I don't waste any time getting this *skit* over with.

"You," I say tapping one of the guys in the group, "I challenge you to a duel!"

"Screw off, Captain Hook," he says whacking the sword with the back of his hand.

I look to Birdie, then back to the guy and pull out several bills from my pocket. I lean closer to the group and speak in a low normal voice. "There's close to a thousand here if you put on a show for my friend over there," I nod in Birdie's direction.

After a few moments of shoving and joking around, one of them finally stands up, turns around, and takes the cash from my one hand and the sword from my other.

"En guarde," he says in a less than enthusiastic voice.

Not sure if that's a pirate term or not, but at this point I'm just glad to get rid of the last bit of cash and end the last fight of the night. The best part of this entire situation is that it's not a kid. Which means Birdie will get the content he's looking for, and then we can get out of here.

And because I'm not fighting with a kid, there's a lot more power behind the hits and stabs he's throwing at me.

Without warning, the guy thrusts my hat, along with the wig, off of my head.

Another guy sitting with the group stands up in his overly tight skinny jeans and faces me. "No way," he says this with a proud laugh. "You're Jax Ferrington."

"That's me," I take the hat and wig that landed on an older couple in the stands.

He hits his friend's arm, the one I was just fighting, with

the back of his hand, then points at me. "That's Dillon Ferrington's brother," his laugh rising with his more than unwelcomed discovery of my identity.

What rubs me the wrong way isn't that I realize he's making fun of me. I get that a lot when I'm recognized by jocks with low self-esteem, like him. But what bothers me is that he's talking about my brother.

He keeps going, "I can't believe Dillon came from a family of a bunch of weirdos like you."

His friend nudges him and tells him to knock it off.

I hope he listens, because I feel anger rising into my chest in the same way I did after I found out Dillon died. This guy obviously knew Dillon well enough to know we were brothers, but that doesn't give him any right to talk to me about Dillon.

He narrows his eyes. I can he's about to throw an insult at me, but what he says is stunning. "Too bad the wrong brother died, huh?"

I drop the hat and sword, then ball my hands into fists. I try to steady my breathing, but I can't settle down. I clench my jaw, knowing that all this tensing is only making my anger worse, but I can't help it.

I can't stop.

A few of his friends are laughing with him now. He must be their leader—a browbeater.

My chest is pounding with rage, and I try to remind myself not to get worked up.

I try to remind myself not to overexert myself, even if it is only emotional exertion.

None of this overreacting can be good for me. And I especially don't want Paloma to see me fumble down a set of bleachers.

He snaps his fingers together and points up at me. "And I heard your mom lost it, and went crazy after Dillon

OD'd."

I don't know why I do it.

I don't know why I didn't just walk away.

But before I know what's happening, I'm laying between the stands and hitting the guy with my fist.

Why didn't he just stop?

Why couldn't I get ahold of my own emotions?

The scuffle doesn't last long, and he gets a few good swings in before his friends pull me off him and the umpires kick us out of the game.

I steam off to my car, surprising myself by the intensity of my breathing.

Before I reach the parking lot, I hear hurried footsteps behind me.

"Jax," it's Paloma's voice, "Wait up."

I slow my pace so she can reach me, but I don't turn around.

She takes my hand in hers. "Hey," she's out of breath, "Those guys were a-holes."

Her PG-rated insult makes me smile. But I also can't help but wonder how much of the conversation she heard between me and those *a-holes*.

"And for what it's worth," she stops walking, which makes me whip around to face her since she's still holding my hand, "You're kind of a hot pirate."

I search her eyes. They are the only part of her that consistently tells me the truth. And right now, they are telling me she's ready.

"Just *kind of* hot, huh?" I close the space between us so that she has to drop her head back to look up at me.

"Don't let it get to your head." She smirks.

My racing heart keeps its pace when my anger melts and becomes instantly replaced by another feeling I can't quite pinpoint.

I take her other hand. "I think you're ready."

Her eyes are darting back and forth between my eyes and my mouth.

Instead of asking me to elaborate on my statement, she says, "I want to kiss you."

I accept the invitation and pull her in closer, kissing her. Because I know what she's ready for. The kiss I give her is slow and passionate, different from the other times we've kissed.

I step back, folding my lips in. Still unable to put my feelings into words.

"What is it?" she says.

"I'm over kissing you."

Her face twists. "What do you mean?"

I pull my hands through my hair and let out a puff of air. "I'm drowning in you, Paloma. You're drowning my heart."

Hopefully she can read my eyes the way I can read hers, and figure out what I'm feeling—since words seem to fall short of defining it.

She bites at her bottom lip, holding back a smile. "You're right," she says. "I think I'm ready too."

I blink in disbelief. It's like she can read my mind.

Before I can respond, Birdie yells from across the parking lot. "Ask her out already!"

I keep my eyes fixed on Paloma as Birdie and Candice laugh at his remark together. They have an armload of camera equipment between them, and the hat, wig, and swords I left behind after the fight.

I drag my fingertips down Paloma's arm. "Ready to be my girlfriend?"

She thrusts her arms around my neck and buries her face in my shoulder.

"Don't break her heart," Candice calls out to me.

I release Paloma from my arms and press my forehead against hers. "I'll take that as a *yes*."

CHAPTER ELEVEN

Paloma

I'm not sure what I was so afraid of. Since Jax and I have been together—

Like *officially* together.

As in, he's my *official* boyfriend.

Things have been great between us.

As if obtaining the title of Jax's girlfriend somehow bonded us more intensely.

I don't even mind that he hasn't introduced me to his mom yet.

After the fight at the baseball game when that guy said Jax's mom went crazy, I decided to let it go.

Not to mention the fact that Mamaw had made a comment about how Jax's mom never got over losing Dillon; I think it's okay not to push Jax into introducing me to his mom. Plus, I know I'll meet her eventually.

For now, I'm marinating in how good I feel being with Jax. Honestly, I don't feel the need to rush anything.

Not even this kiss I'm in the middle of having with him right now.

In the hallway.

At his dad's work.

Jax rests his hands at my waist as he lifts his face from mine.

"I'm enjoying this more than I can explain," he looks behind him, then back to me, "but I have to get some work done."

"I need to get some stuff done too." I admit.

He circles his thumb against the inside of my wrist. "Yeah?" It causes me to shudder. "Like what?"

I draw in a deep breath, trying to focus. "Emancipation stuff."

His thumb freezes, and his voice grows serious. "Can I do something to help you with that?"

I shrug. "I don't think so."

"Is it just stuff with your birth certificate?"

I nod.

"What do you have to do?"

"Apply for it online and pay for it." I'm not sure why this part of the process is so overwhelming for me. It could be the fact that they ask for the father's name when filling out the application, and I don't know who my father is; let alone his name.

I've also been waiting for a moment that Roma and I are at the apartment, awake, at the same time. So I can give her cash and use her debit card to pay for my birth certificate.

"Do you want to use the computer here?"

I hold my phone up. "I can do it on my phone."

He takes my hand and walks me toward the front desk.

"Really," he says. "Just stay and use the computer. The screen is bigger, and it will take you half the time to complete it."

"Fine," I say with a smile. It's not a bad idea.

"And the upside of filling it out here," he flashes me a smile, "is that I can kiss you when I refill the oil containers."

Before I can feel excited about his statement, a cold rush fills my core. As if a giant icicle has been thrust through me.

Not because of what Jax is talking about, but because as we reach the lobby my mother is sitting in one of the chairs.

"Paloma?" Jax says. "What is it?"

My mom lifts her gaze from scrolling on her phone when she notices us.

She stands up with her arms out. "Paloma, sweetie, come here and give your mom a hug."

Hugging her is the last thing I want to do right now.

How did she find me?

Why is she here?

My stomach is twirling in knots.

I take a step behind Jax while keeping my gaze on her.

Jax is understandably confused. He looks from me to my mom and back.

My mom takes my arm, a little tighter than she should, and thrusts me at her sternum to hug her.

I turn my head and give Jax a pleading look, but he still has the most confused expression on his face. He probably has no idea how to handle this situation, especially since the information he has about my mom is very limited.

My mom pushes me away. "Well," she says glancing at Jax, "Don't be rude. Introduce me to your friend."

I can't speak.

I'm in shock. Or denial. Maybe both. I'm not sure. But what I do know, is that she's trapped me once again. Like a bird in a cage. Worse, actually, she's trapped me like a mouse snapped down in a mouse trap. And she's managed to trap me in Dallas, which was supposed to be my hiding place.

Jax takes my mother's hand. "I'm Jax Ferrington."

"April Remirez" She releases his hand almost as quickly as she takes it. "Paloma's mother," she says this with a hiss.

Jax faces me, then my mom again. "I thought Paloma's last name was Smith?"

"It is," my mom says as she catches my gaze.

Jax tilts his head. I can tell he wants her to elaborate. But I know she won't.

This is one of the many questions I've asked her myself to try and get some information about my father, but her lips are sealed tight. And the worst part of it all is that she somehow manages to change the subject so naturally. Another one of her manipulation tactics.

"Your father must be the incredible massage therapist Roma was telling me about." She shifts to one side, examining the office. "He must be busy working now, huh?"

Jax nods. "Yeah, he's with a client. Did you want to book a session?"

Why is he being nice to her? He knows she kicked me out. Why isn't he shooing her away. Now that he's my boyfriend, he can do stuff like that. I think.

I guess in his defense, he still doesn't know the details of her disorder.

She shakes her head. "No," she smiles briefly. "Thank you though. I'm here to take Paloma home."

"I'm not going." I surprise myself when I say this.

There's even a confidence in my voice I didn't realize I was able to access when speaking to my mom.

She gives me the *look*. The one that says *I'm-going-to-kill-you-when-we-get-home*. Then she says, "Yes, you are. You're sixteen. You don't have a choice."

But this time, her *look* doesn't scare me. Because I know I don't have to go home with her. I don't have to experience her wrath or insanity anymore.

"I do have a choice," I say. "And I choose to stay here." I wrap both my hands around Jax's arm, locking myself to him just in case she tries to physically remove me from the building.

Her voice is low when she says, "Get in the car, Paloma."

I don't say anything.

I don't move.

And this sort of gesture makes my mother irate.

"You've had enough fun galivanting around Dallas with this guy." She points to the exit, then says, "Now get in the car before I call the police and tell them my daughter needs to be escorted home."

"Escorted for what?" I say.

She narrows her eyes at me. "For not listening to your mother after you ran away." Even though I'm feeling brave, it still hurts when she stabs me with each sharp lie.

"You kicked me out!"

This sends her into a fit of rage. She tries to take my arm, but I step behind Jax again. I feel him purposely step in her way as she thrusts her arm out at me again.

"In the car, now, Paloma!"

She doesn't acknowledge Jax at all or the fact that he's between us.

And he's not saying anything to her. Probably because he's never seen an adult woman act so childish before.

I'm beginning to feel dread course through me as we spin in circles around Jax. Then a door closes and Pat approaches us from the hallway, wiping his hands on a towel.

"Everything alright?" His expression is in complete confusion.

"Help," my voice is full of panic. "Pat, please, help me!"

My mother backs off and straightens her posture.

Pat lifts his chin slightly, eyeing us. "What's going on here?"

"This is April," Jax says.

I point at my mother. "She's trying to take me away."

"I'm her mother." My mom adjusts her purse strap, as if being my mother is a legitimate reason for her to be acting like a lunatic. "I'm allowed to take my daughter home."

Pat nods, as if he's just connected the dots. Thankfully I disclosed information to him about her during my first massage session with him. So, he knows that she's unstable. And since he's an adult man, I'm hoping he has more authority to get her to leave than Jax.

"I've heard so much about you, it's nice to finally put a face to Paloma's mother." Pat's voice is gentle and steady. "I'm Pat, Jax's dad." He places his hand on my mother's shoulder, motioning her toward the lobby. "Would you mind taking a seat for a minute? I need to wash the oil off my hands, then we can figure out what to do with your situation."

My mom begins to sit, but once she realizes that he's not on her side, she stands straight up. "She is *my* daughter. I have the right to take her home."

Pat draws in a deep breath. He gives me an apologetic look before shifting his gaze back to my mother. "Paloma is filing for emancipation."

My mouth falls agape.

I feel…*betrayed*.

I thought he was one of the few adults in my life I could trust. But now he's telling my mom everything I'm planning to do. I should have known it was too good to be true. Now it's all blowing up in my face.

"Dad," Jax begins to say.

Pat glances at Jax long enough to get Jax to relax and discontinue his statement.

My mom crosses her arms and faces me. "Is that true?"

I nod.

"You can't file for emancipation," she says matter-of-factly.

Pat pinches at his chin. "Actually, she can."

My mom flips her head around to face him.

She opens her mouth to speak, but Pat continues, "She has all the paperwork done and a lawyer."

"What?" she snaps.

Pat gives her a sincere expression when he says, "All she needs is your signature."

I find myself shaking my head. As if I'm saying, *no, no, no,* and watching my entire escape plan burn into ashes before my eyes. It's too late to tell Pat the less my mom knows, the better.

My mom looks at me again, her arms still tightly folded over her chest. "Are you serious, Paloma? A lawyer?"

I'm squeezing Jax's arm so tightly that I feel his pulse in my hands. I release a breath I didn't realize I was holding and relax my grip on his arm.

"If you sign the papers…" Pat begins to say.

My mother pinches her lips together and pulls her brows in. "I'm not signing anything." Then she spins around and stomps out of the building.

She doesn't stop to look back.

She hurries in her anger to her car.

She slams the door shut.

She peels out into traffic; the car she cut off honks at her.

Then, she's gone.

When the desperate feeling for help leaves my body as I realize I'm standing in a safe place again, my breathing intensifies, and tears fill my eyes.

"Paloma?" Jax says, gripping my heaving shoulders.

A woman exits one of the massage rooms. When she sees me, her eyes widen and she says, "Oh…"

Pat places one hand on Jax and the other on my arm. Walking behind us, he quietly says, "Take her to the laundry room until she calms down." He gently squeezes my arm before releasing us, and says to me, "You're going to be okay."

Jax opens the door to the laundry room. We file in as I hear Pat speaking to the client and reassuring her everything is fine.

I feel like I'm going to pass out. My breathing is so intense it's making my ears ring.

I sit on the floor with my back against the dryer.

"Here," Jax hands me a folded hand towel, "like this." He gently holds it against my mouth. "Now try to calm down. You're hyperventilating."

I nod.

Continue to cry.

Continue to hyperventilate.

And hold the towel over my mouth.

Dragging in each breath.

"It's okay," he says. "She's gone."

After a few minutes, the knot in my stomach finally unravels. My breathing begins to steady as I drop the towel from my face and lean my head against the whirling dryer.

It's calming having the steady whir of the machine against my back.

I look at Jax. His eyes are filled with worry and concern.

I roll my head back and stare at the folded sheets and towels on the shelves in front of us.

"I'm okay," I say.

He nods. "I can see why you're doing what you're doing now that I've met your mom."

A small laugh escapes my throat.

"Seriously," he continues. "She's intense."

"She's crazy," I correct.

He slips his fingers between mine and holds my hand. "Has she always been like that?"

Now that he's seen her in action, there's no reason to sugar coat it. "She's getting more out of control the older she gets."

His thumb rubs at the back of my hand. "I'm sorry. That must suck."

"She was okay sometimes."

He shakes his head. "How did you deal with that for so long?"

I sit up to face him. I want to tell him about her bipolar disorder. I want to tell him about the way her meds leveled her out. I want to tell him that I took Lexapro to deal with what happened to me.

I search his eyes.

He smiles. He must sense that I want to tell him something since he says, "Whatever it is, you can tell me. We're tackle buddies, remember?"

This makes me laugh. "That's so stupid, I don't know why I ever called us that." I fold my mouth together and try to muster up the courage to be honest with him.

"There's no rush," he says.

The dryer suddenly comes to a standstill as it rings a

chime, indicating that the cycle has ended.

The room becomes still in the silence.

In a low voice, Jax says, "Would it make you feel better if I told you something about my mom?"

My eyes widen. I just came to terms with being content about not meeting her. Now he's ready to talk about the reason she keeps herself locked up in her room all day. Whatever it is, it can't be worse than my mom.

Before I would have jumped at the thought of learning new information about his mom. But now, I know whatever he tells me is going to need a follow up from me. Which means, I'll have to tell him why my mom put me on Lexapro in the first place.

"Okay," I agree. The word comes out in barely a whisper.

He pulls in a long breath through his nose before he says, "I told you about Dillon."

I close the space between us by scooting closer to him.

He leans the back of his head against the dryer, and I watch his throat roll as he swallows before continuing.

"After everything with Dillon." He turns his head to the side and I hear a crack in his neck. "My, uh…" he laughs in disbelief. "My mom did not deal with it very well."

I place my other hand over his.

"At first, no one thought anything of it." He glances at me. "I mean, she just lost her son. It's normal to grieve something like that, you know?"

I nod.

"But, it didn't go away." He fixes his gaze at the tiled floor. "First, she quit going to church. Then she didn't go back to work." He shakes his head. "My dad took her to the doctor, and they wanted to put her on antidepressants. She wouldn't take them."

My throat goes dry. I know how he feels about pain

killers, but what about other medication? And what is he going to think about me if I tell him I took antidepressants?

I focus my attention on him. Hoping if I am kind and understanding about whatever is going on with his mom, that he will return the favor to me.

"She would stay in her bed for days without moving." He pauses for a moment, then faces me briefly. "It's the reason I knew what to do when I found you stuck in your depressive state. I hate admitting it, but I was the one trying to get her out of bed. Sometimes it worked. Most of the time it didn't. And my dad was grieving too, but he handled the loss better and went back to his life. He thought she just needed more time.

"I started spending more time here." He motions his hand around the room. "I could do my school here on my laptop and keep myself busy helping my dad with the rocks, and laundry."

"And oil and books," I add, smiling.

He grins.

"Exactly." He continues, "So, one day, I forgot my physics book at home. My dad would have been late for work if he turned around and took me back right then. So he said I could take his car back to the house after we dropped him off.

"When I was driving, traffic was busier than I anticipated, and it took me ten minutes longer to get home than it normally would have."

I'm not sure why traffic is important to this story, but I listen and wait for him to continue anyway.

He finally faces me, but when he does, he's not smiling anymore. Instead, his expression is full of sorrow.

"I went straight to my room to get my book. I didn't notice at first, but when I passed by my parents' bedroom, I heard the bath running. I didn't think much of it. I mean,

I knew my mom was home. She was always home. It's normal for people to take baths when they're home alone, right?"

I'm not sure how to respond.

He glances at me. "I was serious when I told you that I understood your depression better than you thought I did." He continues, "Anyway, I was used to her being there in the silence of her sadness. I got used to her quiet presence. I was used to it. Nothing seemed out of the ordinary that day.

"But when I got back downstairs, there was a note with mine and my dad's names on it, written in my mom's handwriting.

"I opened it, and what I read was unbelievable."

He lets out a puff of air, dragging his hand down his face. I don't say anything because I know it's probably hard for him to talk about this with me. I don't know how much he wants to tell me, and I don't want to pressure him. So, I wait.

After a moment, he says, "It was pages. She was saying goodbye to us." His eyes shine. "Pages and pages and pages, just to say she was ending it."

It makes sense why he didn't want me to meet her. He probably felt guilt and shame for outing his mom before she was able to end it. His entire family probably feels guilt and shame that his mom tried to commit suicide. That would explain why she's hulled up in her room all the time.

His hand feels suddenly cold in mine. I'm not sure what I should do. So, I settle for saying, "I'm so, so sorry."

"That's not the worst part." His voice is filled with remorse. "I didn't finish the letter. It only took skimming over the first few sentences to know what she was doing.

"I ran upstairs to find her unconscious, submerged in the overflowing bathtub. Her skin was so blue. I called 911 after I pulled her out of the water. Then I called my dad.

"It all happened so fast. I kept worrying about the flooding water reaching the carpet in the bedroom while I was giving her CPR."

He shakes his head. As if he's still in disbelief over the events he went through with her. "They were able to revive her at the hospital," he adds quickly.

My eyes widen.

He continues, "At the hospital, we learned that she had overdosed on my brother's pain killers. The doctors kept her sedated for two days to help her get rid of everything in her system. But after pumping her stomach and detoxing her, she still didn't wake up."

His eyes peer into mine so intensely I can feel his pain rush through me as he says, "She didn't wake up for three months."

I suck in a rush of air. "Oh my gosh, that's horrible. What happened after she woke up?"

His brows are drawn downward when he says, "She had so much brain damage that she couldn't speak." He looks away. His voice is the most pained when he says, "Or walk, or feed herself, or use the bathroom."

I cover my mouth with my hand. Shocked. I'm shocked because I now realize that his mom isn't hulled up in her room because she feels shame about trying to kill herself. But that she's stuck in her room because she was trying to kill herself and he found her too late.

"It's almost worse seeing her like this, you know? She's not my mom anymore. I don't see her in there anymore." He faces me. "I'm sorry I didn't tell you sooner."

I shake my head. "No, no, I'm so sorry I made it a big deal. I should have minded my own business."

"I still I wish I had told you sooner."

I give him a half smile. "It's okay. You told me now."

He gives me a small grin, trying to lift the mood as best he can after delivering such a horrific story. "It's weird, if I had gotten to her even a few seconds later, she would have been gone."

"That's crazy," I say, unsure of what I can say to help him. "I'm glad you got there in time."

He shrugs one shoulder. "I don't know if this is worse, honestly."

I'm taken aback by his words. Is he saying she's better of dead? I wouldn't even wish that for my mom, and she's insane.

He must notice the shocked look on my face, because he says, "It's not what you think. You have to understand, she was such a beautiful, lively, happy mom. She loved life. And after Dillon, she couldn't get back to the love she had for life again. Then, when she tried to end it, bringing her back only made it worse.

"I mean," he chokes on his words and looks up at the ceiling, as he blinks away the tears filling his eyes. "She has no quality of life now. And my dad, I love him, but he's being selfish keeping her alive when she's not in there anymore."

I keep my voice gentle, "What do you mean?"

He pushes his tears away with the back of his hand before he faces me. "He's hoping for a miracle. And I'm all about miracles, but sometimes things are just what they are. He doesn't see it that way though. And I don't get it. Even after the doctors told him she would never be the same again because of the extent of her brain damage. He's still hoping for a miracle."

Now that I know his heart is heavy with the pain he carries over rescuing his mom, I'm not sure I want to tell him about my mother or about me.

"So," he sniffs, then flashes me a smile. "What's up with

your mom?"

I shake my head and look down at our hands. I feel the warmth return to his palm, before I release my grip around his hand to crack my knuckles.

I laugh, not because anything is funny, but because of what I'm about to tell him is going to sound like nothing compared to what he's gone through.

How does a guy still turn out so great after having experienced losing his brother and almost losing his mom?

"Well," he says, nudging my shoulder with his.

"Well," I echo. "You make it seem so easy talking about your family." I meet his gaze. "And your pain."

He thinks for a moment before he says, "I think the more you talk about stuff, the easier it gets, and the faster you accept it. Not that it goes away or is ever easy to talk about. But that, you're able to move forward again. And be okay again."

I blink in disbelief at his wisdom.

"What?" he says.

A grin spreads across my face. "I can't believe something so wise just came out of your mouth."

He chuckles as he looks down at the floor. When he lifts his gaze to mine again, he brushes his finger down my arm and clasps his hand around mine.

"Why don't we see if there's any truth behind my *wisdom*," he says, rolling his eyes when he says *wisdom* as if he's embarrassed to even use that word to describe himself.

"I don't know what to say." Which is true, I don't even know where or how to begin talking about how messed up my mom is.

"Like I've told you before," his voice is low and gentle. "You just start talking. Just say it."

Why is he always right about everything?

I nod. Suck in a deep breath. And hold my hand over

my racing heart, before saying, "When I was younger, I remember feeling like a burden to her. As if my very presence annoyed her."

Jax's expression falls.

I keep talking so he doesn't feel like he needs to say something nice to me.

"She always wanted me to be quiet, wherever we were. At home. In the store. At the park. In the car. It didn't matter where we were or what we were doing, she wanted me silent.

"I remember we were visiting her friend at a park when I was five or six. Her friend had a little girl my age and we were playing together. We played this game where we would burry our feet in the sand and pretend our toes were worms.

"We were laughing and screaming. And suddenly my mom pulled me out of the sand and demanded I put my shoes on. I can remember the shocked look on the little girl's face. And when I looked at my mom's friend, she started to tell my mom that the park was clean and safe, and that her daughter played without her shoes on at that park all the time.

"I remember my mom squeezing my arm even tighter when her friend said that to her. I started to cry and say that she was hurting me. She dragged me to the car and when her friend tried saying something again, my mother told her to mind her own business." I pull my knees into my chest, feeling like I went right back to being six years old again just by telling Jax that story.

I'm still not ready to hear whatever it is he wants to say to comfort me, so I keep going, "There's so many memories like that. She made friends, but once they saw that side of her, they were gone. Not because they stopped being her friend, but because she pushed them away and pushed them out of our lives.

"Even my grandparents. I met them once, and they were everything I imagined them to be and more. But my mom realized my grandpa was sneaking me candy and she lost it. She accused them of undermining her parenting. And that was the last and only time I ever saw them. I don't even know their names, or where they live, or if they are still alive.

"She did that to everyone, until there was no one. Except me and her. And then, when I was all she had left," my eyes burn, "she pushed me away too."

Jax's voice is gentle when he says, "No wonder you always want to run."

Not exactly the comment I was expecting from him.

"I do not," I say.

He pulls a piece of lint from my shirt sleeve when he says, "You do. And it's okay. It's what you grew up learning to do."

I scoff, "Is that supposed to be more wisdom?"

"Definitely not." He raises one eyebrow. "Well, that wasn't so bad was it?"

"What? Talking about my mom?"

"Yeah."

"Well," I begin to say, but then decide maybe he doesn't need to hear everything about her after all.

"Well?" He tilts his head, confused. "Oh, is there more?"

My stomach growls. I've given so much of my energy to dealing with my mom, listening to Jax, and trying to articulate my mom's issues to Jax that I didn't realize I was hungry.

He looks at my stomach, which makes me feel slightly embarrassed, then his eyes scan the room.

He reaches up to a basket on the shelf and pulls out a

handful of mints. Not the hard candy ones, but the creamy white ones that melt in your mouth. "Here," he says placing a couple into my palm. "It's the closest thing to a snack we'll find in here."

"Or we could find some real food outside of this room." I pop a mint into my mouth.

He gently taps my nose with his finger. "No way, you still have something to tell me. I can tell. So, spill the tea."

I laugh. "I thought only Birdie said stuff like that."

He grins. "I can say stuff like that too. Come on, tell me."

I run my hand through the bottom of my hair, trying to gather my thoughts again.

I'm hoping to buy myself enough time for Pat to come in and check on us, or invite us to lunch, or for someone to interrupt the story telling that's been going on in here for much longer than I'm comfortable with.

"It's okay," Jax says after a moment passes without me speaking. "You can tell me anything. I promise I won't judge you or think any less of you or whatever else you're thinking that is keeping you from telling me."

Since no one is coming to stop this moment from happening, I decide to give in and tell him everything.

"You promise you're not going to think I'm crazy or judge me or leave me?"

He smirks. "Nothing you tell me will ever make me want to leave you."

I don't know about that, but I accept his statement as an understanding for what I'm about to say.

"So, I was in middle school when I found out my mom was diagnosed with bipolar disorder. She started counseling and took medication. She was a completely different person.

"I could sleep at night without her waking me up to

clean the house for hours at one o'clock in the morning. I could trust her to be in a good mood when she picked me up from school. I could count on her to make sure we consistently had groceries in the cupboards.

"It was the best time I ever remember having with her for a consistent amount of time."

My body instantly clams up when I debate on telling him the next part.

"Hey," he says, noticing me tense. "Whatever it is, I'm good with it. I'm not going anywhere."

I nod. I guess I'm just going to have to rip off the band aid and get this over with. "When I got into high school, things were different. People were mean. Teachers didn't care as much about the students. I had no friends."

"What about Candice?" he says.

"She's my friend, but we don't really know each other or talk about real stuff."

He nods. "Got it. Sorry, go ahead."

"So, somehow a rumor spread that I wanted to be a cheerleader. Which I didn't. But a couple of the cheerleaders that were seniors approached me and insisted I join. It was weird people were noticing me. And it sort of felt good to be included. Candice thought it was a bad idea to get mixed up with the popular kids. Even after Candice told me it was a bad idea, I agreed to join them for practice.

"They met me in the locker room and made sure I had a uniform and everything." I suck in a deep breath, and meet his gaze with mine. "This is the part that's hard to say."

He nods, letting me know he understands and won't judge me.

"They told me to try on the uniform, and that I had to wear it without a bra. So, while I was changing, they took pictures of me on their phones and posted them on social media. Literally while I was standing right there. I had no idea.

"And the most mortifying part of it all is that they didn't say anything about it. They acted like nothing. They even taught me a routine after that.

"But when practice was over, they asked for their uniform back and told me I didn't make the squad. It was humiliating. And even more humiliating when I saw my half naked body posted all over the internet.

"I wanted to die."

Jax creases his brow when I say that. I know he probably thinks I'm exaggerating, so I elaborate.

I take both of his hands in mine. Not only am I trying to comfort myself, but I'm trying to comfort him. Because I know what I'm about to say is probably going to hurt him, which is far from what I intended him to feel with this conversation.

My pulse throbs in my chest as my throat goes dry. "I don't mean that lightly, Jax," my voice shudders. "I went home that night and tried to kill myself."

He stands up almost instantly. And since he is still holding my hands, he brings me with him in a less than smooth manner.

"Why?" His voice is pained. Not what I was expecting. I thought he would be angry or storm out of the room. Even after he promised he wouldn't judge me, I still half expected him to be furious.

I tense my grip in his, hoping he won't let go. "I don't know. I was stupid. I was humiliated. It seemed better to never show my face again."

His brow is still creased when he says, "What'd you do?"

"I don't know if what I did was a cry for help. Or if it was real." I tuck a strand of hair behind my ear so I can look at him better. "But looking back, I know now that I wouldn't be better off if I had died that night."

He presses his mouth together and nods. I'm sure this is a lot to process for him. "What'd you do?" he says again, only this time his tone is more understanding.

I shrug. "After my mom went to bed, I went out to the garage. I turned on the car and waited. But not even a full minute went by before my mom found me. I didn't even try to lie when she confronted me about what I was doing.

"She made me sleep in her bed for a month after that. She also kept me home until the school year ended so I could have a fresh start the next year after those cheerleaders graduated.

"And…" I swallow hard, pressing on my cuticles before saying, "she put me on an antidepressant called Lexapro."

Jax's creased brow shifts downward into concern.

"That sucks," he says. "But, I'm glad your mom got you help. And I'm glad something worse didn't happen to you."

"Yeah, I guess." I stare down at my shoes. "But since my mom was so focused on me, she sort of stopped taking care of herself. Her old bipolar habits returned when she became inconsistent with her medication."

I bite at the inside of my cheek for a moment, contemplating on going into the details of my broken relationship with my mom.

I meet his gaze. Noticing he seems to already know the details without me having to say anything more.

"And after that is when she kicked me out," I say.

Jax wraps his arms around me in a hug. "I'm sorry that happened to you," he looks down at me, "And I'm sorry those girls were a-holes."

Just as I was beginning to worry I might cry, Jax makes me laugh.

A knock on the door causes us both to flip our heads around.

"Hey," Pat says, leaving the door ajar as he enters the room. "Feeling better?"

I smile with a nod. "Yeah," I look up at Jax, "A lot better."

CHAPTER

TWELVE

Jaxon

"You sure you want to go with us?" Paloma says.

I turn to look back at Lissy in the backseat. "Do you want me to eat potato soup with you and Paloma today?"

Lissy giggles in her seat. "Who is *that*?"

I throw my thumb toward Paloma. "Didn't you know your nanny's name is Paloma?"

Lissy laughs out loud. "Her name is *Nanny*."

When I look to Paloma for some backup, she says, "Yeah, you didn't know my name is Nanny?"

I laugh.

It's fun getting to see Paloma in her element. She's great with Lissy, and not in an overly animated way that some nannies are like. She's so comfortable with her, and real. That's probably why they get along so well.

We pull into Medieval Times and Lissy can't wait to get out of the car.

"Hold on," Paloma says to Lissy. "We can't forget your princess hat."

Paloma places the pink cone shaped hat on Lissy's head. She's decked out in a medieval dress too.

After we're seated at the bench for the jousting tournament, I lean in to get closer to Paloma so she can hear me over the crowd cheering. "Is she really into this stuff?"

Paloma nods. "Yep," she lifts her shoulders. "She likes Shakespeare too."

"What a cool kid," I say.

Throughout the jousting tournament, I periodically look over to see Lissy clapping and slurping at her stew. But I can't seem to pull my gaze from Paloma for more than just a few seconds.

I'm not sure if it's the way she's picking at her bread roll and eating small bites. Or that she smiles and looks away after she notices me staring at her. Maybe it's the fact that since she became my girlfriend and opened up to me about her past, I've felt more connected to her.

Whatever it is, it sends my heart into a flutter.

But then the flutter doesn't stop, and I realize something a lot more serious is happening.

I stand up and scoot out from behind the table.

"Jax," a look of concern covers Paloma's face. "Where are you going?"

I hunch over and cross my arms over my chest. "Bathroom." I hope she believes my gesture.

"Are you okay?" I hear her say, but I don't look back to acknowledge her. Mostly because I'm afraid if I do, I might lose my focus and topple over.

I bump into a man on my way to the bathroom. "Hey,

be careful," he says, holding the door open for me before he exits.

I can't even apologize.

The room is going dark.

I lock the stall door and lean against the wall to steady myself.

I keep my eyes closed.

Breathing.

Steadying with each exhale.

But even though my lungs are calming down, my heart is still jumping erratically between them.

I slide down the wall until I'm seated on the floor of the bathroom and pull my phone from my pocket.

"Hey, Siri," I say between my labored breathing. "Call Daddio."

"*Calling Daddio,*" Siri replies in her robotic voice, followed by a shrill ring.

It seems like an eternity before I hear my dad's voice.

"Hey, Jaxon," my dad's voice is chipper, which makes what I'm about to say more difficult since I know it's going to change his mood.

I let out a breath, then say, "Dad."

His tone shifts. "Jaxon? Where are you?"

"Medieval Times," I let out another breath, "In the men's room."

"I'll be right there." I hear shuffling in the background as if he's hurrying. "Stay on the phone with me, alright? Keep breathing."

I drag in another breath. "Okay."

...

"Here," my dad says, placing the prescription pills into my hand.

I was fine by the time my dad arrived, so I met him in

the parking lot.

"I handled it," I say, tossing the pills in my mouth and washing them down with the bottled water he hands me.

"You really need to make sure you're not letting yourself get too excited."

"I know."

My dad scratches at his chin. "And maybe don't leave the house without your pills."

"I know."

"And you should probably tell Paloma about this."

"*I know!*"

I feel bad for yelling and immediately soften my voice. "I'm sorry. I meant to say, *you're right*. But I don't want to freak her out, especially after everything that happened with her mom." I give him a look. "We are doing good right now. I don't want to ruin it for her."

He shifts in his seat to face me. "I know it seems like there will be a good opportunity to tell her, but there's never a good time to talk about something like this."

I gently shake the pill bottle in my hand, then smile. "I know."

My dad leans over and pats my shoulder. "Then do the decent thing and tell her before she figures it out."

I nod, then open the car door to exit. "Thanks for bringing these." I hold the pills up before shoving them in my pocket. "See you at home."

"Are you good to drive?"

I raise my brow at him. "I'm good." Then I close the door.

He waves. "Do the decent thing, Jaxon," he calls out of his window.

I'm walking back inside when I wave to him a last time before entering the restaurant again.

When I find my place next to Paloma, she smiles. "I was

about to see if you needed some help in there."

I rub my stomach to make her think she's right about me having trouble in the bathroom. "You wouldn't have wanted to be in there."

Lissy lifts a flower in my direction, "Look, Jax!"

I drop my jaw in animated surprise, the kind of animation Paloma would never do with her. "Woah! What is that?"

Lissy's smile is beaming. "The knight gave it to me. I'm a real princess now!"

I give her a big grin, then shift my gaze to Paloma.

The smile she flashes at me makes my heart skip a beat, I stuff the feeling down and hope my pills can keep the rest of me calm.

I need to be careful knowing that she makes me feel things I can't control, only this time I know that it's more than just my affections for her.

CHAPTER

THIRTEEN

Paloma

I click on the *submit* button and close Roma's laptop.

I finally filled out the form for my birth certificate after I talked to Roma about my mom; who, by the way, had no interactions with my mom.

I'm not sure how my mom figured out where I was.

Or how she knew Roma got massages there.

Or how she knew to find me there.

But I'm not surprised. My mom can find out *anything*.

Roma made the process of filing for my birth certificate easy. She even let me give her money and use her debit card so I could pay for it online.

She also suggested I study for the GED. Which I'm not thrilled about, but at this rate it's the only way I'll have a chance at getting into college.

I get a notification on my phone. It's an email. When I open it, my face falls.

It's a message from Vital Records. It says there's a problem with my request for my birth certificate.

I let out a sigh.

Of course there's an issue.

I should come to terms with the fact that no matter how much effort I put into this emancipation process, it's never going to happen for me.

For all I know, my mom is turning the authorities against me right now and they are probably on their way to pick me up and force me to live with her again.

My phone buzzes.

Jax: Are we still on for this afternoon?
Me: Yep. I have to work a couple of hours today.
Jax: I didn't know you needed a ride to work.
Me: Dipti has a driver scheduled to take me. Today is about you. ☺
Jax: You're the best girlfriend ever. Have fun at work. I'll see you later.

I didn't want to bother Jax with my work schedule. He would have been driving back and forth since I'm only working a few hours while Terra and Claude have a doctor's appointment for the baby.

And I didn't want to have Jax running around, distracted by me all day, since this afternoon is his and Birdie's graduation ceremony.

I can't believe graduation is already here.

• • •

I roll a purple blob of air-dry clay into a ball on the kitchen table while French nursery rhymes gently flow out of the

185

speaker.

"Nanny," Lissy says, as she smooshes an oversized clay eyeball onto what she's trying to make into a ladybug. "I thought you were making me a turtle?"

I look at her. "I am," I say lifting the ball and pressing it between my hands. "This turtle has a purple shell."

She giggles. "Turtles don't have purple shells."

"This one does." I smile at her.

She's wearing her medieval cone shaped princess hat along with her pirate costume.

"Are you excited for dinner with your mommy and daddy tonight?" I say.

She nods. "Daddy is taking me to six flags all day tomorrow so mommy can take a nap."

"Mommy needs a nap all day long?" I let the words fall out of my mouth before I can think about how they might sound.

She doesn't notice. Instead, she hops down from the table and says, "I want to go to the museum."

"We can't," I say with regret. I begin cleaning up the clay noticing she's ready to move on to something else.

"My daddy said you can take me to the museum any time I want to go."

Her daddy needs to learn to remember my schedule. "We can't because I have to leave soon."

The front door unlocks. Terra and Claude are beaming and quietly chattering. I'm assuming the appointment went well.

"No, Nanny!"

Claude and Terra go silent and turn their attention towards Lissy's distressed voice.

I sit on my knees in front of Lissy, holding her hands in mine. I use a quiet voice to try and calm her. "It's okay, we can go to the museum next week when I'm here." She's twisting away from me, I've never seen her like this. "We can spend the entire day at the museum if you want and I'll even pack goldfish and juice boxes for lunch."

The tears drop out of her eyes. "No, Nanny! I hate goldfish and juice boxes." She begins to sob which causes Claude to rush to her side and scoop her up.

"Ma cherie," Claude says, whisking Lissy into his arms.

I look at them helplessly.

I feel like I should be able to calm her without help.

Although, this is the first time she's acted this way in front of me.

Claude gives me a quick grin before he takes her up the stairs to her bedroom; her quiet sobs disappear into the ceiling.

Terra drops her purse on the kitchen counter. She's wearing tight black pants and a crop top that's showing the top part of her belly. I don't know how, but she seems to pull it off.

"How'd the appointment go?" I don't really care how it went, but small talk is better than uncomfortable silence. And she has a way of making me feel uncomfortable whether we are talking or not. I keep my eyes down as I continue sorting the rest of the clay into miniature ziplock bags.

She lets out a sigh that I'm not sure is more tired or irritated, when she says, "My doctor described our little boy as *perfect* so I can't complain."

I give her a stiff smile.

She rummages through the fridge and pours herself a glass of orange juice. I'm happy she's positioned in a way that I don't have to force myself to avoid eye contact. I'm not sure if it's her extreme confidence or the fact that she's ridiculously gorgeous, maybe both, but it makes me feel very intimated by her.

I check my phone after placing the box of clay back in the closet. Because Claude and Terra came home early, I still have fifteen minutes before my driver gets here.

"She's asking for you." I flip around to see Claude standing behind Terra, gently gliding his fingertips down her arms as he begins to kiss her neck.

She shrugs him off of her. "Can you please deal with her? I have a meeting with a client and don't have time for this."

He slumps back against the counter, defeated. "You mean, you do not have time for your daughter."

She turns around and tilts her head. "I don't want to do this right now, Claude. I won't let you ruin my day by trying to guilt me." She looks down at her watch. "I have to go."

Then she sets her drink on the counter, and takes her purse, making her way out the door. Gliding in her perfection as she slips into the car and out of the driveway, as if she's not weighed down by her belly at all.

I don't know why I don't say anything. But as soon as I witness what happens next, I immediately regret not making my presence known.

Claude drops his head back between his shoulders and exhales, a slow deep breath. After a brief moment, he flips around, lunges at the counter and thrusts his open hand at the glass cup Terra left. It crashes against the cupboards, sending shards of glass and orange juice all over the kitchen floor.

I instinctively rush to the kitchen and begin cleaning the larger pieces of broken glass.

Claude meets me on the tile. "I'm so sorry, Paloma. I thought you had left."

His breathing intensifies; *so does mine.*

"It's okay," I say. "I've seen worse." Which is true. I once was in the car with my mom when she ran her car into her boss' jeep in the parking lot. He wasn't in it and she didn't do much damage since we weren't driving very fast. But I think that was worse than this.

Claude joins me in cleaning the glass shards. "She is too busy."

Oh great, and now he's going to confide in me. I didn't mean for my response to be an invitation for him to vent about his marriage problems.

"She's too focused on her career to notice our daughter needs her," he says.

I rise to throw the broken glass in the garbage and retrieve some damp paper towels. Trying to busy myself and ignore the massive discomfort I'm feeling.

"Before we were married, we talked about starting a family." He tosses a handful of glass into the garbage as I continue cleaning.

Trying to get out of here as fast as possible.

"Our dreams were the same." He rubs the back of his neck, keeping his eyes on me as I clean the remainder of the mess. "Once the gallery was established, we would raise our family. *Together.*" His voice rises when he says, "She did *not* keep her promise."

He bangs his fist against the counter when he says this, which makes me flinch. Then he quickly draws his hand back to himself in pain.

My eyes dart from his pained expression to his hand. "Are you okay?"

He pulls his hand away from himself for inspection. When he does, he picks out a bloody shard of glass from the side of his hand. It must have made its way up on the counter when it exploded against the cupboard.

He lets out a groan.

I feel sorry for him. He's upset with his wife's lacking skills in motherhood, and now he's hurt from the glass *he*

189

scattered. I'm not sure which pain is hurting worse right now, but I feel like I should help where I can.

"Here," I open my hand to take the shard and toss it in the garbage.

"I am sorry," he leans his hip into the counter and holds his wrist. The blood is beginning to run down his hand. "It is frustrating because Lissy asks for you more than her own mother. And with a second child—"

"Except for today," I interrupt.

He flashes his eyes at me. He seems surprised at first, then his face falls. "Oh, you must have heard."

I nod. "Yeah, you said Lissy was asking for Terra."

I hand him a paper towel to clean the blood from his hand. "That was not true," he says as he tosses the bloody paper towel in the garbage and opens a cupboard to retrieve the first aid kit.

I feel my eyebrows draw together in bewilderment. "What do you mean?"

He hands me a band aid, and turns his hand in my direction. "Would you mind?"

I shake my head and take the band aid, pulling the tabs and fixing the adhesive against his skin.

I step back, my expression still confused. I don't know if I'm overstepping if I ask him to explain himself. But I don't understand why he would lie about that. If Lissy didn't ask for Terra, why would Claude say she did?

"Merci," he says in his accent, then he flashes me a smile. "She really adores you, you know?"

"Lissy?" I wrap my arms around myself in a hug, as if I'm unconsciously creating a barrier between us.

He nods, still smiling. "I told Terra that Lissy wanted her, because she was asking for *you*."

My eyes widen. *Why would he do that? Why would he say Lissy wanted her mom when Lissy wanted me? Why would he lie?*

"I thought, maybe if Terra comforted her instead, she would somehow want to be present for Lissy." He inches closer to me, placing his hands on my shoulders. "I hoped that it would soften her heart. That she would stop putting her career before her child."

My heartbeat accelerates, not because Lissy has a better attachment with me than her own mother, but because of the way Claude cuts his eyes at me when he says this.

His eyes glisten as he tucks a loose strand of hair behind my ear and inspects my face.

I can't move.

I can't even think.

How did I let myself get into this situation?

Why am I not bolting for the door?

How long can I keep telling myself it's his cultural norm to have no personal space?

He rests his hand on my shoulder. "There is something so familiar about you. Something that makes me feel—" he lets his words linger. As if I'm supposed to know what word to use to finish that statement. The statement that feels mildly inappropriate for him to say to me. I consider his statement for a moment.

Yep, it was completely inappropriate.

I have no idea what's going on in his head!

I swallow hard. I've been lying to myself, telling myself that it's his culture that makes him have no personal space. But right now, with his hands on me and his eyes fixed on me like that, I don't think I can continue to lie to myself anymore.

"You feel it too, no?"

My phone blares and I quickly retrieve it from my pocket. "Hello?" My voice is exasperated, and I take a step back.

It's my driver.

I turn away from Claude as he drops his hands to his sides.

"I'll be right out," I say to the driver. I end the call and tuck my phone back into my pants. "I better go," I say to Claude as I hurry towards the door so he can't block me in like he's done before.

He lifts his bandaged hand. "Thank you for your help, Paloma."

I force a smile.

"We will see you next week, yes?"

I nod. "Yep, tell Lissy bye for me." Then I bolt for the car.

I release an exhale after I'm safely buckled in the backseat.

"In a hurry?" the driver says pulling onto the street.

I pull out my phone to text Jax but then decide this sort of thing is something I should probably wait to tell him in person.

"Yeah." I rest my head against the seat. "I'm going to my boyfriend's graduation."

...

The graduation ceremony was a lot bigger than I anticipated. Who knew that many kids went to online school?

And, of course, Birdie and Jax had their graduation party together at Birdie's mansion house.

"Come on, P.," Birdie calls from the pool. "You can be on my team." He lifts a ball up over his head.

I shake my head. "Play with Jax."

Jax takes a seat next to me on the patio. "I hate watermelon ball." He hands me a fork, hovering his plate in front of me.

I cut a slice of his cake and take a bite. "You hate all

sports," I say with a mouthful.

"That's true," he says, then he flashes me a comforting smile.

I let out a breath of relief. Just being in this environment with these people makes me feel so much more stable than being around Claude does.

"Fine," Birdie says, then he takes a dive down into the water.

When I reach my fork for his plate again, Jax pulls it away.

"Hey," I say trying to stab the cake again. "What are you doing? Share."

He lifts his eyebrow. "Not until you tell me what's going on."

"Nothing is going on," I lie. But I'm only lying because this doesn't feel like the right time to talk about how my employer makes me uncomfortable. Plus, the last time I told him about it, he brushed it off as normal father behavior.

I know how Claude is acting is *not* normal.

But what if Jax still doesn't see it?

"Okay." He stabs his cake and puts the entire piece into his mouth. I can barely understand him when he says, "No cake for you then."

I scoff. "That was so mean," I tease.

He shrugs, trying to chew on the cake without choking.

I feel a warm hand on my shoulder. "I'm happy to see you here, Paloma." It's Dipti, and I feel instantly relaxed being around her.

"Me too, I've been meaning to stop by but with work and everything it's hard."

She nods. "Don't be sorry. I understand." Her eyes search mine. "How is your job going, by the way?"

I glance at Jax, who is cleaning frosting from the corner

of his mouth with his thumb. It makes me laugh.

"It's good," I say facing Dipti. "I love the little girl, Lissy. She starts school in the fall, and I think I'm going to really miss her."

"I'm sure it will be difficult to leave, but that's what makes you good at your job. You're great at taking on challenges." Dipti leans down from her standing position to get closer to my ear. In a quiet voice she says, "And the emancipation process?"

My face falls. I haven't gotten a chance to talk with Jax about it yet and I'm not sure I want to surprise him with the information now.

"What are we talking about?" Birdie says, drying off with a towel.

He's dripping with pool water which makes Dipti step back and fling her hands in the air. "Birdie! Be mindful. The chemicals in the pool will ruin this satin." She flicks off a splatter he dripped onto her sleeve.

Birdie shakes his head, sending water flying in all directions.

Dipti walks away but not before saying, "Retched child." To me she says, "Don't be a stranger," then she turns to mingle with her other guests.

I scoot down, closer to Jax and make a place for Birdie to sit.

"Was it the graduation ceremony?" Jax says.

I turn to face him better. "What?"

Birdie wraps his towel around his shoulder. "I thought graduation was unnecessary."

Jax gives Birdie a look.

"What?" Birdie lifts his arms. "It was! What is the point of bringing a bunch of students together that barely know each other? I don't really care if Rebecca Hills was the valedictorian or not."

"That's not what I mean," Jax says.

"Oh." Birdie shakes his head to one side, trying to empty the water gathered in his ear. "What are you saying then?"

Jax rests his hand on my leg. "Paloma is being weird."

"I am not," I say half joking.

Birdie leans his head down on my shoulder. "Don't be weird P. It's not cool."

"Ew, you're getting my shirt wet!" I push his head off of me.

Jax pulls me onto his lap and pushes Birdie. "Stop harassing my girlfriend."

They both laugh.

Then Jax locks his arms around me. "For real though, what's up?"

I bite at the inside of my lip. "I don't know."

Jax gently tickles my side. "You know."

Birdie taps my knee. "Come on, P."

I let out a sigh, then sink into Jax's grip around me. I want to tell Jax about Claude. But not in front of Birdie. So I settle for telling them my other problem, since I know they are going to bug me until they get some sort of information out of me.

"I applied for my birth certificate."

Birdie claps his hands. "Get it girl!"

I pull my mouth to one side. "But then I got an email saying that they couldn't process it."

Birdie slumps. "Oh, that sucks."

"And it just feels like it's never going to happen for me." I press at my cuticles. "Adulting is hard."

"Yeah, that's why it's called *adulting*. It's not really meant for teenagers," Birdie says, then he smiles. "Maybe mamma bear can help you? I'll ask her if you want me to."

I shake my head. "No, she's already done so much and

I'll never be able to repay her for all the favors she's done for me."

Jax straightens and his eyes narrow. "What if we go to your mom's house and get it?"

I raise my eyebrows, unimpressed. "Walk into my mom's house and get my birth certificate?"

His eyes are bright when he nods enthusiastically.

"I don't think so," I say.

"Why not?" he says.

"Yeah," Birdie says. "Why not?"

I glance between both of them. "You guys are serious."

"*Yeah*," they say, nodding in unison.

I'm shaking my head, realizing my entire body is against this idea. "No, you guys, come on. Be real."

"We are," Jax says.

Birdie tilts his head endearingly. "This is us being so real right now."

My jaw drops, as I let out a laugh of disbelief. "No. What if she comes home while we're there? You guys are eighteen now, you would go to jail for breaking and entering."

Birdie raises his hands. "Oh, I never said I was going with you. I just thought it was a good idea for you to walk into *your* house and take *your* birth certificate."

When he puts it that way, it doesn't seem so insane.

Jax rubs my arm. "That's something even the cops won't be able to argue with."

I finally stop pushing on my cuticles, and roll my eyes. "I guess that wouldn't be a horrible idea."

"Awesome!" Jax says, knocking his knuckles together with Birdie's. Then he says, "When do you want to go?"

I shrug. "When can you go?"

"My schedule is completely free as of…" he checks his phone, "…right now."

I smile. "How about tomorrow?"

When I say this, a rush of terror mixed with excitement blasts through me. Like I'm either going to make a completely terrible decision, or the best choice of my life.

Either way, I'm glad Jax will be there.

CHAPTER

FOURTEEN

Jaxon

"So, you'll be in the house, while I stalk April at work?" Candice says with an expressionless face.

Paloma nods.

"Let me get my keys."

Paloma hugs me as Candice retreats inside her house. "Oh my gosh, I can't believe we're going to do this," she says.

I'm not sure I can either. After witnessing how chaotic her mom was at my dad's work, and hearing the stories Paloma told me; I wouldn't put it past her mom to have surveillance cameras or laser detectors in her house.

But it's worth the risk to get Paloma's birth certificate so she can finally complete the emancipation process.

Paloma fidgets with her hands. "Should we, like…I

don't know. Do we need walky-talkies or something?"

I take her hands in mine. "I think our cell phones will work fine."

She lets out a nervous puff of air. "Right." Her eyes are darting all over the place.

"Hey," I say, trying to catch her gaze. "It's going to be fine."

She bites her bottom lip, then says, "How do you know?"

I shrug. "I don't know," I look up into the clouds, "Faith, I guess?"

She rolls her eyes. "Well hopefully your God isn't too busy to help us out."

I pinch my mouth into a smile as I bite my tongue. I let her comment slide since she's in a high stress state right now.

The screen door slams shut, and Candice meets us in the driveway. "Should I just send you text updates?"

"I don't know." Paloma vigorously runs her hands through the bottom of her hair. "Should we facetime? What if the text doesn't go through and my mom shows up at the house and—"

"Let's do a group text," I say placing my hand on Paloma's trembling shoulder. Then to Candice, I say, "That way if something happens, we will all know in the group text."

Candice nods. "Cool." She opens her car door. "Add me to the group then."

Paloma's eyes look as if they might pop out of her head as her gaze follows Candice's car down the road.

We get into my car, and I wait for Paloma to give me directions to her house. When I realize she's in a panicked trance, I gently shake her leg. "Paloma?"

"Hmm?" She forcibly runs her hands through her hair

again.

I take her hands in mine until she looks at me. "It's going to be okay. Just chill out, alright?"

Her heavy breaths fill the space inside my car.

"You're not alone in this. Me and Candice have your back." I smile, reassuringly. "Okay?"

Paloma closes her eyes and lets out a deep exhale, slow and steady. Then she nods. "Okay."

"Okay." I release her hands and put the car into gear. "All I need are the directions to your mom's house."

She lets out a subtle laugh. "I forgot you're not from here. Just go straight down this road then take a left at the playground."

I back out onto the street, then pull forward.

She's staring at me with a grin when I glance at her.

"What?" I say with a smirk.

"You." Her voice is sweet. "It's weird to think I ever had a life without you in it."

My chest flutters. "Yeah," I say in a breath. "It's wild we ran into each other when we did."

"Literally!" She laughs and laces her hand in mine. "Tackle buddy."

"We'll never live that down."

"Never." She points at the road. "Turn up this cul-de-sac." Her voice shifts downward when she says, "It's the white one at the end."

My chest is still fluttering when I park in front of the neighbor's house. I can't tell if I'm rattled by Paloma's comment, or maybe I'm feeling the intensity of what we're about to do. Either way, I don't want to have an episode here.

Paloma pulls her phone out and sends a text to the group. Candice instantly replies, letting us know she's got her eyes locked on April.

"Ready?" I say.

Paloma shakes her head. "I don't think I can do this."

The fluttering in my chest is making my head start to spin. "We've got this." I exhale heavily, which makes Paloma crease her forehead as she draws her brows together.

"Are you okay?"

I swallow hard. "Yeah." I begin digging in my glove box at her knees. "I just need something real quick."

I ignore her expression as her eyes widen when she sees me open the bottle of prescription pills.

Her mouth falls agape. "What are you doing? What is that?"

I force the pills down with as much saliva I can gather in my mouth and grimace briefly before the pills disappear down my throat.

When my eyes lock on Paloma's, she's covering her mouth with her hand.

"It's not what you think." I reach over to comfort her, but she pulls away. "Paloma, come on. Please don't do that."

She searches my dashboard. I can tell her thoughts are in a million places at once. Then she opens her mouth like she's about to speak but nothing comes out.

I press my palms at my temples. I've never met someone with such extreme reactions to things. Why can't she just ask me what I'm doing? Or what pills I'm taking? Instead, she shuts down in this dramatic way.

I've been patient, but I'm starting to lose my patience. Especially because this has nothing to do with her, but somehow, she makes it about herself.

"I take pills so I don't get worked up about stuff." I grip the steering wheel in front of me. "Okay?"

She swings the door open. Stepping out of the car and

slams the door before she finds a spot to sit on the curb.

I let out an irritated puff of air, before swinging my door open and slamming it in a similar manner.

I pace the length of my car until I feel like I can speak to her in a decent tone.

I sit next to her. "Some things are going to be about you, and some things are about me." I duck my head down to look at her better. Tears are welled in her eyes, which makes me feel like a jerk for getting mad at her.

I wrap my arm around her shoulders. In a soft voice, I say, "I'm sorry I got mad." I touch the tip of her nose with mine. "And I'm sorry I didn't tell you about the pills."

She finally looks at me. Her expression tells me that she's cooling down too. "Why didn't you?"

"I don't know." I shrug. "I guess I was waiting for a good time to tell you."

She gives me a small grin from the side of her mouth. As if she can empathize with my statement. "It's not fun admitting you take prescription pills, is it?"

"Not at all."

"I know the feeling."

I smile. "I know." I feel a little guilty, since I know I'm downplaying the pills. I know if Birdie were here, he would be giving me one of his *looks*. But right now is not the time or place to tell her everything.

"Sorry." She slips my hand from her shoulder down to her waist, scooting closer to me. "I kind of freaked out."

"Just a little," I tease.

She scoffs. "Don't push it," she says with a smile. Then her eyes grow serious. "Can we not keep secrets from each other anymore?"

Our phones go off in unison before I can answer her.

Candice: April on the move.

Paloma's eyes flash at me in terror.

"Get in the car," I say instinctually.

We hurry into the car, and I pull down the street while Paloma is still buckling her seatbelt.

"Where are we going?" Paloma's voice is tense.

I scan the neighborhood. "Is there somewhere we can park and wait until we figure out what she's doing?"

"Go down this next street," she says.

"Which one?"

"Here, on the left."

"This way?" I say frantically.

"Wait!" She presses her hands at her temples. "She might come down that way if she's coming home from work. Go right instead."

I slow the car and turn right.

Paloma nearly chokes on her words when she screams, "Oh my gosh, that's her!"

"Get down. Get down!"

Paloma puts her head between her knees. I place my elbow near the window, and I lean my head into my hand when April passes me on the other side of the street. I'm hoping this covers my face enough so she doesn't recognize me.

It feels like we're moving in slow motion.

To my relief, April doesn't bother glancing at us.

I let out a hard exhale. "She didn't see us."

"How do you know?" Paloma is still crouching down in her seat. "She drove right by you. She would recognize you. She remembers everyone."

I shrug. "She didn't look at me."

Paloma sits up slowly, looking out the back window, then back to me. "Why do I feel like I'm doing something wrong?"

"Maybe because your mom is terrifying?"

She gives me a stern look.

I immediately regret saying that out loud.

"You're not doing anything wrong," I reassure her. Afterall, she's only going into *her* house to get *her* birth certificate.

We get another text. I assume it's from Candice. I leave it up to Paloma to check the message while I'm driving. Perks of group texting.

Paloma responds to the text, then says, "Candice wanted to know if we were okay."

I draw back in disbelief. "Really?"

Paloma tilts her head. "Well, she actually asked if she had enough time to get a milk shake at the diner before my mom goes back to work."

"That sounds more like Candice."

She lets out a laugh. "Right?" She continues texting again. "I'm going to tell her to wait by my mom's house and let us know when she leaves."

I turn onto a street that seems like it might be the downtown of this miniature town. "So, what now?"

"I don't know," her voice sounds a little defeated. "Maybe this was a bad idea."

"Is it safe to park?"

She gives me a confused expression. "What?"

"Is it safe to park? Is your mom going to appear out of nowhere again?" I scan the street then glance at her. "Because I want to make sure I'm looking at you when I say this."

"Say what?"

I raise my brow. "Paloma…"

She must realize what I'm trying to say to her, since she says, "Oh," she begins pressing at her fingertips. "Yes, it's safe to park here."

I pull into a parking space, put the car in park, and shift in my seat so I'm facing her.

She makes a slight snorting sound when she laughs. "You really needed to park for this?"

I nod with a grin. "I did."

"Okay, go on then."

"This—"

She lets out a bigger snorting laugh through her nose, then looks at me in surprise. "I'm so sorry, I don't know why this is so funny."

I give her an unimpressed expression. She must know I'm only joking since she continues to laugh.

"Okay," she says after a few deep breaths. "I'm sorry. I'm sorry it's hard to take you seriously when you're being so…"

"Serious?" I say.

She laughs again. "Yes," she covers her humungous grin.

I can't help but laugh in response to her. "You're all over the place today."

She's still smiling when she says, "What do you mean?"

"I don't know, you're up and down, happy and sad, then bursting in hysterical laughter."

Her expression grows more serious, but not in a bad way. She seems sure of herself when she says, "I feel like I'm more of myself today than I ever have been."

"Really?" I take her in with my gaze. Because I don't want to forget the first time she felt certain about herself.

She waits a moment before answering with a proud grin. "Yeah."

"How so?"

She scans the trees lining the sidewalk in front of us for a moment before she says, "I'm feeling my feelings for the first time." She faces me. "Like, I'm not trying to stuff my feelings, or downplay how I'm feeling, or pretend I'm cool. I'm just being me. Honest with myself," her eyes are darting between mine, "and honest with you."

"I'm glad." And I really am.

Normally, when she's mad at me, like she was about the pills, it would take at least a day until she decided to talk to me again. "And I'm glad I got to be the one to see the *real* you for the first time."

She scoots closer to me. "Me too." Then she places her hand behind my head and pulls me in for a kiss.

Before I can really enjoy what's happening, a voice outside the car pulls Paloma from me.

"No way," a guy says.

Paloma let's out a laugh of disbelief. "This is too perfect," she says with sarcasm.

"Already moving on to your next victim?" he says.

Victim?

I begin to roll my window down to say something, but Paloma slaps her hand around my arm. "Jax, please don't."

"Who is that?" I ask.

She shakes her head. "Just leave it alone."

I look at the guy again. She doesn't have to tell me who he is. I can tell he's her ex-boyfriend she told me about.

I roll my window down the rest of the way. "Hey bro, you got a problem or something?"

"Yeah, *bro*," he mocks. "You should know your girlfriend is crazy."

I look at Paloma, her eyes are begging me to stop. I face the guy again. "Yeah, I know."

He blows raspberries at us and continues walking away as he mumbles, "Whatever."

Paloma's expression fills with excitement as she rolls her window down. "That's right! He knows I'm crazy!"

Her maniacal laughter returns.

"Okay, Paloma," I say. "We better go before more people find out you're back in town."

I'm not sure if she didn't hear me or if she's having too much fun antagonizing her old boyfriend, since she lifts herself out of the window and yells, "Walk away, Levi! You're just jealous!"

He's already crossed the street, but finds it necessary to say, "Jealous of what? How crazy you are?"

I decide to leave before Paloma draws any more attention to us with her newfound power in using her voice.

As we pass Levi, Paloma yells, "Jealous that I'm happier without you!"

I can see Levi flip us off, but I don't say anything about it since Paloma is too pleased with herself and oblivious of what's happening around her.

No wonder she has a skewed perception of religion.

"That wasn't weird at all," I say.

Paloma keeps her head by the window, letting the subtle wind blow her hair around her face. "Let's go get it."

I know what she's talking about, but to be make sure, I say, "Your birth certificate?"

"Yeah."

"Do you want to wait for your mom to leave first?"

"No."

"*No?*" Maybe she has lost her mind. "I thought you didn't want your mom to find out that we're in town?"

She faces me. "Who cares. What is she going to do?"

I want to say that her mom could do a lot. The woman is off her rocker. Worse than any *Karen* I've ever encountered. But instead, I turn around and back track my way to her mom's again.

We pass Candice's car at the end of the street, but she's too busy on her phone to notice us. When we park in front of the white house, Paloma doesn't miss a beat before she makes her way up the steps to the front door.

I fumble out of my car to follow her. "Paloma," I don't know why I'm whispering. "What's the plan?"

"No plan." Her eyes are fixed on the door as she rings the doorbell. "Just living in the moment."

I'm all about living in the moment, but sometimes a plan is good to have too. Before I can ask any more questions to formulate my own plan, April swings the door open.

"Paloma?" April's expression shifts into surprise.

"Mom." Paloma crosses her arms. "Can we come in?"

April steps aside.

"Hi, April," I say, trying to seem as normal as I possibly can in the second most awkward encounter I've ever had with her. "How's it going?"

She ignores me and instead gives her attention to Paloma. "What are you doing here? Are you moving back? Where are you going?" Her concerned tone grows hard in a matter of milliseconds. "I'm talking to you."

"Nope." Paloma makes a beeline for a bedroom off the kitchen. "I'm not moving back."

April throws her hands up in confusion before they both disappear into the bedroom. "Then what are you doing?"

I debate on taking a seat at the couch. Their home is quaint and modern. Alarmingly clean too.

I decide not to sit, and instead take a step in the direction of the bedroom where I can see Paloma's shadow rummaging about as April stands helplessly behind her. I'm sure it's shocking for April to see Paloma with a new sense of confidence.

Suddenly, Paloma emerges with a large file box. It makes a thud when she drops it on the living room floor.

"Tell me what's going on." April's voice sounds unsure now.

Paloma throws the lid off the box and begins searching through papers. Since I already know what she's hunting for I decide to examine the photos on the wall. There are only three pictures, so it doesn't take long.

One of baby Paloma held in April's arms. They both look genuinely happy. It's a small candid photo.

The second, looks like one of those stale Sears family portraits. April has a stiff smile, and Paloma's smile doesn't match her sad eyes. It makes me wince; she couldn't be more than seven or eight years old and already has the dark sorrow of lonely pain in her eyes.

The last one is a school photo of Paloma. It looks recent, but I don't recognize the girl staring back at me at all. Not because of her chopped haircut, but because she's a girl carrying the weight of the world on her shoulders. The same girl with the broken soul I met at the mall.

I look back at Paloma. She's on her knees, hunched over the box, sifting through papers. Knowing exactly what she wants and going after it with certainty and determination.

I meet her on my knees. I'm proud of her. I don't know if she feels it for herself, but I'm proud enough for the both of us.

She smiles and hands me a folder to search through, while she takes a thick manilla envelope.

I can't even help her because I can't stop looking at her. She's come a long way from that girl in the photo hanging on the wall.

I finally pull my eyes from her and flip the folder open.

"Please." April's voice sounds desperate. "Please, just tell me what's going on. Are you in some kind of trouble?"

I sort of feel sorry for her, but this doesn't seem like something I should explain for Paloma. So instead of overstepping, I stay quiet and begin scanning over the papers in the file. Half aware of April's desperation to get her daughter to communicate with her, and half aware that I think I've just found the document we came here for.

I scan the document then say, "Paloma?" Yep, this is definitely her birth certificate.

She slaps an envelope and loose papers against her legs, then facing April, she says, "You know what, mom. Fine."

"Paloma," I repeat.

April slumps down on the edge of her couch. "I only want to help you."

"Really?" Paloma rises to her feet, unphased by the papers falling from her legs into a mess on the floor. "Now you care? Now you want to help me?"

April nods, her brows are drawn apart in a pained expression. "Yes, and if you want to get emancipated, I will do whatever I need to do to make that easier for you."

Paloma thrust her hands at her hips. "Are you joking?"

"No, of course not." April looks sincere, *I think*. "Whatever I can do to help, please, just tell me."

Paloma crosses her arms. "Well," she stares at her mom for a moment before saying, "You could sign the forms."

April swallows hard. "Okay."

"Okay."

I lift up the document when I decide they are done talking. "So, you don't need this anymore?"

Their eyes shift to the document in my hand.

April's eyes widen, and she quietly says, "*No, no, no,*" under her breath.

Paloma's firm expression turns into relief as her eyes light up. "You found it," she says, snatching it from my grip. Which is what I was hoping she would do, since I know what the document says.

And because I know what it says, I know Paloma

probably won't be as happy as she is right now after she reads it.

April stands up. "Paloma, wait, I don't know if you—"

"I thought my last name was *Smith*," Paloma's expression is full of confusion, but her voice sounds dark.

April clasps her hands in front of her mouth. "I was trying to protect you."

"Protect me from my father? Protect me from the truth?"

"Protect you from yourself, and all the questions I knew you would have. And from being hurt by knowing who your father is."

Paloma's mouth falls agape. Instead of defending herself any further, she faces me and says, "Let's go."

I don't waste any time opening the door and following her out. I don't have to ask if she's okay. I know she's not. I know the information on her birth certificate is an unexplainable blow. I'm sure she's confused, and frustrated, and thinking about all the *what if's*.

"Paloma, *please!*" April is standing at the bottom of the porch steps.

Paloma marches to the car.

I can see Candice still parked at the end of the road. She lifts her hands in confusion, like she's asking what the deal is. She's probably wondering if she can get that milk shake yet.

I wave her off, letting her know she can go.

When I look back at April's tear-streaked face, I can't help but have compassion for her. Even though she's chaotic and insane. Even though she wasn't a great mom, she's still a person with a heart and soul.

So, I lock my car.

Paloma pulls at the door handle. Quickly realizing it's not going to open, she looks up at me. "It's locked," she says.

"I know."

She draws her brows together. "Unlock it. Let's get out of here."

I give her a gentle expression. "You should talk to her."

"Why?" I can hear the disgust in her voice.

I look behind her at April's brokenness. "Just look," I say.

She turns around, then back to me. "That's not real. Can't you see she's trying to manipulate me?"

"Look again," I say gently.

She forces air from her nose, then turns around.

"*Please,*" April repeats.

Paloma lets out a groan and approaches April. "Mom, I love you, but keeping this from me," she holds up the document, "is worse than anything else you've ever done to me. *Ever.*"

"I thought I was doing the right thing." April sniffs back tears. "I didn't want your father to take you from me. He's not the man you imagined."

Paloma lets out a laugh full of disbelief and hurt that could crack the sky. "Well, *surprise,* he's exactly the rich, smart, and loving father I imagined he would be."

April cocks her head to the side. "But—"

"But, what? You think I don't know who he is?" Paloma points to her birth certificate. "Here's some news for you, *mom.* I've been working for Claude Laurent since I moved to Dallas."

CHAPTER

FIFTEEN

Paloma

I can't stop reading his name.

Claude Laurent.

How cruel is the universe?

I mean, out of all the places I could have ended up. How did I find a job working for my father?

My stomach twists into a knot when I think about the last time I was with him. I wonder if he would look at me like that, or speak to me in that way, or touch me if he knew I was his daughter.

I could puke I feel so disgusted.

I wish Jax were here. He seems to have insight on these things. Although I'm not sure I want to tell him more than he already knows.

He has a scheduled tour at Baylor University today—

not that he's going to apply. I think he's trying to make his dad happy despite the fact he's already decided to go to college in Dallas.

And I'm supposed to be getting ready for work right now.

Part of me wants to avoid this entire situation and bail on work altogether. But the other part of me wants Claude to know the truth.

...

I punch the code with my finger, into the buttons on the door and let myself in after the deadbolt unlocks.

The house is quiet. Odd.

I scan the livingroom, then the kitchen.

"Hello?" I make my way up the stairs and down the hall. "Lissy?"

I hear footsteps on the marble floor below the staircase and rush to meet them.

"Paloma." It's Claude's footsteps. And I'm met by his cheerful French accent. "I was in my office and did not hear you come in."

My beating heart is jamming my throat.

"Lissy is playing a game."

I nod. Which is all I *can* do.

He smiles. "She wanted you to find her." He turns back to his office while still talking to me. "Hide and seek? Marco Polo or something? She's been very quietly waiting for you to arrive."

He flips his head to me once more before disappearing into his office. "I'm sure you know it. Anyway, Terra is out, and I'll be back this evening."

"Okay." I manage to scrape the words passed my lips.

He emerges from his office with a satchel and his keys. Without looking back he opens the door and says, "Au revoir, ma cherie!"

I'm not sure if his statement was for me or Lissy. But what I do know, is that my father just walked out the door in oblivion to the fact that he's my father.

I had planned the entire thing out while Dipti's driver silently chauffeured me from Roma's apartment to Claude's house.

I was supposed to find Claude playing with Lissy in the living room.

I was supposed to hand the birth certificate to him, and he would say, *Oh what is this? A birth certificate, yes?* His happy French accented voice would turn into confusion when he realized that it was *my* birth certificate.

Then when he read that the mother is April Rimerez and the father is *Claude Laurent*, he would burst into tears and try to hug me.

But I would say, *No, you didn't try to find me all this time.*

Suddenly a thump in the bathroom pulls me from my thoughts.

It's probably better if I wait to show him my birth certificate anyway. Plus, now I'll have more time to think of a better way to present the information to him.

"Marco," I say, opening the bathroom door.

"*Polo!*" Lissy's voice is muffled.

I open the towel cabinet, but she's not there.

I pull the shower curtain back, even though I know she's not going to be there. "Marco?"

"Polo!"

I thrust open the cupboard under the sink. "Found you!"

Lissy jumps into my arms with a belly full of contagious giggles.

"That was a good hiding spot," I say.

She scratches at a mosquito bite on her arm. "I was

hiding there for a really long time, Nanny, and now I'm hungry."

"I bet." I take her hand in mine. "Let's go make you something to eat."

"Cookies?"

I shake my head, and widen my eyes. "Better."

"Cake?"

I shake my head again. "Even better."

"What's better than cookies and cake?"

I hunch down in front of her once we reach the bottom of the staircase. "Gelato."

Her face beams with a smile. "Botolino Gelato?"

I nod. "Yep!"

After we devour our ice cream, we play in the tree house for hours.

Lissy wanted to build a fort, so we essentially moved the contents of her entire bedroom into the treehouse. We're both sticky and hot from the humidity but I don't mind, because even though Lissy doesn't know it yet, we're basically two sisters playing together. And I can't wait to tell her.

"Nanny?"

My eyes are closed and I'm laying on a pile of stuffed animals. We are playing zoo-keeper and she's decided it's nap time.

"Hmm?" I say, wishing this was a real nap time.

"Can you write a story for me?"

I turn to my side, placing my head on my hand. "Sure. What do you want the story to be about?"

She taps her head and scrunches her face to the side in thought. "Two friends."

I smile. "Okay, that sounds like a great story."

She begins to pull a spiral notebook and a handful of crayons from her bag. "Sorry, Nanny, but it's a sad story."

I frown. "Oh?" Now I'm curious what she's thought up in her mind.

She hands me the paper and a yellow crayon. "Write this," she says, then she clears her throat. "Once upon a time…"

I scribble across the paper mumbling the sentence to myself. "Okay. And then?"

She takes two of her stuffed animals and pretends they are walking. "There was a fishy and a bumble bee."

I nod. "Were they friends?"

"No," she says, then pouts her lip before continuing, "The fishy wanted to be best friends with the bumble bee. But the bumble bee had to do lots of paperwork."

I tilt my head when I look up at her.

"Write it, Nanny," she says as she points to my frozen hand, before continuing. "The fishy lived in a fishbowl and the bumble bee buzzed around all over the place because she was too busy to have a home."

I do as she says and keep writing. "And then what happened?" I say.

She lets out a small sigh. "Well, the fishy asked the bumble bee if she wanted to play. But the bumble bee would always say, *later*. Every time, the fishy says, *please come and play with me pretty bumble bee*, but she says, *later, later, later, later*.

"And one day the fishy decided he was going to be so brave."

I'm trying to write as quickly as she's talking.

"The fishy swam to the bottom of his bowl. And he waited all day long until the bumble bee finally flew over his fishbowl. When he saw her, he swam so so so fast and jumped out of his fishbowl!"

I look up at her as she throws her toy fish over the side of the treehouse. A gasp escapes my mouth, but I don't say anything.

Lissy is staring down at the bumble bee toy in her hands, ignoring the fact that she just abandoned her fish toy in such an extreme way. Her voice is sad when she says, "And the bumble bee was so mean, she didn't even see the fishy trying to play with her."

My mouth falls agape.

Maybe we've been reading too many dramatic Shakespeare plays. Or maybe this is more personal. This story feels a lot more like a depiction of her relationship with Terra. Or maybe the relationship she's seen between Terra and Claude. I don't know, but one thing is for sure, poor Lissy is feeling the lack of attention from her mom.

"So, what happened to the fish? Did he find a new friend?" I say, hoping for a positive turn of events to her story.

Lissy looks down at the grass where the fish toy is lying. "The fishy died."

My eyes widen. *Yep, definitely too much Shakespeare for a five-year-old.*

"And so did the bumble bee," she says quickly, tossing the bee down to the grass to meet the fish toy.

This officially shows me that it doesn't matter if you're rich or poor or middle class. All families are messed up. Or maybe all kids just want to have attention from their parents?

I don't know.

I'm a little worried that her parents might find this story so I shove it into my pocket so I can throw it away later. Especially because it's written in my handwriting.

But Lissy notices what I'm doing and tries to retrieve the crumpled paper from my pocket. "Nanny, that's my story. Stop! You're ruining it!"

"I'm sorry." I don't stop her from taking it. "But it was

hard to see with the yellow crayon. Maybe we can write another story with a darker color?"

"I have a better idea," she says.

"What?"

"We could eat gelato again." Her eyes meet mine with a smirk.

I rub a dirt smudge off her leg. "That sounds like the best idea ever."

The rest of the afternoon goes by quickly. Lissy is so tired by bedtime, she doesn't make it through *Two Noble Kinsmen* before she falls asleep.

I close the book and place it on her shelf. But instead of retreating to the couch, I watch Lissy's gentle breathing and her sleeping face. She looks so much like Terra. I wish she looked like me, or that we both looked like Claude. Maybe then he would have been able to just look at me and know I was his daughter.

I hear the front door close, and suddenly I wish Claude wasn't my father at all. I wish my father was a stranger I didn't know. I wish that I wasn't in this mess. I wish I didn't have to have this conversation with Claude at all.

I finally get up, dim the lights, and crack Lissy's bedroom door.

I suck in a rush of air when I see Claude reheating the onion soup the cook made for dinner.

"She's asleep," I say.

He's tasting the soup with his finger when he turns to face me. "Ah, good." He motions for me to take a seat. "Where did you find her?"

I tilt my head. "What?"

"The game," he says with a mouthful.

I blink. "Right, uh, she was under the sink cupboard in the bathroom."

"Good hiding spot." He takes another bite.

My pulse is racing, because I know what I'm about to do next is going to change everything.

"Claude," my voice is not the confident tone I imagined it would be.

He gives me a look of anticipation.

"There's something I have to tell you."

His expression shifts. "Is everything okay?"

I swallow hard, trying to get my throat to open, trying to gain the strength to say what I need to say. "Uh," I can't look at him. "I think you're my father."

He drops his spoon to the table. "I do not understand."

I retrieve my birth certificate from my bag and hand it to him without a word.

He scans the document, his chest rising and falling with each breath.

"How long have you known?" he says.

"Since yesterday."

I always imagined my father would come and rescue me from my mom. I thought he would be the one to introduce himself to me. But that's not the way the world works, I guess.

Instead, I'm standing here, watching my father read over my birth certificate in…disbelief? No, he looks more…*relieved?*

"I thought this." He's still holding the document, but his eyes are looking intensely into mine. "I thought this was true."

I crease my brow. "You thought what was?" Even though he speaks English, there's still seems to be a language barrier between us.

He moves around the counter, invading my personal space in the same way he's been doing since the day I met him.

He sets the document down, taking both of my hands

in his. "When I saw you, I had this connection."

Here we go again with the touching and connection stuff.

"I thought I knew you, I thought to myself, could this be my Paloma?"

I'm standing now. "Wait, you knew about me?"

"Of course I did."

I pull my hands from his, crossing them over my chest. "Why didn't you say anything?"

"You told me your name was Paloma Smith." He runs his hand through his hair, then hugging his arms around himself, he says, "My Paloma's name is Paloma Laurent. When you said your name was Smith, I convinced myself it could not be." He lifts his arms and shrugs. "How would I recognize you? You were only a baby when I saw you the last time. But there was something still so familiar about you."

"What?" I'm not following any of this information.

He gives me a confused look. "What did April tell you?"

I shake my head. "Nothing. She lied and told me my last name was Smith my whole life. And she wouldn't talk about my father…about you, at all. She refused to have any conversation about you."

His eyes glisten, and his voice is soft when he says, "I am so sorry."

The words come out before I can stop them. "Why didn't you ever come see me?"

He looks equally confused and heartbroken. "After the divorce—"

"You were married?" I knew my mom was keeping secrets about my father, but she didn't even tell me she was married to him.

"We were married right after you were born, and divorced six months later," he says with a grim voice.

It's as if his eyes are locked on mine. I can't look away

AURORA STENULSON

even though I hate that I'm watching a grown man's eyes fill with tears.

"Something changed in her. She became possessive of you and very angry at me." He pushes a tear away. "And after the divorce, she convinced the judge I was a horrible person. I was supposed to have supervised visits with a social worker so I could see you, but that did not happen because your mom took you and left."

I clasp my hand over my mouth. How could she do this to me? And to Claude? How could a judge believe her lies?

I don't stop him or resist him when he pulls me in to hug me. "Back then I had no money, or resources to find you. I was not even a legal citizen yet. I felt so helpless," he puts his hands around my face and looks at me, "but I have thought about you every day. And now I know the connection between us was real."

It doesn't bother me that he says this, because now I realize everything he's been doing has been because he sensed I might be his daughter.

He wraps his arms around me to hug me again, and I can't help but sob into his shoulder when I hug him back.

"*What is this?*"

I don't have to look to know who it is.

We turn to face Terra who is standing in the kitchen. One hand holding her heels and the other placed on her hip, or where her hip would be if her belly wasn't protruding with her and Claude's unborn baby.

I can't speak. Honestly, I don't know how to explain this. She's just walked into her house where her husband and nanny are crying and hugging in her kitchen.

"Terra, come, you will not believe this," Claude begins, but he's quickly cut off by Terra.

"Oh no, you're wrong." Her eyes narrow as she takes a step closer to us. And suddenly I'm very aware of Claude's

222

arm around my shoulders. "You see, I think I will believe you when you tell me that you're having an affair with our nanny."

I gasp.

Claude releases me and approaches Terra. "No, no, you do not understand. I would never do that to you, or to our family."

She thrusts her shoes in his direction, but he shoulders the blow. Then she tries pushing him, but he stands steady in his firm stature, which only seems to frustrate her more.

"I'm pregnant, Claude," her voice is pitchy, like she's about to scream. "How could you do this to me?"

I want to leave, but I don't know how to get around them without moving into the line of fire.

"I have done nothing." He tries to comfort her by holding her arms. "I love you. Paloma is not my lover, she is my daughter."

They are both looking at me now, and I wish I could disappear.

Terra must misread my silence, since she flips her head back to Claude and slaps him across the face.

I cover my mouth in shock.

Terra marches out the door, Claude following closely behind her and begging her to believe him.

"Liar!" She screams, before slamming the door, rushing to her car, and peeling out onto the road.

Claude has his back to me. He has one hand in his pocket, and is rubbing his eyes with the other.

I take the document from the table and shoulder my bag. "I'm sorry."

He inhales deeply, his voice is low but still has the hint of that positive tone he seems to carry with him when he says, "I should be apologizing. She does this sometimes," he waves his hand in a circular manner, "convinces herself

I am having an affair. It is the same story when she was pregnant with Lissy."

I hand him my birth certificate. "Maybe this will help?"

He glances down at the paper, then back to me. "Maybe."

"You can make a copy, or take a picture. I can talk to her, if you think that would help?"

He grins from the side of his mouth. "She should not need evidence. I know I am honest, and deep down she knows too. She might only need more time to accept that." He drops his head back and chuckles to himself before facing me again, like he can't believe he's having this conversation with me right now. "Do not worry about it. We will be fine."

I nod. "Okay, if you're sure."

The lights of the driver's car shine through the window as he pulls into the driveway.

Claude squeezes my shoulder affectionately. "Even though Terra is confused and upset, this is one of the happiest nights of my life."

Before opening the door to leave, I put my hand over his, and smile. "It's one of the happiest nights for me too."

CHAPTER

SIXTEEN

Jaxon

"This is ridiculous."

I kiss Paloma's cheek. "You can do it."

She groans. "I feel stupid."

"You're not stupid," I lean my chin against her head, "Just hit submit so we can hang out."

She groans again.

I reach around her and hit the submit button on my laptop.

She flips her head around and her mouth is wide open in disbelief. "Why did you do that?"

"You were taking too long."

She hits my arm playfully. "You're the worst."

"I think you meant to say," I clear my throat so I can talk in my best Paloma voice. "*Thank you, Jax. You're the best boyfriend ever. I'm so glad you finally did what I couldn't do, and submitted the GED application for me so we can go to college together."*

She slumps back against my headboard. "I do not sound like that."

I flop over and close the space between us. "You really do though."

She pretends to bite my shoulder.

"Let's eat, I'm hungry." I rise to my feet and take her hands in mine to help her off the bed.

"What if I fail the GED test?"

"You won't."

"What if I do?"

"Then," I turn to face her, "you'll take it again. And again, and again, and again. Until you pass and get into college." I touch the tip of my nose against hers. "With me."

"You're way to optimistic. Just like Claude."

"How's that going?"

"Work?"

I raise my brow.

She shrinks. "I know you didn't mean work..."

"Well?"

"I don't know." She pushes at her nails. "He's been trying to organize brunch with me. But after everything with Terra, I don't want to be around her until I know she's cooled off."

"Makes sense." I tap my dresser in thought. "You know, you could still hang out with Claude without Terra. And get to know him better...as your dad."

A smile curls up the side of her mouth. "I know. I guess I could do that." She moves to my door. "I miss Lissy too. I'll call and set something up with them later."

"Good idea."

We exit my bedroom, but halfway down the stairs I realize Paloma's not behind me. She's standing in the hall in front of my mom's bedroom.

I walk back up the stairs. I know she's been curious about my mom.

And since she found her birth certificate and told Claude he was her father, she seems to be interested in family relationships more than ever.

"Do you want to meet her?" I say.

She sucks in a rush of air. "Can I? I mean, will she know I'm there?"

I shrug. "I don't know," I open the door to my mom's bedroom. "Let's find out."

Paloma's eager expression quickly fades when she sees my mom. She stands at the foot of her hospital bed for a moment, before saying, "Can I touch her?"

"Sure."

"Will she feel it?"

"I don't know," I rub the back of my neck, "I guess I haven't tried."

She tilts her head. "You haven't touched her since she's…"

She lets her words linger without finishing her sentence, but I know what she means. She can't believe I haven't held my mom's hand or hugged or sat next to her since she's been in this vegetative state.

"She's not awake, so I don't think it matters."

Her face twists. "She hasn't been awake at all?"

I shake my head.

"What about that guy that was here helping her stretch?"

I think for a moment. "The physical therapist?"

"Yeah, wasn't she awake for that?"

I nod. "She was, but she's gotten much worse in the last

few months. I haven't seen her move or open her eyes in a while."

"Do you ever talk to her?"

I shake my head. "Not really."

"Why, not?"

I pull at my hair on the top of my head. "I don't know." I lock eyes with Paloma. "I guess I don't see any reason to."

Paloma moves to the edge of the bed and sits next to my mom. "If her heart is still beating, she's still in there." She faces me with unsettled widened eyes. "Right?"

"I don't know." I watch Paloma take my mom's hand in hers and a rush of guilt plagues my core. "We should go."

"Can I say something to her first?"

The irritation begins to rise in my voice. "Sure, but then we should really go. Okay?"

She nods and turns back to my mom. Her eyes scan over the wires, breathing tube, and machines crowding the bed.

"Hi, Mrs. Ferrington, or Bethany. I'm not sure what you want me to call you." She glances at me, then back to my mom with a smile. "It's nice to finally meet you. I hope you can hear me, because I want you to know that you have an amazing son. Jax is honest, and thoughtful, and kind. He's been a rock in my life and I'm really grateful that you taught him how to love people so well."

I cover my mouth with the side of my fist. I like to think I try to obtain all of those attributes she described. But am I really as honest as I think I am?

"Anyway." Paloma rises from the bed, resting my mom's hand at her side again. "I'll see you later."

We head down to the kitchen, but I'm not as hungry as I was before Paloma decided to talk with my mom.

"Thanks for that," she says, tossing a grape into her mouth.

"Yeah, no problem." I pluck a grape from the vine, but feel too much shame to eat right now. "You know she's not there anymore, right?"

She gives me a disappointed expression.

"I'm not trying to be insensitive."

"You kind of sound that way."

I raise my eyebrow. "I just mean," I blow out a puff of air, "that's not my mom. She's just a body that's literally being kept alive by tubes and machines."

She shrugs without looking at me. "For someone that believes in a God of miracles, you sound pretty un-believing right now."

"I'm being realistic." I don't know why this is making me upset. "I just don't want you to get your hopes up."

"Well, too late, because I think a part of her is still in there. Even if the machines are doing all the work right now."

"You and my dad, both."

She places her hand over mine. "Hey," she says. When I look at her, she gives me a soft smile. "It's okay if we don't agree. Maybe you're right. Maybe she is gone. But maybe your dad isn't ready to say goodbye yet. But when he is, you won't be so shocked when she's gone, right? Wouldn't you rather spend a little more time with her here like this, than not at all?"

My irritation melts at her insight. "I thought I was the one with all the wisdom and advice."

She moves closer to me and reaches her arms around my torso to hug me. I don't know why her statement hits me so hard, but I'm thankful she said the words out loud that have been swirling around in my head.

"It's okay to feel stuff," her voice is muffled against my

shoulder.

"I know," I say with an exhale.

My phone rings.

"It's my dad," I say, showing her my phone screen.

While I'm on the phone with my dad, I keep my eyes on Paloma as she digs through my cupboards and fridge to gather the fixings for a sandwich.

I smile, not realizing when the switch happened where she became so comfortable in my kitchen. But happy she's there.

I end the call.

"My dad needs me to go down to his work and help out for a few hours," I say.

She faces me with an eager expression. "I can help you," she says.

"Paloma." I sit next to her.

"Hmm?" She's taking enormous bites out of her sandwich. It's kind of cute.

"Can you stop eating for a second, so I can say this to you?"

She places her sandwich on the plate. With a mouthful she says, "You know, you can just tell me things. You don't have to pull the car over, or get me to stop eating, or—"

"*You're perfect.*"

Her eyes widen.

"You are," I say. "You're perfect. You're beautiful. You're brave and smart. You're my absolute favorite person."

Maybe this is too much for her.

She just found out she's been working for her biological father. She completed her emancipation paperwork. She applied for her GED. She met my mom. And now I'm throwing this at her.

I wipe a crumb from her face. "Too much?"

She shakes her head.

"Then why aren't you saying anything?"

Her eyes flick between mine, before she says, "You're my absolute favorite person too."

CHAPTER

SEVENTEEN

Paloma

I slap the study guide against my legs.

"You're doing great," Jax reassures me. "Let's take a break."

"I want a gap year."

He tilts his head. "A gap year?"

I toss the study guide on the floor. "Yep." I sit cross legged on my bed. "Lots of people do that. After they graduate, they just take a year off."

"What would you do with your gap year?"

I shrug. "Not study for a stupid GED?"

He laughs and leans over the pile of books on my bed to kiss me, then his face grows serious. He looks like he's about to tell me something serious.

"What if we weren't together?"

232

I scrunch my nose. "I would hate that. I can't even imagine it."

He stares into my eyes for a moment. "There's something I—"

Roma gently knocks on my door before opening it, sending Jax jumping to the other side of the bed with a book open in his arms.

"Hey," Roma says. "I'm heading off to work."

"Okay," I say. "Have a good shift."

She enters my room, taking several steps closer to me. Which is odd behavior for her.

"I just got off the phone with Candice." She straightens her scrub top over her stomach. "Mom's not doing well."

I feel my smile fade. "Oh no," I'm not sure what else to say, so I settle for, "Is she okay?"

Jax sits up. He looks at Roma, then me, then back to Roma. "Should I go?"

Roma holds up her hand and shakes her head. "No, you're fine," She says to him. Then facing me, she says, "I'm going to make some calls and see if I can get mom into a nursing home. It's time."

I raise my eyebrows. "Wow. Okay." I'm not sure why she's telling me this. It seems like the only time we have a conversation, it revolves around something intense.

She presses her mouth together. "So I think I'm going to ask Candice to move in with me so she can finish high school here."

I nod with excitement. "Absolutely." But does this mean I have to move out? Roma only has two bedrooms in her apartment.

"Okay, I just wanted to make sure you're prepared."

My face falls. "I understand."

She checks her phone. "I thought you would be more excited to share your room with her. You two were good friends, weren't you?"

I let out a breath of relief. "Yes. I mean, *yes*! I misunderstood what you were saying. I would love to be roommates with her."

Roma smiles. "Good."

"As long as she's okay with it."

Roma puts her phone in her oversized purse. "Well she'll have to be unless she wants to live in foster care."

I let out a nervous laugh. "Good point."

She turns to exit my room. "See you later," then she points to Jax and says, "And no sleep overs."

"Yes, Ma'am," Jax smiles. "Wouldn't do it if I could. I have to meet Birdie in the morning for a shooting."

She stares at him blankly.

"Not like a gun shooting," he waves his hands in front of him, then pretends to hold a video camera. "Like a film shooting. For our next YouTube video."

"On that note, I'm going to leave now," she laughs on her way out at his comment.

I lay across my bed on my stomach. "That's awesome, right?"

He sets the textbook down and moves closer to me. "That we're making a video?" He cocks his head to the side. "Or that you and Candice get to be roommates?"

I nod.

He scrunches his face to one side. "Well…"

I push his leg playfully. "Hey, she's my best friend."

"I thought I was your best friend?"

"You're my best friend boyfriend, slash tackle buddy, slash GED study partner, slash tutor, slash—"

He kisses me again. "You're my best friend girlfriend, slash tackle buddy too."

I'm certain my giddy smile looks ridiculous right now, but I don't even care because I'm the happiest I've ever been.

He picks up the study guide off the floor. "But if I'm going to respect Roma's curfew, and get enough sleep before the *video* shooting, we better get back to studying."

I take the study guide from him, and groan. "Fine," I say, scanning the next question.

• • •

I've never heard that sound before.

It's unexplainable.

Like the sound you make when you come up for air after swimming too far down in the deep end of a pool.

When my eyes finally open, a rush of cold chills runs through my body as my heart begins pounding in my chest.

"Jax." I shake his arm.

We must have fallen asleep studying. The lights are still on, and the study guide is open on my lap.

"Jax," I repeat as he continues gasping for air.

I can't think straight, my hands are clammy, and my pulse is throbbing through my entire body so hard it's the only thing I can focus on.

"Jax, you're scaring me." I try pulling him up into a seated position.

He doubles over, clenching his arms around his stomach.

I scramble for my phone. "I'm calling your dad."

His arm is heavy when he thrusts my phone out of my hands. "Don't," he manages to say between his gasping.

"You need help." I rush out of my room. "I'll drive you home."

I quickly gather our shoes at the front door and hurry back. By the time I return he's not in my bed anymore. I hear vomit splatter violently in the toilet.

I rush to the bathroom, crouching next to him in one

swift motion. "I'm seriously calling your dad."

He holds his hand up. "No, don't," he says before cradling the toilet and puking again. His entire body heaves forward violently.

"You're not okay."

I'm not sure what he's trying to be tough about. He can't deny that something is wrong. First, he's waking up gasping for air, then he's puking in the bathroom.

His breathing is heavy when he says, "I know what's going on. I just need my pills."

"I'll get them." I'm sure they are in the glove box where I've seen them on occasion when he's taken them. I reach into his pockets and take his keys. "I'll be right back."

It feels like the front door won't open fast enough to let me out. And the elevator seems even slower as I wait to reach the first floor. I drop the keys twice trying to get his car to unlock before digging in his dashboard for his prescription. On the way back up the elevator, I wish I had called his phone and left it on speaker near him so I could have at least known what's going on right now.

I can't help but think what's happening is somehow related to him passing out on the stairs at his house. Who gets dizzy for no reason like that?

When I reach him in the bathroom, he's laying on the rug. He seems a little more calmed down, which is reassuring.

I fill a cup with water and quickly take a pill from the bottle. "Here," I say, squatting behind him to help hold his head up.

His throat rolls as he forces the pill down with a sip of water.

"I need two," his voice is raspy.

I repeat the action again, giving him a pill and water while propping his head up.

I pull the towel from the rack and wipe the perspiration from his face. "You're okay." I'm trying to be calm, but really, I'm completely freaked out.

He said his pills were to help him when he's feeling *worked up*. I assumed he meant it was for anxiety. But I'm starting to wonder if *worked up* means something else for him.

His hand is cold when he places it on my trembling leg, his breathing is labored when he says, "Hey, I'm fine." He looks up at me. "There's nothing to worry about, okay?"

I nod.

But I don't believe him.

And I'm afraid if I ask what's really going on, I won't like the answer.

He scoots back against the bathtub, and I move around him to get his shoes. "I still think we should go to your house where your dad can help you."

"Paloma—"

"It's one thing to have the stomach flu or something. But—you couldn't breathe, Jax. You really scared me."

He twists at the ring that seems wedged on his finger. "Alright," he meets my eyes with his, "We'll go."

In an exhale I say, "Thank you."

"Can you get my phone? It's in your room." He glances his weary eyes toward my bedroom then blinks hard before looking back to me. "I should let my dad know what happened."

"Sure." I smile.

I leave his shoes near his feet and retreat to my room. I look on my bed, under the textbooks, and pull my covers off, but it's not there.

I make my way around my bed to the other side where Jax was and crouch down to find his phone under my bed. I notice a missed call from Pat. I'm sure he's wondering why Jax hasn't come home yet. Afterall, it is after midnight.

When I return to the bathroom, a wave of fear sends a chill down my spine.

I'm unable to move.

It's like my brain is overridden. I can't even think.

Jax's phone vibrates in my hand. It takes me a minute to pull my gaze from Jax's unconscious body and check his phone.

When I read the text message from Pat, I realize how heavy I'm breathing. Another text comes in on his phone:

Daddio: R u coming home?
Daddio: Haven't heard from u. Check in.

I slowly kneel next to Jax. His phone is in my trembling hands.

What am I supposed to do? I don't know if I can touch him. What if I touch him and hurt him? But what if I don't touch him and make it worse by not doing anything?

The phone goes off again, only this time the vibrating continues because Pat is calling.

I answer.

He says, "You were starting to worry me. Where are you?" His voice is full of relief. It breaks me, because I know he thinks Jax is going to respond to him.

I can't speak. My throat goes dry, and my eyes burn with tears.

"Jaxon?"

My heavy breathing turns into hyperventilation.

Pat's voice fills with concern when he says, "Jaxon, do you need me to come get you?"

The words burst from my mouth, "There's something wrong with Jax. We fell asleep studying and when I woke up, he couldn't breathe—he got sick and then passed out in the bathroom. I don't know what to do now!"

"Paloma?" Pat's voice is gentle.

I place my hand on Jax's chest. Still not knowing what to do but not afraid to touch him anymore now that his dad is on the phone.

But when I do, what I feel unnerves me.

"Paloma, where are you?"

I ignore his question. My words come out in a shudder, "Oh my gosh, his heart is beating so fast." A loud sob bounces off the bathroom walls when I say, "What do I do? I'm so scared. Please tell me what to do!"

"It's okay, Paloma."

How is he so calm?

"Right now, you need to take a deep breath. You can't help him if you're worked up, so I need you to calm down."

I do as he says and suck in a deep breath. It helps but my voice is still rattled. "Okay," I manage to say through my panic.

"Good." He sounds ready to give me some instructions. "I know it's scary. But just breathe. You're not alone, I'm right here and I'm not getting off the phone until I see you both at the hospital."

Hospital? I knew this was more serious than Jax was letting on about. But how could he pretend like he was fine when he needs to go to the hospital? And why isn't his dad more freaked out right now? They are either have a lot more faith than I realized, or this isn't the first time this has happened.

"Paloma? Are you there?"

I put the phone on speaker and place it on the bathroom sink. "I'm here. What should I do?" My hands are hovering over Jax, unsure of how I should use them.

I can hear Pat rustling around, like he's gathering things before he leaves. "Where are you?"

"Roma's. In the bathroom."

"Good. Get a cold washcloth and put it on the back of his neck, but make sure he's breathing first."

I hover the side of my head by his nose and watch his chest rise and fall as his breath fans past my ear. "He's breathing."

Pat exhales. "Good."

I quickly run a washcloth under the sink. "Is he going to be okay?"

I hear his car start. "Yes, we just need to get him to the hospital."

I place the washcloth behind his neck, then unlace his shoes. But when I try sliding his foot into one of his shoes, it seems as if they've grown twice in size.

"His shoes don't fit," I say.

"What?"

"His shoes. They don't fit anymore."

He makes a humming sound, as if he's thinking, then he says, "Are his feet swollen?"

I blink. Pulling his sock off, I don't recognize his foot anymore because it's so swollen. I've never seen a swollen foot before, but his looks like someone infused it with water until it resembled a balloon.

"Yes. They're huge." Which is an understatement since I don't know how his toenails aren't popping off.

"It's a symptom," Pat says quietly to himself.

It's quiet for a long moment. The only thing I can hear is his wavering breath, which leaves me feeling uneasy when he says, "You need to use your cell phone to call the ambulance right now. I'm not getting off the phone with you." He inhales then blows out a nervous exhale. "Ride with them to the hospital. You don't need to be driving right now."

"Is Jax okay?"

When he doesn't respond after a moment, I take my phone out of my pocket and call 911.

"I'm calling the ambulance now."

CHAPTER

EIGHTEEN

Paloma

You don't get a real education in school.

I'm realizing this as I watch the little line turn into mountains on the screen attached to the machine that's monitoring Jax's heartrate.

In school, you learn algebra, and chemistry, and history, and even things that make you squirm like anatomy.

But your teachers won't prepare you for real life. They don't make classes about *sudden illness*. Or *bipolar parents*. They don't make classes about *fatherless homes*. You can't take an elective in *hospitalized boyfriend*.

It doesn't matter if I pass my GED test. How does any of that information prepare me for the hardships of life? Or the inevitable crises that seem to plague the world.

The nurse gently opens the door. She scans the room

and smiles at me. "I just need to check his urine output."

I force a smile. But really, I'm boiling inside.

This is what I mean, I don't want to hear about my boyfriend's urine output. Because that means there's a tube connecting his bladder to a pee bag hanging off his hospital bed.

It makes me angry.

And sick.

It also makes me feel stupid that Jax never said anything about this. It makes me feel stupid that I didn't connect the dots sooner. It makes me feel stupid I let him into my life but he was still keeping me out of his.

The nurse smiles at me again before she leaves but I ignore her. I can't fake another smile.

My phone lights up on the bedside table next to Jax.

Pat: Be there in an hour with lunch. How does tex-mex sound?

Awful.

Me: Sounds good. Thanks.

Pat had to leave earlier to check on his wife and cancel his appointments for the week at his office.

I sent a text to Claude letting him know I wouldn't be able to come by for a while. Which is probably for the best since Terra thinks I'm a harlot. He was understanding but also eager to get together soon.

I look at the cat face decorating the hot air balloon wallpaper on the wall above Jax's bed. If I was a kid, that sort of decoration wouldn't make me feel better. Especially if it was hovering over my bed.

In the last eight hours, I've learned Jax has something

called Dilated Cardiomyopathy. Or DCM for short. Apparently, it's a rare heart condition. And the episode I witnessed last night has happened before.

When I googled DCM during his surgery last night—or early this morning I guess—I found several news reports that said teenagers have died from DCM.

That's just perfect.

I can't believe my eighteen-year-old boyfriend had surgery to get a pacemaker implanted into his body.

His doctor said he'll need a heart transplant if he's going to live past twenty.

It's unbelievable.

Someone else has to die in order for Jax to live. How is that fair? You would think science and technology would have come further than this by now. How have they not invented a plastic heart to keep people alive? They've turned everything else about a person into plastic.

Jax makes a slight coughing sound and adjusts himself with his eyes still closed. I don't get too excited because he's been making some noises and movements off and on all morning.

He rolls his head to the side.

I watch him more closely, since this is a new kind of movement.

His eyes are heavy when he looks at me, and I feel a sense of relief when he speaks. "What happened?" His voice is dry.

I quickly send a text to Pat letting him know Jax woke up, then I page the nurse.

I sit on the edge of his bed. "You had surgery."

He lifts his arm to inspect himself, but winces in pain. "Agh, what is that?"

I help him drink from his water cup. "Try not to move this arm." I set the cup down and gently open the top of his gown, revealing the foreign object protruding from under his skin. "They gave you a pacemaker and you're not supposed to lift your arm until it heals."

He tilts his chin down to inspect his chest. "How long is that going to take?"

I shrug. "I think the surgeon said six weeks, but I'm so sleep deprived right now I might have misheard."

He lifts his hips to adjust himself. "And my heart?"

My mouth tightens. I want to shake him and ask him why he didn't tell me about this. I want to say, *What about your broken heart? How could you forget to mention you knew your heart was drowning in itself?*

Instead, I draw in a calm breath. "You need a transplant."

"What?" Even though his eyes are heavy, I can still see the panic surface over his expression. "Already?" His face twists then he coughs out a sob and squeezes his eyes with his hand.

I'm so conflicted right now. I want to demand answers from him. I have so many questions. But he also just had surgery, and I'm sure the pain medication is messing with him. Not to mention he almost died last night. I want to comfort him and feel what he's going through with him.

But I can't.

I'm still to upset and hurt that he kept this from me.

There's just too much to process and I need a minute to think everything over. I need sleep.

The nurse finally arrives. "Well, good morning." Her sing-song voice instantly annoys me. Even though we're at the children's hospital, his nurse doesn't have to talk to him like he's a six-year-old. But she does. "You might be feeling a little groggy, like clouds are in your head. But that's totally normal, okay?" Her eyes are wide and full of expression.

Jax presses his tears away with his palm as he nods.

"Yeah, I feel pretty out of it right now."

She nods with an overly animated smile, as she draws out her words, saying, "Totally normal."

I leave the bedside for a chair so she can better inspect him.

She lifts the covers and moves his gown around. "Everything looks as good as it can after surgery." She replaces the blanket and shows him the various buttons on his bed. "You know the drill?"

He touches one without pressing it fully. "This one calls you." Then he does the same motion to another button connected to a wire. "This one makes the pain go away."

Her eyes get big as her smile widens. "That's right, good job, buddy."

Okay, this is getting to be too much for me, and I didn't just wake up from surgery.

"I'll bring a menu in when the doctor gives you the okay to eat." She opens the door to exit. "Until then, just press that button if you need me."

Jax nods.

I swear glitter follows behind her when she dances out of the room. Who is that happy and chipper in such a depressing place?

I scoot my chair closer to him after she's gone. With a severe look on my face, I say, "Why didn't you tell me?"

He closes his eyes and rests his head against the pillow. "I can't do this right now."

He can't do this right now?

I'm the one that had to wait with his unconscious body, not knowing if he was going to make it before the ambulance got to him.

I'm the one that's been waiting for him to wake up to have this conversation.

The least he can do is give me an honest answer.

"It's not fair to me that you kept this a secret." My eye catches the device protruding from under his skin. "This is serious, Jax. You should have told me."

He opens one eye and looks at me. "I wanted to. I was waiting for the right time."

I scoff, in disbelief. He's being so selfish right now. I don't care that he just got out of surgery, he's known the entire time we were together. He couldn't figure out a time to tell me before now? "Well in case you haven't noticed, there's never a *right time* to talk about difficult things. Like you always tell me, you just have to say it."

I push myself out of the chair. When I swing the door open to go outside for some fresh air, I'm met by Pat and the surgeon.

"Paloma," Pat says with a bag of food. "I have a couple of tacos with your name on—"

"I just need a minute," I say moving passed him.

Pat sees Jax in distress and says, "What happened?"

Before the door closes completely, the surgeon reassures Pat, saying, "It's normal to feel a lot of emotions after surgery." I'm not sure if he's talking about me or Jax and the emotionally distressed state I left him in.

When I'm finally outside of the hospital, I search for a bench. I may as well find a nice place to hang out since I'm stranded here for who knows how long.

The only bench in the shade is preoccupied by someone. But upon further inspection, I realize that the person sitting on the bench is Mamaw.

CHAPTER

NINETEEN

Jaxon

"I wish she would have waited to tell you about the transplant," Dr. Peltz says as he clicks the top of his pen then places it in the pocket of his white lab coat.

I wince when I reach for my water cup.

My dad quickly takes the cup and hovers it in front of me with his attention still on Dr. Peltz. "He would have found out eventually."

Dr. Peltz scratches the side of his jaw. "True. But typically, I like to wait until patients have recovered a little more before breaking that kind of news to them."

I sip water from my straw, then say, "Yeah, but your patients are usually little kids." My entire chest feels like it's on fire. "I can handle it."

I click the morphine button again, hoping it will kick in

soon. I can't seem to keep my emotions under control, so hopefully if I can fall asleep, I won't have to feel them.

"True." Dr. Peltz's phone rings. He checks it briefly then looks at my dad. "Since he is technically an adult, I can make a referral—"

"No." My dad faces Dr. Peltz with a hardened expression. Drawing in a breath he says, "Why would we do that when you've been his doctor through this entire journey? You know his history. You've held his heart in your hands for crying out loud." He scratches his chin with his thumb. "No," he's shaking his head. "I'm not comfortable with a change like that. Not when he needs another surgery."

I press my mouth together when he says *another surgery*, trying to keep myself from falling apart like I did when Paloma told me about the transplant.

"I understand." Dr. Peltz checks his phone again. "In the meantime. We'll keep you here until after we get an x-ray and make sure the wires are set correctly." He looks at me. "And when you're ready for a meal, I would stick to fresh fruit and vegetables. Steamed is fine. But you want foods easy to digest and high in nutrients right now."

I nod, hoping he leaves before the emotions I'm trying to force down erupt out of me.

"We'll talk more about nutrition before you go." He checks his phone again, then smiles at my dad. "He looks great for post-surgery. Go ahead and let the nurse know if you need anything."

My dad pats the Dr. Peltz's shoulder. "Thank you, Dr. Peltz."

Dr. Peltz draws the curtain behind himself as he exits.

As soon as the door closes, I press my hand over my eyes. And I can only use one hand because I'm not supposed to lift my other arm. Not that I want to right now since it causes excruciating pain in my chest when I do.

"Hey," my dad's voice is gentle and sympathetic, which causes me to crack out a sob. "You heard what he said, you look great. And the pacemaker will help while we wait for a transplant."

"I'm fine." I press the tears away. "It's just the drugs."

My dad chuckles lightly. "I'm sure that's what it is." He holds my knee for a second, as a form of comfort.

Even though the drugs are affecting me, they aren't the culprit of my emotional instability. I still feel a sense of guilt I can't shake. Guilty for keeping this from Paloma. I did try telling her about it last night, but everything with Roma and the news about Candice moving really distracted us.

I also feel guilty because if I don't get a transplant and end up dying, I'll leave my dad here.

Alone.

He's already lost Dillon. Mom is essentially gone. And then I would go.

I'm not afraid of death.

I know where my soul is meant to live.

But leaving my dad alone is unthinkable.

The thought of it hurts worse than the incision pain.

"I guess you won't be eating any of this." My dad pulls a taco from the bag he brought, and digs in. I'm surprised the smell isn't bothering me more. He finishes his bite before saying, "Want me to get you something from the cafeteria? Dr. Peltz said to stick with fruit and vegetables. I can swing by the grocery store if you'd rather."

"I'm good," I say with an exhale, trying to regain my composure.

I reach my arm to grab my water, but quickly wince at the pain it causes. I groan, then let out a frustrated breath. I hate the feeling of helplessness I'm enduring right now.

"Do you want to page the nurse and get a pillow to rest

your arm on?"

I shake my head.

"I'll go talk to the nurse about an extra pillow."

I roll my head to face him. "I don't need it."

"You don't have to be tough, Jaxon." He smiles. "Afterall, I used to bring you your *wubby* every time you got hurt when you were little. It's okay to ask for help when you're hurt, okay?"

He would bring up my baby blanket right now to remind me that I'll always be his kid. No matter how old I am.

I force a half smile as he exits the room, then I rest the side of my head against my pillow. I stare at the remote, wondering if it might help my mood if I turn the TV on. But I quickly decide against it, since that would mean I would have to move. And right now, moving my body is not an option.

The door clicks, and I roll my head to the other side of my pillow anticipating seeing my dad come back so fast.

"That was quick," I say, "Can you leave a nurse a tip? Or maybe a good review for—"

I don't finish my statement.

Because my dad didn't walk through the door.

It's Paloma, followed by the rap of Mamaw's cane against the vinyl floor.

"Mamaw." I don't even mind that the tears are beginning to pool at the edges of my eyes again. "What are you doing here?"

She frowns, as if she's disappointed in my question. "You don't think I would come see my own grandson after what happened?"

I laugh as she gives me a gentle hug against my head.

I feel instantly comforted by the way she smells.

She releases me and walks around the bed. "What are

they trying to do to you in here?" She opens the blinds over the window. "I already feel depressed, and I've only been in here for two seconds."

The light spills in through the window. I can instantly feel the sunshine against my face. The warmth feels so good.

"That's better, isn't it?" Mamaw squeezes my foot as she finds a chair to sit in. "So, Paloma tells me you gave her a scare last night? That wasn't very nice of you, Jaxon."

I let out a small laugh. "Ouch!" I draw back in pain. "Don't make me laugh, Mamaw. It hurts too much."

She reaches for the morphine button. "What good is this if you're still hurtin'?"

I grimace, holding back my laughter and bracing myself. "*Please* don't make me laugh."

She takes my hand in hers. "Alright, I'll try."

My eyes begin to grow heavy. The morphine must be working.

Finally.

"It's going to work out," Mamaw says. "I'm prayin' for a transplant."

Just before I drift off, I hear Paloma scoff. As if she's astonished by Mamaw's comment.

CHAPTER TWENTY

Paloma

I spent three days in the hospital with Jax.

And then I spent seventeen hours with him at his house.

Then I realized he wasn't going to apologize for keeping his heart condition a secret from me.

Or maybe I realized I couldn't be around him until he's fully recovered. Physically, he's getting better every day. But mentally, he's not the same and refuses to talk to me about anything serious.

And, I'm *hurt*. And angry.

How could he let me feel so much for him? How could he pretend like he wasn't a ticking time bomb? Who does that? Who strings someone along that they claim to care about, and then forget to even bother saying sorry after they almost die?

Maybe I'm being insensitive.

But this isn't only affecting Jax. It's affecting me too.

And I can't keep hanging around Mamaw and Pat. They won't stop talking about trusting God.

I just had to get out of there.

And for the first time, I was able to call up my father and ask him to rescue me.

That's how I got to Roma's apartment.

Which is where I am now.

Only when I went to change my clothes, my bedroom wasn't my bedroom anymore.

"Finally you're here," Candice says opening a box. "I don't know where to put any of my stuff."

Right. Candice is moving in.

"Wherever." I scoot a tote to the side on my way to the closet. "There's space in the dresser and closet since I didn't bring much."

"Cool," she says tossing an armload of black and gray t-shirts on my bed.

Our bed.

Because I haven't been home and I don't own many clothes, I quickly realize the only clean shirt in my closet is an oversized sweater.

I flip my head around to Candice. "Since we're sharing a room, and bed, and bathroom…"

She doesn't make eye contact when she says, "Mmhmm…"

I was hoping she wouldn't make me ask. "Can I borrow something to wear? I've been in the same clothes for four days."

She scrunches her nose. "Ew." Then she tosses a crop top and jeans at me.

I hold the top against my torso then give her an unimpressed look. "I'm going to have lunch with Claude so I think I should probably wear something that *doesn't* show of my body."

She tilts her head. "Who is Claude?"

I let out a puff of air. "My dad."

"I'm never going to get used to you saying that," she says tossing me a less revealing shirt. "How's that going anyway?"

"Good, I guess." Not really, but I don't have time to give her the details about Terra. Plus I don't have it in me to be disappointed by her lack of compassion for my life if I were to tell her. "He's actually waiting downstairs for me, so I better go."

She walks over to the window. "Seriously? He's here?" She says this in her typical monotone.

"Yeah," I smile. "Maybe you can meet him after you get settled in."

"Deal," she says with her back against the wall as she peaks through the curtain like a sniper.

I lift the clothes before hurrying out for a quick shower. "Thanks for these."

Before I can shut the bathroom door, Candice is in the hall. "Hey," she says resting her head on the bedroom door frame and looking at me. "Sorry about Jax."

I smile. "Thanks." I didn't think she had a compassionate bone in her body. But my inaccurate assumption has me feeling relieved. Like I might be able to count on her for some sort of emotional support after all.

• • •

In the last forty-five minutes, I've learned so much about Claude; *and* myself.

He has so many stories from when I was a baby too.

"It sounds like you and mom had a really great relationship," I say, setting my teacup down.

He took me to *teatime* at an immaculately aesthetic French restaurant. I can't get over the romantic way the music is flowing from the speakers, or the perfection of the white and gold chairs strategically placed throughout the room.

"We did," he smiles. "I really enjoyed her."

I stir my tea. "So, I guess I can't really be your nanny anymore."

He tilts his head. "Why is that?"

As if he needs an explanation. "You know, after everything with Terra. It would be weird."

He waves his hand. "She is okay. I explained everything to her. She has no problem."

I doubt she's completely over it. She saw us hugging in her kitchen and heard Claude tell me he had a connection to me.

He must sense my doubt, since he says, "She knows you are my daughter. She knew I had a child before, and she knew of the circumstances that kept me from being in my child's life. But now," he lifts his hands toward me, "you are here, and no circumstances are between us."

I force a smile, still not trusting Terra or her hormonal outbursts. "I still don't think I can come back as your nanny though. Plus Lissy will be in school soon."

His tone grows serious. "Yes, perhaps you are correct. But I know Lissy will want to continue to see you."

"Have you told her, yet?"

He rubs at his forehead for moment. "Terra wanted all of us to tell Lissy."

That surprises me.

"When you are ready," he continues saying. "We will tell Lissy, together."

"That sounds perfect." I smile.

He clears his throat. "And if you are looking for more

work, I do need a secretary at the gallery."

I raise my eyebrow. "I might have to take you up on that."

The waitress approaches, placing our food at the table. Claude says something to her in French, which makes me wonder if all the waitresses speak French here.

Claude sets his teacup on the saucer. "She was very fun." He smiles. But by his somber tone, I'm assuming he's talking about my mom again. "We had a lot of fun together." His smile drifts into a frown. "Until she was not herself."

"I know what you're talking about." I finish chewing the delicious bite of duck in my mouth before saying, "She's bipolar."

"Bipolar?" He tilts his head, narrowing his eyes.

His expression has me wondering if he knows what bipolar disorder is, so I decide to explain. "She has intense mood swings." I lift my fork up and down. "Like really high and really, *really* low. And sometimes," I swirl my fork around like a tornado, "she's mean and all over the place. But she can't help it." I tap the side of my head. "The chemicals in her brain are messed up."

His expression fills with remorse.

I finish the last of what little vegetables I was given on my plate.

I say, "She's not all bad—"

"I am so sorry," he interrupts, placing his warm hand over my arm. "I did not know she was struggling. Believe me when I say I would have tried harder if I had known what happened to her was not her fault, but something possessing her mind and emotions."

I'm not sure I would call it that, but I can also see how this moment is an epiphany for him, so I let him continue.

"Your confusing life is my fault." He covers his mouth

with his hand for a moment, then holds my hand with both of his. "You deserve a better life."

I focus on the golden wedding band on his finger, avoiding his tearing eyes. "It's fine." I immediately suck in a rush of air, realizing what I just said. And if Jax were here, he would gently coax me into admitting the truth, instead of settling for the minimizing phrase I've grown so accustomed to using.

I shake my head. "I mean, it's not fine."

I squeeze my eyes shut, and when I open them Claude's entire expression seems to be trembling as he tries to smile though his tear-streaked face.

"What I mean," I continue to explain, "is that I didn't grow up with an ideal childhood, but that doesn't mean I'm going to pout about it now. I've accepted that my mom is imperfect. I've accepted my dad was shut out of my life by my mom. I've accepted I never learned to ride a bike. Like I always say, it's the hand I was dealt. There's no point in trying to figure out *why* I had the childhood I did. All I can do is move forward."

Claude is still smiling through his tears when he says, "I am proud of you, Paloma. So much wisdom and understanding for such a young lady."

I pat his hand, reassuring him that I don't hold anything against him.

"There is one thing I do not understand," he takes the blinding white napkin from the table and wipes his face. "You never learned to ride a bike?"

I contain my belly laughter, which instead comes out as a sort of snorting sound through my nose. "That's the thing you're having trouble understanding about my life?"

He laughs. "Surprised, yes?"

"Not really." I tuck a loose strand of hair behind my ear, then lean into the table. "I guess I've been waiting for my dad to teach me how."

His eyebrows rise. "Yes, I agree." Looking past me, he smiles at the waitress to invite her over so he can get the check. "First, we must get you a bicycle."

• • •

Turns out learning to ride a bike was a lot easier than I had anticipated.

Claude took me to Bike Works to make sure I had the perfect size bike without too many gadgets and gears to confuse me. Then we spent the afternoon at White Rock Lake where he held on to the back of my bike seat, until I was comfortable enough and ready for him to let go.

Who knew getting to know my long-lost father would be so easy?

Candice is on her phone when I walk into the apartment. "No, you can't mix the blood thinners with the Aricept." I'm assuming she's talking about her grandma's medication to whoever is on the other end of the phone call.

She faces me while she's sprawled out on the couch. Then pointing to her phone, she rolls her eyes as if she wants me to know she's talking to an idiot. Then her face shifts when she sees my bike.

I walk my bike to my room; *our* room, remembering we share this space now as I find that she's still only partially unpacked.

"Daddy bought you a new bike?" she says behind me.

I lean the bike against the wall. "Yeah, and taught me how to ride."

"How was that?"

I push a pile of her shoes to clear a spot to sit on the bed. "It was good." I scrunch my nose and raise my eyebrows. "And a little weird."

She shoves a pile of clothes off the bed so she can sit next to me. "So, what about all those creeper vibes you were feeling before?"

I forgot I had told her about that. "I think the mix of his French-ness as well as the fact that he admitted that he felt like I was his daughter, makes it okay." I almost feel nervous. Like I'm giving an oral presentation when I say this.

She gives me a look. "Serious?"

I let out a slightly irritated breath because she needs me to explain this. "I mean, it feels more like he was in my space like a dad is to his daughter."

She raises her brow.

I narrow my eyes at her. I can already feel her wanting to ask me how I would know what that feels like. "He's not a creeper anymore." I let the words come out quickly to get her to let it go.

She looks at her phone. "Okay, if you say so, then daddy's not a creeper."

"Thank you." I pull my legs under me and sit cross legged to face her better. "So, who were you talking to on the phone?"

She scoffs and rolls to her back. "The CNA at the nursing home."

"How's your grandma doing anyway?"

She shrugs, holding her gum between her teeth then pulling it with her fingers partially out of her mouth until the long string of gum snaps.

Apparently, she doesn't want to talk about whatever happened with her grandma. It must be serious enough to make Roma decide to move them both to Dallas.

"Are you going to enroll in school before summer is over? Or get a job?"

Flinging the gum string around her finger, she says, "I'll

go back to school in the fall." She rolls over to her stomach again and looks up at me. "I should probably get a job too, huh? Tia is kind of a tight wad."

I laugh. "Probably a good idea."

She pokes my arm with the sticky glob of gum covering her finger. "What about you?"

"What about me?" I say pushing her hand away.

"Well, now you have a new dad that used to be your boss. Won't it be weird if you keep working for him now?"

"Lissy starts school soon, so they don't need a nanny for a while anyway." I don't feel like explaining the details of why I won't be working there anymore to Candice right now. "But, Claude told me I could work for him at the gallery if I really needed a job."

She nods. "See if daddy can get me a job too."

I begin to unfold one of her t-shirts to hang in the closet.

She turns to her side, propping her head up with her hand. She abruptly repositions herself and says, "I almost forgot." She exits the room and returns with two envelopes.

I hang her shirt. "What's this," I say taking the envelopes and reading the return addresses.

One is from the Dallas Community College.

And the other is from the District Attorney.

"Well, open it," she says.

I tear the envelope from the college open first. "I've been accepted, pending my GED test scores."

She tosses a pair of socks at me. "Look at you, college girl."

"Not yet." I give her a smug smile.

"And the other one?"

I hesitate before opening it. Each time I receive any sort of notice or information from the court office, it's always bad news.

Candice flops her palm out in front of me. "Want me to open it?"

I search her face. Maybe it would be better if she delivers the news to me verbally. I don't want whatever the letter says to leave a permanent scar on my eyes. I hand her the envelope.

She tears it open and scans the paper.

"Well?" I press at my fingertips. "Good or bad?"

In one breath she says, "You've been granted emancipation."

I take the paper from her and read it in disbelief. "How? I was supposed to have a preliminary meeting with the judge first."

She shrugs. "Maybe you're mom signed the paperwork and gave her consent after all."

Why would my mom do that? I know she said she would do anything to make the process easier for me. But I didn't believe she was telling the truth.

I fold the paper and stuff it back in the envelope. "I can't believe she would do that for me."

"Maybe she's not as vile as we thought." She spins her gum around her finger again, which is beginning to make me a little irritated.

"How long do you think until we can't stand each other anymore?" I say.

"You know," she finally joins me to hang her clothes up in the closet, "I was just thinking about that."

"What'd you come up with?"

She holds a pair of pants next to herself then hands them to me. "You can have these." Then she dumps out a garbage sack full of more clothes that we can hang up. "I'll probably try to kick you out when you start bringing Jax over again."

I force a laugh. But I'm not sure when I'll invite Jax over again. Or if I will at all. He hasn't texted or called once since I left his house. And it's not like we talked much when we were together the last few days.

Since his surgery, he acts like my presence is too painful, or annoying, or irritating. I don't know exactly what he's feeling, because he won't talk to me.

It's as if he's taken all the love he poured into the cracks of my heart, and replaced it with the misery that's consuming him.

CHAPTER

TWENTY-ONE

Jaxon

"You're depressed."

I flop my arm over my eyes to keep the light from blinding me. "I am not depressed."

Birdie pulls the blankets down to my feet. "Good, then get up and let's roll."

"Do you not understand I just had surgery?" I know the surgery isn't what is keeping me in this bed. It's been weeks since the surgery. I know that Paloma's absence and lack of compassion for my recovery is bothering me, but not enough to keep me in bed all day. And I know that the fact that I need a heart transplant is chipping away at my will to live, one day at a time. Which is probably where my lack of enthusiasm for living manifested from. But no amount of revelations or insights are going to get me out of this bed.

Birdie rapidly flicks my light on and off. "Do you not understand that the doctor said the sooner you get up and moving, the better off you'll be?"

"I don't want to go, Birdie. Just leave me alone." My tone is harsh, but I don't have the vigor to apologize.

I hear Birdie walk down the stairs as if he's in a hurry. Good.

Maybe he will finally leave me alone.

His energy has been draining and the daily visits have become more than what I can handle.

I curl myself back up into myself. Both physically and mentally.

I wish there was a way to know if I was getting a transplant or not. Or if the transplant would even work.

Even knowing the end date of my life would be nice. Then I would know how many more days I had to sleep away until my life was over.

Before I know what's happening, I feel a rush of icy cold-water splash across my body.

I sit up, instantly, gasping for air.

"What are you doing?" I pull my soaking shirt off, expecting to see Birdie with an empty cup.

Instead, Mamaw is standing over me with a pitcher in each hand, and Birdie is chuckling to himself in the doorway.

"*Mamaw?*"

She sets the empty pitcher on my bed and hands the full pitcher of water to Birdie. "We won't be needing that one anymore."

Birdie takes the pitcher and heads down the hall, still chuckling and snickering. I'm surprised he wasn't recording. That would have made an instant viral reel for his channel.

I pull a clean shirt from my dresser. "Mamaw, why did

you do that?"

Before I pull my shirt on, she places her stiff wrinkled hand over my pacemaker. Forcing me to stop and catch her hazy blue gaze. She seems concerned.

I wait for her to speak.

"I'm not so sure this thing works." She smiles like what she's saying is a joke.

I don't know how to respond to her.

She says, "Well, isn't it supposed to give your heart a jump start when you're sittin' around moping?" She laughs at herself.

I nudge her hand away and finish pulling my shirt on. "That's not how it works." I frown, still waiting on an explanation about the fact that she tossed water on me.

She must sense I don't think any of this is funny, since her denture grin falls flat. "I've been around long enough to know when someone needs help," she says.

I rip the wet sheets from my bed and bunch them into a ball in my arms. "And you thought throwing freezing cold water on me was going to *help*?"

The corners of her mouth curl up and the wrinkles around her eyes return with her smile. "Yep."

"You couldn't ask me to get out of bed?"

"Nope."

"Mamaw…"

"Jaxon…"

I shift my weight to one side. "Why couldn't you ask me to get up? Why did you have to throw water on me?"

She shrugs and takes the sheets from my arms. "Tryin' to *talk* you out of bed wasn't workin' so I thought a cold shower might help."

"A cold shower?"

She turns to leave my room. "Yep, it always worked on your Papaw."

I can't believe Papaw didn't try to kill her for doing that to him.

Birdie returns to my bedroom with the same chuckle he left with. "Mamaw passed the vibe check," he says, cupping his face in his hands as his laughter grows. "The only thing that would have made it better is if she had thrown that extra pitcher of water on you."

He cracks himself up.

"Yeah, that would have been awesome," I say with intense sarcasm.

"Come on, Jax, you know she was right." He flicks my light on and off again. "Nothing else was going to get you out of that bed."

"I just had—"

"*You just had surgery,*" he mocks in a whiney little girl voice. In his regular voice, he says, "Yeah, I know. But you're recovered and you know it." He points to the side of his head. "The rest of your recovery is in here."

Maybe he's right.

Maybe I'm obsessing over the transplant.

I was hoping we would get a call sooner than this.

I was hoping I would be able to get the transplant over with and move on with my life.

And I was hoping to have a normal beating heart in my chest by now.

It just feels like I'm stuck in limbo.

Waiting.

"I know." I open my dresser again for a pair of shorts. "I just want everything to go back to normal again."

Birdie is still flicking my light on and off like a four-year-old. "With your heart? Or with you and P.?"

I hold my hand over his to stop him from flicking the light again. "Stop. You're going to give me a seizure."

"Because I asked you about P., or because I asked you

about your heart?"

"Because you keep messing with my light." I push past him and head down the hallway. "I need *something* but I don't know what." It's like my skin is crawling and I need to get out of my house.

I hear Mamaw watching TV downstairs.

I'm sure my dad is working, maybe he needs some help. I can still do laundry and clean the massage tables for him.

But that doesn't feel like what I need to be doing right now either.

Being in the house is making me feel claustrophobic.

Before I go downstairs, I open my mom's bedroom door. The machines are whirring. The sound of the oxygen rushing in and out of her lungs through the tube in her throat is almost calming. I can't even let myself think about the fact that her heart would fit perfectly behind my sternum.

Birdie meets me in her doorway. "She looks so peaceful," he says.

He's right. She does. Not like a sleeping peaceful person, but more like a dead one. Which is terrible to say. But it's a fact. And a fact that I can't shake.

Despite my own thoughts about my mom, I remember how Paloma seemed so hurt when I told her I hadn't spoken to my mom since she's been connected to all the tubes and wires. And despite the fact that I don't believe my mom is there anymore, I decide to talk to her anyway.

"I had another surgery." I hear Birdie quietly gasp when I say this to my mom. "It went okay, I guess. I'm recovered and have a pacemaker until I get a heart transplant. Just wanted you to know. I'm also feeling a little agitated being stuck at home so much."

"He's just stir crazy," Birdie interjects.

I turn my head over my shoulder to give him an

unimpressed eyebrow raise for interrupting this vulnerable moment I'm having. Facing my mom again, I say, "I'll be back later."

I shut the door and we head downstairs.

"Where are we going?" Birdie says.

I take the keys from the table and open the door. "I'll be back later, Mamaw."

She waves her hand above her head without pulling her eyes from the TV. "Bye, honey. Have fun."

In the car, Birdie is rapidly texting on his phone. He slaps his hand around my arm before I put the car into gear. "Should you be driving?"

"My doctor cleared me weeks ago." I put the car into drive.

"Where are we going?" Birdie sounds uncertain.

"To the arboretum."

"For what?"

I glance in his direction. "Fresh air."

...

Not even ten minutes of walking through the tulip garden, and I'm winded. It's as if my entire body has atrophied since my surgery.

The only thing making me want to continue walking is the music coming from the amphitheater. If I can just get there, I'll be able to sit and regain my strength to make it back to the parking lot.

"Do you want to take a break?" Birdie points to an open bench near a bridge.

I shake my head. "I'm good. I'll take a break at the concert."

"Are you sure? You're dragging."

I turn to face him. He looks concerned, which makes me concerned since Birdie doesn't worry about anything.

"Alright," I say reluctantly. "But honestly, I could keep going."

"I have an idea." He claps his hands. "Stay right here." He scans the area. "I'll get us some water," he says, then he disappears into the crowd.

I twist at the ring on my finger, keeping my hands from reaching into my pocket and texting Paloma.

At this point, I don't know if she will ever forgive me. I should have kept my distance. I shouldn't have promised I would never hurt her. I didn't mean to hurt her. But I don't know how to get back to where we were. I don't even know what to say to her.

"Hey."

Her voice melts me.

And when I look up to meet her eyes, her presence stifles me; as if I'm engulfed in her *everything*.

"Paloma." I begin to stand, but she places her hands on my shoulders to lower me back down to the bench. "I don't know what to say."

"I'm sorry." Her expression is full of anguish.

I tilt my head. "No, I'm sorry. I should have told you the truth from the beginning."

She touches my mouth with her fingertips. "Shh," her eyes search between mine. "I don't know how to say this."

I smile. "Yes, you do. You just have to stay it."

She lets out a quiet laugh from her nose. "I knew you were going to say that."

"You set yourself up for that one." I drag my hand down her arm. "Tell me," I say in a quiet voice.

She presses her mouth together. Her eyes are fixed on mine, full of something intense and painful.

"The truth is," she says, "if you had told me in the beginning, I don't think I would have been able to handle it. I think I would have run away from you."

"Paloma," my voice is still quiet.

"I'm not done."

Every part of me wants to stop her. To take back my encouragement to get her to tell me. It feels like she is trying to say goodbye and now that she's right here. Now that she's consuming me with her existence, I can't let her leave.

Ever.

She takes my hand in hers. "After the surgery, I was so angry that I forgot to think about how scary this must be for you."

"*Paloma.*"

She holds back a smile by pinching her mouth together "Can you stop talking so I can say this to you?"

My eyes widen at her confidence. "Yes," I say, my eyes widen. "Sorry, continue."

She rolls her eyes. "Even though the right thing to do would have been to tell me, I'm glad you didn't. Because everything that happened, it all let me grow closer to you. It gave me time to *trust* you."

I concentrate on the bright green specks in her eyes.

She bites her bottom lip for a moment. "It gave me time to realize you're everything to me. And I don't want to live my life without you."

For the first time, my heart does a backflip in my chest but it quickly returns to its normal rhythm. I can finally love her without drowning in the erratic beat of my heart.

I pull her hand to my chest. "Feel that?"

She nods.

"Until this heart stops beating, I'm going to be here for you."

Her breathing intensifies, and her eyes shine. "Please don't die," she says as she flings her arms around me.

I hold her close, feeling torn about the day we met. If

she had kept walking through that mall instead of stopping to hug me, she would have saved herself so much heartache. But in the same breath, I wouldn't have gotten the opportunity to see her grow into the self-assured person she is now.

I feel something run into my leg.

When I look up, Birdie is shoving a wheelchair in my direction.

"Look what I found," he says with a proud grin. Oblivious that I'm kind of in the middle of something with Paloma. He pats the seat. "Now we won't have to stop if you need to rest."

Candice is standing behind him with an armload of water bottles. "Here," she says, stretching one out to me. "I'm thrilled we ran into you." Her sarcasm is so thick.

"Has anyone ever told you how *pleasant* you are?" I say with a stiff grin.

Her face stays flat when she says, "All the time."

Birdie taps Paloma's shoulder. "P. you didn't tell me you were granted emancipation. Congratulations, girl."

My mouth falls open. I lift my arms at my sides. "What the heck, that's awesome!"

She smiles. "Yeah, I guess my mom signed the document. I didn't even have to go to court or anything."

Even though it's only been weeks since we've seen each other. I feel like we haven't talked in a decade.

Everything about her has matured.

She seems more certain of herself than ever.

"Come on," Birdie says, running the wheelchair into my leg again. "I'll push you around."

"I'm not sitting in a wheelchair," I say matter-of-factly. I push the chair away with my shoe.

Candice plops into the chair. "I'll keep it warm until he changes his mind," she says to Birdie.

Birdie takes off running with Candice, who is unphased by his squealing enthusiasm.

I peer down at Paloma with an affixed expression. "They set us up, didn't they?" I take a sip from my water, then hand it to Paloma.

She shrugs. "I sort of told Birdie to let me know when you decided to emerge from your cave of darkness."

"Seriously?"

She takes a drink and hands the bottle back to me. "Seriously. You really think he wanted to hang around with you that entire time?"

I stand and take her hands in mine to help her up. "You never called."

She laces her fingers between mine. "*You* never called either."

"Alright, that's fair." I pull her close and wrap my arm around her shoulders. "Well thanks for waiting on me."

She tilts her head to look up at me as we follow the sound of Birdie's happy screams down the path. "What made you get out of bed anyway?"

"Well, actually," I kiss the top of her head, "Mamaw threw a pitcher of ice water on me."

"*She didn't.*" She sounds flabbergasted.

"Believe me, I would still be in bed if that weren't true."

She laughs in disbelief. "I can't even picture Mamaw doing something like that."

"Apparently she made a habit of throwing cold water on Papaw when he wouldn't get out of bed too."

"I'll remember that for the next time you decide to stay in bed for the rest of your life."

I bend over, pretending my body breaks. "Please don't."

She pulls us down the walkway with laughter.

We make our way to the amphitheater where Birdie is sitting on the grass hill next to Candice who is still perched in the wheelchair.

I follow Paloma.

The band is playing acoustic music and it fits the sunset atmosphere we're in perfectly.

We sit on the grass and Paloma relaxes her head against my chest. The sun illuminates her face in a way that makes me want to hold her and never let go.

I close my eyes, wishing I could capture this moment and pause it forever.

Because I know when the sun finally sets, and the music stops, and we return to our lives, I'll constantly be running out of heartbeats.

I'll constantly be one heartbeat further from this moment.

I'll constantly be one heartbeat closer to the end.

I'll constantly be one heartbeat in need of a transplant.

And nothing makes me want a transplant more than the way I feel about Paloma right now.

CHAPTER

TWENTY-TWO

Paloma

"Laurent Gallery, this is Paloma." I say into the receiver. I took Claude up on his offer, and I've been answering calls and filing paperwork at the gallery for a week now.

It's a mindless job, but I don't mind since I'll be starting college classes soon.

After I took the GED, I signed up for the courses I need for my generals. Jax decided to apply at the community college too. He's in all the same classes with me and told me I can be his tutor after his transplant surgery.

Which is still an unknown date.

Either his heart fails him, and he dies.

Or his heart fails him, and he gets an emergency transplant.

Apparently transplant lists are a long list. A list where people wait on someone to die so they can have their organs stitched into their body.

It makes me sick to think about.

So, I don't think about it.

Instead, I answer phone calls and file paperwork at the gallery.

And I find it a perk that I get to see Claude when he comes in for a meeting with a client.

And I look forward to going to class with Jax in the fall.

"Paloma?" The voice on the other end of the phone is familiar.

"Yes?"

"Can you lock up the gallery and come to the house?"

"Terra?" She sounds frantic. I was expecting an agent, or artist, or someone from another gallery to be on the other line. I haven't even spoken to Terra since the night she saw me and Claude hugging. He told me she believed the truth, but I've been actively avoiding her since she didn't seem interested in my company.

I clear my throat. "Is everything okay?"

"*No.*" She lets out a quiet sob when she says this.

Where is Claude to help her? "Is it the baby?" Maybe she's in preterm labor and needs a ride to the hospital. But why is she calling me?

She chokes on her words. "I can't find Lissy. Please, can you get to the house immediately?"

My heart thuds against my chest. "I'll be right there."

I hang up and organize a few papers before flipping the *open* sign to *closed* and locking the doors.

I text Jax before getting on my bike.

Me: Can you meet me at Highland Park?
Jax: Yeah. Everything okay?

Me: Yes, I'm good. Lissy is missing. I need a ride to the Laurent's and I'm on my bike.

Jax: I'll see you there.

I like to ride my bike from Roma's to the gallery since it's not that far of a ride. But Claude's house is not in riding distance from the gallery.

I get to Highland Park as fast as I can and feel more grateful than ever that Claude, *my dad*, taught me to ride a bike.

I see Jax's car in the parking lot.

He must see me too, since he gets out and opens the hatchback of his car to fold the seats down.

"Here," he says taking the bike and lifting it into the back of his car.

I get buckled in the car as quickly as I can, and while Jax pulls out into traffic I realize how intensely I'm breathing.

"Claude couldn't give you a ride?"

I blow out a rush of air. "He wasn't at the gallery."

"Oh?"

I wipe the perspiration from my forehead with the back of my hand. "Terra called and asked me to help her find Lissy. She sounded terrified."

"I hope Lissy's okay."

I smile, knowing what Lissy is probably doing. "I'm sure she is. We used to play hide-and-seek all the time."

"Oh, yeah?"

"She's literally the best hider. She can sit in silence forever. It's unreal for a little kid."

He flashes me a smile. "Have you seen her since…" he lets his words linger for me to answer.

I've been consumed with everything going on in my life, I sort of forgot about Lissy. Not *forgot*, but didn't prioritize thinking about her.

I shake my head. "Not yet."

"Why not?" He doesn't sound judgmental when he says this, but I still feel a sense of guilt wash over me since she is technically my sister. And Claude wanted me there when they told Lissy that I was her sister. Which means she still doesn't know.

"I don't know," I say.

He shakes my leg. "You can tell me."

I let out a groan. "It's just," I try to gather my thoughts into words for a moment, "everything with Terra."

"You're still not over that?"

"I don't know if *she* is."

He laughs.

"I'm serious Jax."

He side eyes me before pulling off the freeway. "I know you are. That's why it's funny."

"How do you figure?"

He gives me a look before checking his rearview mirror.

I know what he's about to do, so I say, "You don't have to pull over on the side of the road to say whatever it is you want to say to me."

He checks his side mirror, then turns his blinker on before pulling into a gas station and parking.

"Jax." I flip my head in his direction. "I'm in a hurry."

He adjusts himself in his seat to face me. "Listen to me."

"*I am!*"

"Good." He strokes the side of my face with his thumb. "You're going to encounter difficult situations in your life. You can't avoid it."

I fake a smile. I don't want him to think I'm not listening for fear that he might keep us in this parking lot even longer.

"It's your choice to either move through the fear," he

leans in closer. With a theatrical tone he says, "Or let it consume you into *a cave of darkness.*"

I can tell he's partially being serious, and partially mocking me. "At least I'm not hiding in my bedroom," I say.

He kisses the side of my face five times before putting the car back into drive. "How did I fall for such a sass?"

I push his arm playfully. "Don't say that you sound like an old man."

His smile shifts into a line. "But for real." He inches down the street where the Laurent's live. "You're going to face a lot of scary stuff in your life. I only want to make sure you don't give up when you're drudging through the middle of fear."

"I won't give up."

"*Ever?*"

I face him with a sincere smile. "Ever."

I'm not sure if he's referring to the fact that I'm about to be face to face with Terra for the first time since that night in her kitchen. Or if he's talking about his next surgery, and worried I'm going to react in the same way I did when he got his pacemaker.

Either way, his pep talk has me ready to face whatever is on the other side of the Laurent's door.

He puts the car in park. "Do you want me to come with you?"

I face their entrance, then flip my head back to him. "Would you?"

He smiles and meets me on the other side of the car.

I lock my hand in his before ringing the doorbell.

He says, "You don't walk in anymore?"

I draw my eyebrows together. "Not since I was promoted from Claude's nanny, to Claude's daughter."

He tilts his head in confusion. "I feel like that gives you

even more reason to walk in without knocking."

"Hush," I say with a smile.

The door flings open, and I can tell Terra has been crying.

"Come in, come in," she says, quickly filing us in.

I point to Jax. "This is my boyfriend, Jax."

He shakes her hand. "You must be Terra."

She smiles and nods at him, then shifts her gaze back to me before she breaks.

"I can't do this." She covers her face and sobs into her hands.

I feel sorry for her.

Her belly is enormous and trembles with each sob.

That can't be good for her baby to experience that sort of stress.

She pulls her hands from her face and looks at me. "If something happened to her, I would never forgive myself."

My face falls.

She's so desperate right now, I don't even know how to respond to her.

I'm used to the Terra that's put together. That's beautiful in her anger. That's confident in her lack of empathy. That's focused on her career.

This Terra...*cares*.

"Why don't you sit down," Jax says, placing his arm around her shoulders. I know this is an intense moment, but I can't help but fall for him a little more as I watch the way he comforts Terra in her distress.

Jax looks back to me as he helps Terra sit on the couch between her sobs. "You got this?"

I nod with certainty.

I kick my shoes off, set my bag on the entryway table, straighten my posture, then cup my hands around my mouth. "*Marco?*"

I creep lightly up each marble step.

"Marco?" I call out again.

Terra's sobs soften, and she whispers something to Jax. "Marco?"

I hear a muted giggle upstairs, which consumes me in instant relief that Lissy is somewhere in the house and not hiding outside or lost roaming in the neighborhood.

I step silently down the hallway. "Marco?"

"*Polo!*" Her voice is muffled, but I can tell from the direction her voice is coming from that she's in her parents' bedroom.

"Marco?"

I open the door to the master bedroom and stand in awe at the chiseled sculptures of nude Greek gods, along with the bizarre paintings covering the walls. The only painting that my eyes don't avert from is a deep shaded purple and dark red painting of a rose above their headboard.

"Marco?"

Lissy's giggle becomes clearer now that I'm in the bedroom. And knowing that a five-year-old has been hiding in here for hours, makes me want to avert my eyes from the artwork displayed in every inch of the room.

I duck my head under the bed. "Marco?"

Despite how clean it is under their bed, I hear the voice of Lissy call back to me. "Polo!"

I don't understand. It sounds like she's right under the bed, but I don't see her anywhere.

Just then, a tiny hand waves at me from up inside the box spring.

"Lissy?"

She crawls out of a hole in the bottom of the thin cloth covering and scoots closer to me. "Nanny!"

I take her hands in mine and pull her the rest of the way

out from under the bed. "How did you get in there?"

She throws her arms around me and hugs me. "I cut a hole so I could hide."

I squeeze her. "You really scared your mommy."

She pulls back to look at me. "I didn't want to get in trouble for using scissors on mommy and daddy's bed."

I pull her close again. "It's okay, Lissy, I'm just glad you're okay."

Terra hurries to my side and takes Lissy from me. "Oh, sweetie, you scared mommy to death."

Lissy touches Terra's face. "Mommy, why are you crying?"

Terra forces a smile. "I'm just so happy you're okay." She faces me. "Where was she?"

I look at Lissy.

She gives me a pleading look.

I face Terra again. "She was in your bed the whole time."

"She was?" Terra looks down at Lissy. "You were in mommy's bed?"

Lissy nods with a massive grin.

It's not exactly a lie. Technically she was *in* their bed, but not in the way Terra thinks. I'm not their nanny anymore. I'm bound by the bonds of sisterhood now. And I'll never tell on *my sister* for cutting a hole in the bottom of their bed.

I turn to face Jax, who is standing in the doorway with a grin plastered to his face.

I smile back.

Then he points to the armless sculpture in the corner and grimaces.

I hold back laughter, so as not to offend Terra in her moment of relief.

The front door opens, and Claude's warm accent

reverberates up the stairway and into the bedroom.

"Daddy!" Lissy squeals in excitement.

Terra releases Lissy, then stands to her feet and frantically wipes at her makeup around her eyes. "Don't say anything to him about this." Her voice is stern and she's avoiding my eyes.

I might be bound to the secrets of sisterhood, but I'm not bound by any oath to keep Terra's secrets.

"Why don't you just tell him the truth?" I'm shocked when the words leave my mouth. I've never once stood up to her or even made a suggestion that wasn't in alignment with what she wanted.

She flips her head in my direction. "Excuse me? Don't confuse my appreciation for your help as an invitation for you to tell me what to do."

I wait for my throat to tighten, or go dry. But when it doesn't, I realize she has no real power over me. Sure, I'm in her house, but I don't have to be here. I didn't have to help her either, but I wanted to. She can try to scare me away with her insecurity. But I now realize that her confidence and composure is all a front for her own self-loathing.

Instead of running scared when she's afraid like I have done when I'm faced with fear, she becomes a stone-wall. Pretending like she's tougher than anyone else. Pretending like she doesn't have any real emotions.

I take Jax's hand when I meet him in the doorway, and to Terra, I say, "You could tell him you were playing hide-and-seek and leave it at that. Or I can tell him you lost Lissy and called me to help you find her. Both of those statements are the truth. But no matter what, he's going to wonder why I'm here."

She looks stunned.

I take her silence as an opportunity to go back

downstairs.

Before we reach the living room where I can hear Claude speaking to Lissy in French, I notice several suitcases by the front door.

Claude's face lights up when he sees me. "Paloma, I was not expecting you." He reaches his arm out to me. "Come. Come, there is someone I want you to meet."

"Grandmere and Grandpere are here!" Lissy says jumping up and down on the couch.

"*Grandmere*?" I say searching Claude's face for an explanation.

But before he can speak, an older couple face me from the chaise. The woman smiles and glides over to me with open arms. "Bonjour, ma cherie," she smells like intense perfume and new car. She says something to Claude and Lissy that I don't understand. And apparently, she doesn't speak English.

The older man meets us in the hug, wrapping his arms around us silently.

Jax lets go of my hand and takes a step back to hold his phone in our direction and snap a photo.

"Hi?" I manage with uncertainty.

The couple release me but continue to stare at my face endearingly.

Claude places his hand on my back. "These are my parents. I have told them all about you."

"Your parents?"

He nods. "Yes, and that would mean they are your grandparents, yeah?"

I smile. "I guess so."

Lissy laughs. "Grandmere and Grandpere can't be Nanny's grandmere and grandpere, daddy."

Claude picks Lissy up from the couch. "And why not?" he asks.

She searches our faces, and when her gaze meets Claude's she whispers to him, but still loud enough for the rest of us to hear. "Because Nanny isn't my sister."

Terra files in behind us and rests her head on Claude's shoulder. I'm not sure how to take her posture or lack of eye-contact.

"She must be your sister then, yes?" Claude beams a smile in my direction

I suck in a rush of air when he says this.

Lissy looks at me. "How can Nanny be my sister?"

Claude kisses her cheek. "Because she is my daughter."

Lissy eyes widen with her smile. She wriggles out of Claude's arms and jumps at me, nearly toppling me over. "Nanny, did you know that you're my sister? I never knew that!"

I laugh. "Yep, I'm not your nanny anymore, but I'll never stop being your sister."

Lissy holds my hand and jumps up and down. "Now I'm going to call you *Sissy* instead of Nanny."

Claude and Terra smile at each other.

"Lissy and Sissy," Jax says with a laugh.

I face him, he's still holding the camera up like he's taking a picture.

He winks, before I turn back to face the Laurent's; before I take in the sight of my family.

My family.

CHAPTER

TWENTY-THREE

Jaxon

"Just pick one," Birdie's voice echoes in the open room.

"I thought this was your job." I scroll through my phone, searching for the next charity foundation to donate our YouTube channel money to.

"Nope, it's your turn." Birdie reverses his mini hummer, his knees up to his chest, and spins in a circle just in time before Paloma tries to crash her mini hummer into him.

"Cheater!" Paloma yells at Birdie.

Birdie lets out hysterical laughter. "It's not bumper cars, P."

They look ridiculous driving in kid-size hummers.

I hold up my phone. "How about Scholarship America? They help kids go to college."

Paloma swerves into Birdie at the last second, hitting his car hard enough that she tumbles out.

I jump down from the table where I was seated and help Paloma to her feet.

She's laughing.

So is Birdie.

"Are you okay?" I say, more as an automatic response than real concern since I know she's fine.

Paloma nods, with a giant grin.

I face Birdie. "Can you two take a break and help me pick a charity?"

Birdie pulls forward. "That one sounds good," he says, then he parks and climbs out of the mini hummer.

Paloma snatches my phone from my hands. "No," she says in protest to Birdie's comment. "You don't want to settle." She begins scrolling through the list of charities. "You have to choose one that's important to you. It should be special."

"Special?"

She doesn't respond to me, making her way to the door and exiting without looking back.

Birdie's eyes wander from where Paloma was to the hummer in the middle of the room. "Was she planning to come back? Or…?"

I tuck my hands in my pockets. "You should probably park it yourself."

Birdie pinches his mouth together. "Right," then he mumbles something to himself before getting in the tiny car with his knees crammed up to his chest.

Aatmay shuffles through the door and gives me a brief, "Hello," before going through another door in the large room.

I can't help but wonder what's going on in his mind as his son drives the hummer down the court. Or maybe this is just a normal day at their house.

I make my way over to the door Paloma exited from. "I'm going to see if Paloma found a charity yet," I say.

Birdie waves at me, reversing the mini car as fast as he can toward one of the miniature parking places.

I find Paloma seated at the bottom of the winding staircase.

Still scrolling.

I take a seat next to her.

Without looking at me, she says, "None of these are good."

I pull back and raise my eyebrows. "Really?"

She rolls her eyes. "I don't mean they aren't *good*. They just aren't…" she lets her words trail.

"What?"

She shifts her gaze to meet mine. "It should be a charity that matters."

My forehead creases as my eyes widen. "I think most of those matter."

"You know what I mean."

The sun shining through the window is making her eyes glow. I can feel a ridiculous grin on my face, but what she doesn't know is that I'm smiling because I'm falling for her.

I've *fallen* for her.

Fallen for the girl that fell into my arms at the mall. Although, she's nothing like that girl anymore. She's more. She's *better*.

Which is something I didn't think was possible.

She smiles back at me. "What? It should be important."

"Yeah," I can't stop looking at her, "you're right."

She smirks. "Jax."

"Yeah?"

"Why are you looking at me like that?"

How do I tell her what I'm feeling?

How do I say that she feels like the missing part of me?

How do I tell her that my heart feels like a magnet to hers?

How do I tell her she revived my drowning heart? That she made me want to knock my heart condition and live a long life. A long life that I want to spend with her.

"I wish there was a word for me to use so I could tell you why I'm looking at you the way I am." I'm not sure if I'm feeling so sentimental because I'm uncertain of the days I have left with her. But I honestly don't know what word to use to describe the way I'm feeling.

She pinches her mouth together. "Just tell me."

"I don't know how."

She faces the phone again. "Well, unlike you, I have patience and don't push people. So, when you find the right words, you can tell me."

She has no idea.

I kiss her shoulder, then rest my chin there to look at my phone with her. "Okay, well, we've already donated to half of the charities on that list. Maybe we can donate to one of the *important* ones again?"

She leans her head on mine. "Maybe you could make your own charity?"

Before I can tell her that's a perfect idea, my phone rings.

I sit up.

Her expression changes when she sees the name. "Dr. Peltz?" she says looking at me with concern. "Why is he calling?"

She hands me the phone.

"I don't know."

I answer and put it on speaker.

"Hey, Dr. Peltz."

He clears his throat. "Hi, Jax, how are you doing?"

I shrug, not that he can see me. "Good," but the word comes out more unsure than I mean it to.

Paloma tucks her hand in mine.

"Good, good," he clears his throat again. "Are you sitting down?"

My pulse begins to intensify.

Why is he calling?

He usually calls my dad.

He has called me personally three times since I've known him.

Once to tell me my scans didn't look good, and I needed to come in.

A second time to let me know he was switching my prescription, and I needed to come in.

And the third time is right now.

I let out a slow breath. "Yeah, I'm sitting." I glance at Paloma, who looks as if her lungs have cut off the oxygen to her brain.

I prepare myself for bad news, since that's all he's ever delivered. Even if it is small bad news. Bad news is just that; bad news, no matter how insignificant.

"Well, I'm calling because…" he chuckles to himself.

How is he laughing?

Why is he laughing?

He says, "Jax, we have a heart for you."

I let out a puff of air from my gaping mouth.

"What?" I say in disbelief.

Paloma covers her mouth with both of her hands.

Dr. Peltz chuckles again. "You're getting a heart, I need you to come in."

My eyes burn with tears of—happiness. Disbelief. Shock. Uncertainty. Honestly, I'm submerged in emotions.

I hang up.

Paloma throws her arms around me. "Oh my gosh,

you're getting a heart."

When she pulls back and looks at me, I hold her face in my hands. "I know how to say it now."

"What?" Her confused expression shifts into a smirk. "Why are you looking at me like that again?"

I search her eyes for a moment before saying, "Enamored."

She scrunches her face. "Enamored?"

I fold my mouth together, then say, "Yeah, I'm enamored by you."

Her eyes shine.

And then, "I love you, Paloma."

CHAPTER

TWENTY-FOUR

Paloma

"Don't go to the light," I say.

Jax pinches the elastic of the shower cap thing on his head. "I wasn't planning on it."

"And don't worry, everything is going to be fine." I move out of the way as the nurse starts an IV line.

He gives me a smug smile. "Didn't you just warn me about getting too close to the light while I'm under?"

My chest shudders, ridden with anxiety.

Tears burn in my eyes. "Just don't give up in there no matter what happens, okay?" My emotions are all over the place. I'm trying to be encouraging. Encouraging and supportive to him, while trying to convince myself he's not going to die on the operating table.

He reaches his hand out to me and I take it in both of

mine. "I won't," he says. "I promise."

Dr. Peltz enters the room, followed by Pat and Mamaw. "Are you ready to go?" he says. He's decked out in scrubs and his expression tells me he's more than eager to cut into Jax. Which leaves me feeling a little dizzy and uneasy imagining Jax's body open on a table.

Jax nods reassuringly. "Let's do it."

Dr. Peltz clasps his hands then rubs them together. "Alright, that's what I like to hear." He smiles at Jax, then faces Pat and Mamaw, and says, "We'll take him in for anesthesia and get him prepped and ready for surgery now if ya'll are ready."

Pat nods and hugs Jax. "This is the day we've been waiting for."

"Hopefully your gray hair slows down after this," Jax says playfully. He's more than optimistic right now.

Pat heads for the door and Mamaw hugs Jax, then kisses the top of his head. "I'm so proud of you, Jaxon. You're such a strong young man."

"Thanks, Mamaw."

She shakes his arm. "I have faith you'll be fine in surgery, just like you've survived the last decade with this condition."

I'm not sure if she's trying to convince Jax, or herself that he'll be okay in surgery. Or maybe she really does believe he'll be fine. Either way, I wish I felt as certain as Mamaw right now.

Everything seems to be happening so fast, I can barely process it.

Dr. Peltz meets them in the hallway to talk more. Probably about his surgical plan, or post ops, or whatever surgeons talk to the family about.

"Hey," Jax says gently, "look at me."

I pull my gaze from the small window on the door

where I see his family, back to him. His eyes are bright and full of life.

"I'm not afraid," he says, as if he can read my mind. "We'll be able to swim, and go to six-flags, and get massages together." I should be the one telling him I'm not afraid. I should be reassuring him. But I can't. I can't pretend like everything is okay when I don't feel like it's okay.

I don't know if it's because I'm nervous, or trying not to cry, but I laugh. Only it comes out of my nose, making a snorting sound.

Jax pulls me closer to him. I sit on the side of his bedside and curl next to him. "We'll finally be able to do all the exhilarating things I haven't been able to do because of my heart," he reminds me.

A rush runs through my stomach. "Promise?"

He kisses my face. "Promise. And you won't have to worry about me passing out when I run up a flight of stairs."

The nurse unhooks a wire and reorganizes his IV tube route. "You two are so sweet." It's a different nurse than the last time we were here for the pacemaker surgery. *Thank goodness.*

Jax faces her. "She's my girlfriend." He says this with a proud grin, flashing her his full smile.

"I gathered that," the nurse says securing one of the guards on the side of the hospital bed. "Sorry, but we should probably get going."

I climb off the bed and move out of the way so she can pull the guard up on the other side.

She wheels the bed around so that Jax is facing me. My heart sinks. He's so certain and happy. But this could be the last time I ever see him. Dr. Peltz said that since he's had surgeries before, he's going to have to take his time and the surgery will take six hours or longer.

I hold the door open as the nurse wheels him into the hall.

Mamaw and Pat hug him once more before heading toward the waiting room.

My throat is dry.

I'm torn.

I'm excited he's getting a heart that will give him a normal life. But I'm worried too. I'm so worried he's going to die on the operating table. Or he'll reject the heart after surgery and die. Or the heart will last a year and then he'll die.

I'm worried he's going to die. And that scares me.

The one person I've handed my heart to could be the same person that crushes me in the most unimaginable way.

I press my mouth together, trying to keep the tears from rolling out of my eyes.

Before Jax reaches the only-doctors-allowed-passed-this-point door, he lifts his arms up inviting me in for a hug, in the same way he did blind folded at the mall.

I hurry toward him and hug him one last time. "I love you," I say with my face buried into his neck. "So much."

The puff of air he releases sounds like a laugh of confidence. "I love you," he shifts his head to meet my gaze, "More than you know." His eyes are piercing blue, so full of certainty. As if he's about to do something as safe and mundane as brushing his teeth. "Do me a favor," he says.

I hope those same blue eyes full of life return in six hours. "Anything," I say.

His grin shifts to one side of his mouth. "Tell Birdie we're fighting."

He kisses me, and the only reason he stops is because

the nurse continues pulling his bed away. "Sorry, this is as far as you can go," she says to me. "I'll come back with updates every hour."

I dig my eyes into her. "Promise?"

She twists her face.

Jax notices her expression and says to her, "Just say, *promise*, back to her."

The nurse blinks. "Promise…" She says this with confusion and uncertainty, but I'll take it.

Before the doors close, I say, "Why are you and Birdie fighting?"

"He's late!" he calls out.

Then the double doors shut.

They're shutting me out of the next six hours of Jax's life.

And I resent those doors for doing that to me.

I meet Pat and Mamaw in the waiting room.

Pat is sitting with his phone in his lap as he scrolls through whatever he's looking at.

Mamaw keeps her eyes on the TV.

There is a couple, probably in their mid-thirties, clinging to each other in the corner of the waiting room. The woman looks as if she's been crying for years. I'm sure their son or daughter is on the other side of those dreadful double doors that shut loved ones out.

There's nothing beautiful or romantic about either of our situations. Nothing glamorous. Only raw, painful, and ghastly emotions infuse this entire waiting room as we are all forced to wait patiently for good news. While hushing thoughts of anything horrific happening in surgery inevitably swirl around in our minds.

"I'm here!" Birdie is winded when he reaches us. His eyes flash around the room. And he's holding a coffee carrier with four drinks. "Oh no," he says biting at his bottom lip. "Did I miss the salute?"

I nod. "They just took him back. And Jax wanted me to tell you that you two are fighting."

He rolls his eyes then makes his way over to Pat, handing him a coffee. "I brought something sweet. Mamabear always says that a warm belly warms a burdened spirit."

Pat sips at his coffee. "Thanks, Birdie. Your mom is a smart a lady."

Birdie tilts his head and grins. "She really is." He taps Pat's arm. "I'm going to tell her you said that. That'll just make her day."

Pat laughs to himself as Birdie holds a coffee out to Mamaw.

"Don't worry," he says in a low voice. "It's decaf."

Mamaw scrunches her nose and begins to say, "I don't drink decaf—"

But Birdie hurries over to where I'm pacing.

He twists his face like he's disgusted. "She's such an old bat," he says as he hands me a coffee. "This one is for you."

I look at him endearingly.

But I must hold my gaze too long because he says, "Stop acting like he's gone, or I'm going to cry."

I inhale sharply. "I'm sorry." I swallow my emotions down. Birdie has a way about making life feel lighter and brighter, and I don't want to ruin his mood with my sappiness. "Thank you," I say lifting my cup.

"You got it, P. You're my girl," he says as he winks at me.

I take a sip.

It's like a warm blast of strong-smooth espresso mixed with carmelly-swiss-vanilla and dark chocolate happiness that burst against my taste buds.

"Wow," I say. "What is this?"

He shrugs. "I don't know," he sips his coffee. "Mmm, mine is good too."

I shift my weight on one hip. "Birdie…"

He takes a seat as far away from Mamaw as possible. "I really don't know, P."

"You bought it."

"Can you sit, you're making me feel uneasy."

I sit next to him.

He sits up in his chair and leans toward me while keeping his eyes on the large window in front of us. "I told the barista to make beautiful sunrays of hope in a cup for my bestie who is about to have one of the hardest days of her life."

I give him another stupid endearing grin. "You said that to her?"

He forces his coffee down rapidly, which makes a gulping sound. "I mean, the barista was a guy—but yes, I did say—"

I wrap my arms around his shoulders. "I love you, Birdie."

He lets out a squeal that causes Pat, Mamaw and the sad couple to flip their heads around and look at us with concern.

"You guys," he says to the room, "this girl is ah-may-ZING!"

I don't even mind that he's being loud.

"Love you, sweet boo," he says hugging my arm.

After a moment, I notice Mamaw is the only one still looking at us. But it almost looks like she's…

Yep, she's glaring at us.

I don't want her upset with me. "Mamaw?" I say. "Are you okay?"

She scrunches her nose and purses her mouth. "My grandson is in there and you're hugging on this loudmouthed-knot-head."

Birdie's jaw drops and he lets out an offended scoff.

"Mamaw," I say, trying not to laugh. "Birdie is just my friend."

"*Best* friend," Birdie says with attitude.

Pat leans over to Mamaw and says something that makes her raise her eyebrows, then turns her attention back to the pamphlets on the table.

Birdie taps his knee, then whispers to me, "How long is this going to take?"

I shake my head in silent laughter. He's the best person to sit with me through something like this. I'm not sure anyone else could put me in a better mood.

"Six hours," I say quietly.

"Six hours!" Everyone looks at us again. I'm starting to feel like Birdie isn't a *waiting room* type of person.

I quietly, "Shh," but I can tell he's about to say something else.

He lets out another offended scoff in Mamaw's direction. "What are you—" He rises, then snatches the pamphlet from Mamaw's grip. "*How to prepare for the loss of a loved one,*" he reads. Then facing her he says, "Don't fill your mind with this nonsense."

Mamaw draws her brows together, then opens her mouth to say something.

I grasp Birdie's hand before she can defend herself. "We should go for a walk." I don't want to get on Mamaw's bad side either. Leaving the room seems like the best option at this point to salvage whatever relationship I have left with Mamaw.

First me and Birdie take turns racing down the hallways and staircases. The floors are painted with colorful waves that make racing an easy game.

Until a woman tells us to stop, because *this is a hospital.*

Not even ten seconds later, we see a couple of kids racing on the colored waves. I'm not sure if they got the idea from us, or if they thought of it themselves. Either way, it makes me feel better when I see them run by the woman and ignore her when she tells them to slow down.

We go downstairs and stare at the wall of screens until our brains hurt from the stimulation and blue light.

After further exploration, we find another waiting room with a giant tree in the middle of the floor with a climbing wall surrounding it.

We don't even have to say anything to each other. Birdie just gives me a knowing look and that's all it takes before we are rushing over to sit against the plastic tree trunk.

"Why do they make a children's hospital so fun?" Birdie asks while slightly out of breath.

I look through one of the holes of the climbing wall in front of us and watch a toddler peek his head through the hole and then hide again. "It's a children's hospital," I say smiling at the toddler peeking at me again. He giggles and runs to his mom's lap.

Birdie adjusts himself on his side and faces me. "Exactly. How sad would it be if you were a sick kid in such a fun hospital where you can't even experience all the fun?"

This doesn't seem like an issue that would bother Birdie. There must be something more that's going on with him. I shift to sit closer to him. "Jax is going to be okay. We have to keep thinking that."

The toddler runs back and peeks at me again. "And I think the fun stuff is for the healthy kids that come to visit. And it probably gives the sick kids something to look forward to when they're better."

Birdie taps my arm. "When did you get so wise, P.?"

I press at my fingers. "I'm not."

"You so are." He checks his phone. "Have you gotten any updates? It's almost been five hours."

I take my phone out of my pocket. I must have been having so much fun with Birdie that I didn't feel it vibrate because I have six texts and four missed calls.

The first three are from Pat.

The nurse said surgery is going good.

They are moving quicker than anticipated.

Everything went well. They are closing up. Are you two coming back soon?

"The surgery went well," I say, "Pat texted me forty-five minutes ago saying it was almost over. They have probably closed Jax up by now, right?"

Birdie's face lights up. "Well let's go!"

"Hang on." I quickly check my other messages.

Two texts from Candice.

Hey.

Wanna get some In and Out with me?

Shoot. Everything happened so fast I didn't even think to tell her about Jax's surgery.

The next text is from Terra.

Call me ASAP.

Normally that wouldn't unsettle me. She's an abrasive texter. *She's an abrasive person.*

But what unsettles me, is that the four missed calls are

all from her.

What if she went into early labor and needed me to watch Lissy?

Or maybe Lissy is playing hide and seek again, and Terra is just freaking out like last time.

"Ready?" Birdie says.

I crease my brow. "Yeah," my eyes are locked on the four calls from Terra.

He makes his way to his feet. Then reaching his hand out to help me up he says, "What is it?"

Locking eyes with him, I say, "There's something weird about how many times Terra called me."

Birdie leads us out, holding the door open for me.

I continue, "She also told me to call her ASAP." I give him a concerned look. "I should call her, right?"

"Probably," he says.

I tap her number, walking in stride with Birdie. "I hope Lissy's okay. And the new baby."

Terra answers on the second ring. "Paloma, where have you been all day?" Her voice is panicked.

I'm taken aback by her interrogation. "I uh," I don't even know how to casually tell her where I've been. "I've been at the hospital. Jax had surgery."

She ignores my comment about Jax. *She's so self-absorbed.* "I tried calling you earlier."

Is she *mad* at me?

I don't even work for her anymore.

Did she not hear that I've been busy worrying about my boyfriend at the hospital all day? I think this has more precedence than whatever she's freaking out about.

I feel my defenses rising.

"What did you need, Terra?" I'm not surprised by the tone in my voice.

But the look on Birdie's face when he hears my

response tells me I might be coming off a little harsher than I intended.

"I thought you might want to know." Her voice cracks on the last word, then she draws in a shuddered breath before saying, "Claude's been in an accident."

I stop in my tracks.

My chest tightens.

"Is he okay? What kind of accident?" I hear the same panic she answered her phone with rise in my own voice.

Birdie backtracks and stands in front of me. His face shifting to concern.

Terra chokes the words out. "He was in a car accident." She sniffs, but she's not trying to hold back the fact that she's sobbing. "He didn't make it."

I drop my phone and double over with a weep of disbelief.

Is she certain he didn't make it?

How does she know?

Is she with him?

I *don't* believe this.

I *won't* believe this.

I *can't* believe this.

Birdie places one hand on my shoulder. "P.? What happened? What is it?" He picks up my phone, placing it against his ear. "Hello? Hi, this is Birdie, P.'s—I mean, Paloma's friend."

I barely hear Terra's muffled voice.

Then Birdie kneels next to me. To Terra he says, "I'm so sorry…Which hospital?…Medical City, okay…Yes, I'll make sure she's okay…Take care."

He tucks my phone into his pocket.

I've never felt so broken.

I've never felt so torn to be in two places at once.

I'm over the moon that Jax's surgery went well.

303

I want to be here for him.

And at the same time, I'm shattered that the father I just got to know has been ripped out of my life in an instant.

I can't breathe.

Birdie places both of his hands on my shoulders. "I'm so sorry, P."

When he says this, it makes it more real.

Like the fact that Birdie knows that Claude is gone, that my father will never be in my life again, makes it official.

It's not a bad dream.

It's *real*.

And the fracture in my heart *hurts* so bad.

I can't cry, because I can't catch my breath. I'm gasping for air. The dizziness takes over and I collapse to my hands and knees.

My hands are cold, and my entire body feels like I just fell into a freezer.

I barely notice a doctor stop in the hallway to speak with Birdie. I have no idea what they're saying. All I focus on is the colorful lines in the floor, and the fact that I'll never get to tell my dad that I love him.

I never said it.

I didn't know I loved him, until right now. Until he wasn't in my life.

I'll never be irritated by his lack of personal space again.

I'll never hear his warm accented voice again.

I'll never see his face at the gallery again.

The next thought breaks me.

I let out a sob and the tears finally flood from my eyes.

Claude and Terra's baby will never know him.

It hurts worse than any pain I've ever felt.

"Paloma." Pat's voice is gentle next to my ear. "Come on, let's get you out of this hallway." He helps me to my feet.

I feel like I'm floating across the floor.

I can't breathe.

I'm so dizzy, I might fall over any second.

"Here," Pat says motioning us into the open elevator.

I have no idea where Birdie is, or what's happening around me. I'm completely inside of myself. Everything that's happening to me is the most intense compilation of broken emotions I've ever felt at once. From my tears to my heart, to every cell forming my body—I feel it all.

We file in but I'm not sure how much farther I can go before I'm going to literally pass out.

Pat hits a button on the wall, then the elevator stops.

"Okay," he says.

What happens next should surprise me, at least a little, but it doesn't faze me at all.

Pat hugs me.

"I'm so sorry, Paloma."

I cover my face with my hands and break down into his shoulder.

He doesn't tell me to hush.

He doesn't push me away.

He doesn't tell me it's going to be okay.

He just waits in the moment and repeatedly says, "I'm so sorry."

I realize I've been crying for an entire Ed Sheeran song playing in the elevator when I step back and lean against the elevator wall. I wipe my face with the neckline of my shirt and draw in a deep inhale.

Pat's giving me a bereaved expression when I finally look up at him.

He doesn't say anything.

But I don't want to talk about Claude again. If I do, I'm afraid I'll never stop crying.

"How's Jax?" I say. "Sorry, we ditched the waiting

room. He and Mamaw are kind of—"

"Don't worry about it. Jaxon is fine, he can wait." He scratches at his chin. "I'm concerned about you right now."

I sniff. "I'm good." I roll my eyes. "I'm not good, but I will be. I just want to see Jax."

Pat forces a grin, but his eyes are still full of concern. "Are you sure?"

I blow out a rush of air. *I do not want to keep crying.* "I'm sure."

He nods, looking back to the wall. "Okay," then he presses a button, and the elevator begins to move again. "You know," he says. "Greif comes and goes. It's like an aftershock that hits you at the strangest times."

I bite my upper lip to keep from crying again.

He lets out a laugh to himself. "The hurt never goes away. But instead, it becomes a part of you. It hurts less with time and after you accept it." He keeps his eyes on the changing number of the elevator. "But it never fully goes away. I want you to know that, because I wish someone had told me what it would be like losing someone for the first time."

I know he's talking about Dillon. And probably a little bit about his wife too. I hope I can talk about death in such a normal way one day, just like Pat is able to talk about the way death continues to sting.

Like it's a normal part of life.

Because it is.

The elevator stops and the doors rush open.

Pat pushes himself off the wall where he was leaning. "Well, let's go check on Jaxon," he smiles briefly before exiting.

I follow behind him.

"Is he awake?" I ask.

Pat turns down another hallway. "I'm not sure. He was still sleeping when Birdie called."

"Birdie called you?"

He glances back at me. "He's a good kid."

I smile. Then I feel guilty leaving Birdie downstairs. He was already worried about Jax, then I probably exacerbated that worry after he witnessed my breakdown.

When we reach the room, Birdie and Mamaw are gathered around Jax.

And they are laughing.

I find a place on the edge of his bed.

I force a smile. The last thing I want to do is deliver bad news after his surgery again.

"Hey," his voice is hoarse. Probably from the breathing tube. "I was worried you ran off on me."

I hold his hand. "I would never."

Everyone chuckles.

Mamaw places her hand on my shoulder, and I feel the pain rising inside of me again. Like the way she is touching me is telling me she knows about Claude.

I try not to look at Jax.

Birdie must notice my instability and redirects the conversation. "So, I've been thinking about a new video series."

Jax smirks, his eyes still only partially open. "You couldn't wait until I was out of the hospital first?"

"Don't worry," Birdie says. "It won't require much action."

Mamaw makes a grunting sound before saying, "Well, are you going to tell us what it is?"

We all laugh at Mamaw's vigor.

Birdie presses his palms together at his chest. "So, I was thinking." He looks at Jax. "When you're feeling up to it, of course." Birdie flashes his eyes at the rest of us with a smile. "We can visit the kids staying at the hospital, and let them share their stories with us."

The room goes quiet.

I search the various expressions on their faces.

"Will they let you do that?" Pat says.

Birdie shrugs. "I don't see why not."

"It's a great idea," Mamaw says.

Her comment causes Birdie and Jax to share a look.

"Alright," Jax says. "Get me a wheelchair."

CHAPTER

TWENTY-FIVE

Jaxon

I wake up from the twelfth unintentional nap I've taken since my surgery.

I check the time.

It's 5:20 a.m.

Paloma is curled up fast asleep on the couch.

I vaguely remember my dad and Mamaw leaving last night.

I also remember that Birdie mentioned a new idea for our YouTube channel that seems like one of the best ideas he's come up with yet.

I notice Paloma's phone light up next to her face. I contemplate trying to get out of bed, but when I shift to the other side, the familiar ache from surgery returns.

My throat hurts.

The fluid from the IV in my neck is cold.

The bandage on my chest itches.

It feels like if I make any sudden movements, I might tear my ribcage apart and undo all the work Dr. Peltz has done to fix me.

Paloma's phone lights up again, only this time her eyes flutter open. She looks at her phone, then slides her other hand over to text with both hands.

Before she clicks her screen off, the glow from her phone reveals a somber expression on her face.

"Hey," I manage. Somehow my throat feels drier than when I woke up after surgery.

She rolls over to face me. "Hey, how are you feeling?"

"Sore." I peel the tape holding the bandage in place over my sternum to inspect my incision.

She sits up and wraps the blanket around her shoulders. "Are you ready to get out of here so we can go for a swim at Birdie's?"

The incision is long, but doesn't look as terrible as it feels. "Oh man, I don't know if I'll—"

Her soft cry stops me from finishing my sad attempt at humor.

"Hey," I say, attentive to her sudden onset of apprehension. "Come here."

She scoots next to me, careful not to pull any wires out of place.

"I'm going to be okay," I reassure her.

She releases what sounds like a frustrated exhale. "It's not that."

I push her hair out of her face. In the most gentle way possible. "Tell me," I say.

Her mouth falls into a deep frown that dents her cheeks in the corners of her mouth. Like she's about to burst into tears.

It breaks me.

Before she can tell me what it is, the night nurse comes into the room.

"Good morning," he says in a quiet voice. "How's it going?"

Paloma wipes her face and returns to the couch.

The nurse checks the monitors, my incision, the IV bag, my legs, then asks how my pain is.

"Uh, three," I answer, unfocused, because my attention is on Paloma.

"Good," he says. "Keep resting. You're healing well and should be getting up and walking tomorrow."

"Awesome," I say.

He scribbles something on the markerboard on the wall in the room. With his eyes on the board, he says, "Do you need anything before I go?"

Even though the lights are dim, I can see Paloma's sad expression. And it's piercing my heart that's literally being held together with staples and stiches.

"Nope," I say.

He heads for the door. "Alright, I'll be back in another hour or so to give you your antibiotic and talk about switching you to a less intense immunosuppressant. If you need anything before then, just let me know."

Before he's completely out the door, I say, "Actually..."

He turns around and leans his shoulder on the doorway.

I gently cough, which hurts my sternum more than I anticipated. I wince, placing a hand over my chest. "I was wondering if you knew who donated my heart? I'd like to thank the family, if that's possible."

He smiles. "I'll find out for you."

As soon as he's gone, I reach my arm out to Paloma. "Come here, tell me what happened."

Her shoulders fall with her exhale. "I don't know how

to say this, Jax."

I search her face. She's sad. I can tell that much. But I don't recognize the broken expression on her face.

I tip her chin up with my finger, so she meets my eyes. "You just say it."

Her eyes flash between mine, and I can tell whatever she's about to say is going to hurt. "Claude died in a car accident yesterday." The words spill out of her.

I feel my mouth fall open in shock.

I want to ask her if she's sure, but it would be pointless. Of course she's sure he died. She wouldn't be this upset if she wasn't sure.

I know the disbelief I'm feeling is from the sudden shock of hearing it for the first time.

I don't want to believe it's true.

But I know it is, and I hate that Paloma is feeling the heartache of loss right now.

I hold her as best I can without disrupting the wires and monitors on my body. She tucks her head under my chin. "I'm so sorry," I say. "I'm *so* sorry."

What a horrible day it must have been for her yesterday. She was juggling all the emotions she had worrying about me dying on the operating table. Then she found out her father died.

I wish I could hold her tighter.

I wish I could hug her pain away.

I wish I could carry it for her.

· · ·

"How do you feel about a shower?" my dad says.

I lift my arm and sniff. "I smell fine."

Paloma scrunches her nose. "You don't smell fine."

"I showered two days ago."

My dad unzips a bag and begins stacking my clothes in

a pile. "You need a shower."

I look to Paloma for some backup, instead she says, "You really do need a shower."

A smile spreads across her face. It's the first genuine smile I've seen since Claude's accident. Terra decided to cremate him and made arrangements to have a funeral this weekend. That's all I know so far. Paloma doesn't want to go, but I know she'll regret it if she skips it. Once it's done, *it's done*. And I don't want her to have to carry that kind of regret.

I twist my body to one side of the bed and gently place my bare feet on the cold floor. "Fine." I take the clean clothes my dad hands me. "I'm going home today, I don't know why I can't shower in my own bathroom."

"Go," Paloma says with a laugh.

It's been five days since my surgery. I've been taking a handful of prescriptions daily, the nurse freed me of my catheter, and I haven't rejected my new heart. So that's good news.

I'm not supposed to get my incision too damp, so I shower as quickly as my sore body will allow. When I return from the bathroom, I'm shocked to see Terra.

"Hey," is all I manage to say when she looks at me.

The last encounter I had with her, she was in a state of distress and barely made eye contact with me.

"Hi, Jax," her voice is low and calm, unlike the high-pitched screaming she was using at her house the night Lissy was hiding.

I don't have a moment to filter my words, so they just come out. "Why are you here?"

I probably should have started with something like, *Are you okay? I'm sorry about your husband...*

My dad cocks his head. "Jaxon," he says this as a sort of reminder for me to watch my phrasing.

I'm feeling a little weak after the shower, so I find a place next to Paloma on the couch. "I'm sorry, I didn't mean to sound rude." I scan their faces but stop when I see the way Paloma is looking at me. It's as if she could equally burst into tears and laughter. Honestly, there's something strange about the way everyone is looking at me right now.

Terra brushes the air with her hand. "It's fine. I'm sure it's a surprise to see me here."

That's an understatement.

She takes a few steps in my direction. "I wanted to tell you myself."

I search her expression, but I don't know what to say.

She continues, "The heart beating in your chest," she folds her mouth together and her eyes shine, "it was Claude's heart."

My mouth falls agape.

Paloma takes one of my hands in hers, and Terra kneels in front of me.

I don't know how I should feel right now.

Shocked.

Weirded out.

Happy.

"Can I…" her eyes are darting between my eyes and my chest. Like she wants to ask me, but can't quite bring herself to utter the words in this strange situation we're both in.

I look at my dad, who gives me a nod from his chair on the other side of the room.

Before I can overthink what I'm about to do, I place her hand on my chest which causes her to gush out a quiet sob.

I'm the only one in the room not crying at this point.

The door to my room clicks open and the nurse from

the other night makes his way in. "I was coming to talk to you more about your donor," he says this before realizing what's happening in the awkward scene of this hospital room. "Oh." He looks mildly embarrassed. "I guess I'll come back later."

My dad rises. "I think we've figured out what you wanted to tell us." He places his hand on the nurse's shoulder and walks out with him.

Terra pulls her hand up to cover her mouth. "I can't believe his heart is still beating." She sits back on the edge of the bed.

"How did you find out it was donated to me?" I ask.

She takes a tissue and presses it at the corners of her eyes and rests one hand on her belly. "Well," she exhales sharply, "When they asked what I was willing to donate, I told them they could take anything that would keep someone alive. But all I asked was that they tell me where his organs were going."

The room grows still for a moment.

Paloma takes the pause as an opportunity to share. "All they told us was that his heart came from a healthy forty-two-year-old male."

I nod. "I was going to write a thank you letter and send it to the organ hospital for the family—for you."

"We never put two and two together," Paloma says.

Terra smiles. "I didn't either. At first, anyway." She rolls her shoulders back and grips the bottom of her belly with both hands. "They told me his liver was going to a thirty-year-old-woman in Oklahoma." She looks up at the wall, like she's digging in the back of her mind. "His skin would be used for graphing in New Mexico and Louisiana. His kidneys went to Washington. On and on they went, telling me where each part of him would continue to give life to others."

Then she looks at me. "But when they told me there was a teenage boy just down the road at the children's hospital, that needed a new heart. I just had to see who it was."

The room goes quiet again.

I don't know how to feel.

I don't know what to say.

The last few days have been emotional.

Crazy.

Unbelievable.

I mean, I'm still alive because of Claude. And the worst part is that I can't even thank him for it.

"Well," she says. "I better get going. The funeral's not going to plan itself." She glances at Paloma. "I hope to see you there."

Paloma nods. "I'll try."

"You're invited too, of course," she says to me.

"We'll be there," I say. It's the least I can do to pay my respects to the man who gave me my life back. Who just so happens to be the man who gave life to Paloma too, in more ways than one. I feel more indebted to him than anyone else.

Terra ever so slightly waddles to exit the room.

I rise to my feet and meet her before she's gone. "Terra." She looks surprised when she faces me. "Thank you."

Her expression shifts into a smile. "Thank you, Jaxon."

Then she leaves.

When I sit with Paloma again, she places her hand to the left of my chest.

I place my hand over hers. "Do you need a turn too?"

She laughs, kisses the side of my face, then gently replaces our hands with the side of her head. Pressing her ear against my chest.

"I can't believe that's his heart," her voice is quiet. "A part of him is *literally* still alive in you."

CHAPTER TWENTY-SIX

Paloma

I catch myself pushing on my cuticles and instead of allowing myself to continue, I fold my hands together.

Candice nudges me with her shoulder. "I thought we were going to a funeral, not a concert.

I didn't realize how many people knew Claude. I've never been to a church this size before. And I've definitely never been in a crowd this large before.

I knew Terra was good at putting on events. She was Claude's gallery events coordinator before she started representing artists. But Candice is right, this does feel like a concert.

"Sorry, we're late," Birdie says, filing in behind Jax.

"It's okay," I say to Birdie. Then I give Jax an are-you-serious look and say, "I told you not to come. You should be resting at home."

He places his arm around the back of my chair when he sits down. "Was I supposed to take his heart and skip his funeral after his widowed wife invited me?"

He has a point.

Birdie peeks his head in the direction of me and Candice. "What's with the lights?"

Candice's eyes widen. "I know, right?"

A band gathers on the stage and plays music that only half the crowd knows the lyrics to.

This is turning out to be the strangest funeral service I've ever been to.

The speaker is surprisingly fantastic. He makes us laugh, and cry, and remember all the good parts of Claude. He even includes my name as one of Claude's daughters, which I know is Terra's doing.

As the service ends, Birdie helps Jax, who insists he's fine, up from his seat.

Candice shakes my arm. "You've got to be kidding me." She's whispering but it's still spitting out of her mouth when she says it.

"What?" I say. But when I flip around to see what she's talking about, I don't need her to answer my question.

Because I see that she is talking about my mom.

Even though I'm emancipated and know she has no control over me or my life. Even though I stood up to her and told her off when I took my birth certificate. There's still something about her that makes me uneasy.

After the way we left things at her house, I'm not sure how she will react to seeing me.

To my surprise, she walks past us.

I scrunch my forehead at Candice and she says, "That was weird. What do you think she's doing here?"

Jax gives me a look and talks out of the side of his

mouth. "Paloma, isn't that your mom?" He's not being as discrete as Candice was.

Birdie perks up at his comment. "P.'s mom? For real? She's here?" He thrusts his body back and forth until he makes a complete circle. "Where? Where's P.'s mom?"

Jax hits Birdie's arm with the back of his hand. "Shush," he nods in the direction of my mom. "She's the lady holding the book and the flower."

Birdie nods when he finds her in the crowd. He purses his lips, then says, "You don't really look like either of your parents."

"Thanks? I guess," I say.

Birdie taps Jax's arm. "And that's not any flower, that's a rose."

Jax scratches at his sternum. "I've never seen a flower that color."

Birdie drops his jaw. "It's a *rose*."

It reminds me of something I've seen before. It takes me but a second to remember. Yes, in Claude's bedroom. The painting of the rose was the same deep purple and red color.

"I don't understand why she would come here," Candice says.

"I do," I say.

They turn to face me as I watch my mom approach the front of the room where Claude's family is mingling.

I continue, "She's mourning too."

I'm sure she's doing more than mourning. She's probably feeling guilty for keeping him out of my life. And for ruining his life when she took off with me. There's also probably a part of her that regrets leaving him. A part of her that wishes her disorder hadn't become her identity. A part of her that wishes she could have spoken to him one last time.

I begin to step toward the front of the room. "I should probably say something to her."

Jax slips through the crowd behind me. "I'll go with you."

"What is she doing?" Candice says.

At first, I think she's talking about me. But then—

No way.

She wouldn't.

Oh my gosh, she is.

My mother is approaching Terra.

"Hello," she greets her, "I wanted to say that I'm so sorry for your loss." She sounds sincere.

Terra gives her a rehearsed smile. "Thank you so much." My mom hands the notebook and burgundy rose to Terra. "What's this?" It's weird my mom seems more bereaved by Claude's passing than Terra. Everyone deals with grief differently. I guess.

My mom encourages her to open the notebook by lifting the cover. "In France, it's tradition to set a notebook on a table covered in a black cloth outside the front door of the mourning family's home."

Terra nods with raised eyebrows.

My mom continues, "It's for anyone that wants to write their condolences in it when they stop by."

Terra smiles, without a clue that she's talking to my mother. Who is also Claude's ex-wife. "Well, thank you so much." She doesn't bother asking how she knew Claude. Even in mourning, Terra's still only focused on her job. And right now, that's having a meet and greet with thousands of people at her husband's funeral.

"And this," my mom says handing her the rose, "was his favorite color."

Terra twists the stem of the rose between her fingers, examining it with a curious expression before turning to give her attention to someone else.

I wonder if she'll leave that painting above her bed.

My mom makes her way down the aisle toward the exit but locks eyes with me before she's even halfway there.

I don't know what to do.

Squeezing Jax's hand in mine, I feel my pulse begin to race.

"Paloma," she says as she shifts through the crowd. "I'm so sorry," she says to a man when she knocks his arm with her shoulder. She quickly returns to approaching me. The concern on her face looks real. She tilts her head and lifts her arms. But she seems unsure of her gesture. "Can I hug you?"

I nod, releasing my grip from Jax's.

She wraps her arms around me and the familiar aroma of *mom* returns. Giving me that uneasy feeling, but at the same time it holds a sort of comfort over me. Like despite all of her insanity, she's still the person that raised me and took care of me.

Even my senses can't deny it.

"Hey, April," Jax says next to me.

My mom releases me and faces Jax. "Hello."

He touches his chest. "I have Claude's heart in here."

She gives him a repulsive expression. As if what he said was morbid and out of line.

"It's true," I say, noticing she's probably about to say something regretful to him because she doesn't understand that he's telling the truth.

She flips her head back to face me.

I tuck my hand in Jax's as a form of security for me. "Jax needed a new heart because he had a rare condition. It's crazy Claude was in the accident when Jax was next in line for a transplant."

She draws her brows down. "You're serious?"

I look at Jax.

He looks at me.

"It's kind of a miracle," I say.

My mom smiles. "I'd say so." She looks at Jax, then back to me. "Can we talk?"

I suck in a rush of air. I'm not sure I want to be alone with her. I don't really know how to talk to her by myself.

Jax let's go of my hand.

When I peer at him with a don't-leave-me-alone-with-her look, he smiles and says to my mom, "It was nice seeing you, April," he tilts his head, shrugging his shoulders, "despite the circumstances."

She forces a smile. "You too." Then she faces me again. "Can we step outside?"

I nod.

When we walk down the aisle for the exit, Terra is talking to Jax.

Candice's eyes have never been bigger when we pass by her and Birdie, still sitting in their seats. I give her a knowing look, so she doesn't try to come and rescue me from my mom.

Once we're outside, the words burst from my mom as if the pressure from holding them in has finally released.

"I'm so sorry I didn't tell you about Claude before." She clasps her hands together and looks at the ground. "I'm also sorry that he's gone. And I'm sorry for putting you through everything I put you through in your life and especially the last couple of years. I'm back on my meds now and started therapy again. I don't know how to undo all the hurt I've caused you. But apologizing seems like a good start."

I never thought I would hear her own her issues like that. I'm not sure what to say, so I quickly ask myself what Jax would tell me to say.

"It's okay." When I speak, she looks up with eyes full of anticipation. "I forgive you, mom."

She smiles and her eyes shine with joyful tears. "Can I hug you?" she says.

I let out one of my snorty nose laughs. "Yes, you don't have to keep asking."

She hugs me again. Only this time, I hug her back.

"Sissy-yy!" I don't even have to look to know Lissy is running toward me.

She clings to my waist while I'm still in mid-hug with my mom.

My mom releases me. "Who is this?"

I wrap Lissy in a hug. She's so cheerful and happy for just losing her dad. She's also probably still too young to understand the finality of death.

"This is Lissy," I say with a chipper grin. Just being around Lissy makes everything a little less grim.

"Hi, Lissy," my mom says. "I'm April, Paloma's mom."

Lissy shakes my mom's hand and says, "Hi, I'm Lissy, Paloma's sister."

My mom slaps her hand to her chest and sucks in a rush of air.

Lissy faces me. "If April is your mommy, does that mean she's my mommy too?"

I laugh. "No, Terra is your mommy and April is my mommy and Claude was our daddy."

She twists her curls with her finger and scrunches her nose. "That doesn't make any sense."

Another little girl calls out to Lissy. I set her on her feet and she runs back inside of the building.

"Wow," my mom says. "I knew you were working for Claude, but it's very surreal to see his other daughter in real life."

I let out an uncertain laugh. "Try finding out you've

been babysitting your sister for months."

She smiles, knowing I'm half joking.

"Well," she says. "I should go."

"Or you could stay." She did say she's back in therapy and on her meds so I know I don't have to worry about her freaking out any time soon.

She waves her hand through the air. "No, it's not my place." She looks toward the people filing out of the door. "This is your family. And your life." She waits a moment before facing me. "You're still my daughter, and I still love you. So, if you want to call or visit, I'm always here for you. Okay?"

I give her a pained smile. Knowing everything is changing. "Thanks, mom. I will."

She hugs me once more before she heads for the parking lot.

The uneasiness I felt before is replaced by a sadness. But also by something I've never felt before with my mom.

I feel *peace*.

I know things are different now. But it doesn't mean I have to cut her out completely. I'm sad she's going home to her house where she lives alone. But I'm happy to know that the next time I visit her, I won't have the desire to sneak into her house.

Our relationship is different.

But that's okay.

I know now that the perfect family doesn't exist.

And knowing that I can see my mom on my terms, when she's doing what she can to be healthy, is the best news I could receive all day.

CHAPTER TWENTY-SEVEN

Jaxon

"We're closing in on the end of the series," I say, pulling my socks on. "The kids at the hospital are great. They always want to share their stories with us." A laugh escapes my throat. "It's their parents we have to convince to let us film."

My phone vibrates and I pull it from my pocket. It's Birdie, impatiently waiting for me outside.

"Was Birdie always this Type-A?" I say, taking a few steps closer. "Anyway, I'll let you know how it goes tonight." I adjust the blanket by her feet. "I love you, mom."

I squeeze her hand gently before exiting the room.

After my heart transplant, it seemed like a second chance at a full life. Before, with the pacemaker, it was almost like I was counting down the days, counting down every thud in my chest until the last beat of my heart would end my life.

To repay the debt I feel I owe Claude, I've decided to live more fully. I've decided to accept that my dad's never going to take my mom off of life support. I'm okay knowing she's probably never going to wake up, and I'm choosing to talk to her in case she does. I've promised God and myself that I'll live a full life. I'll live the longest life this heart gives me. And I won't take it for granted.

It's been three months since my surgery.

Three months since Claude's accident.

Three months since Mamaw moved in with us.

Three months since I decided to attend the same college as Paloma.

Three months since the miracle of a lifetime.

"Jax!" Birdie thrusts the front door open as I bolt down the stairs. "Do you not know how to read a clock?"

I slip my shoes on. "I'm sure there's a reason we are running a little late."

"Not this again." Birdie smacks his palm to his forehead. "Not the everything-has-some-underlying-meaning-to-it superstition spiel. And honestly, in this case, you're running late because *you can't read a clock*!"

"There is a reason. We're probably avoiding some sort of—"

He throws his hand up in front of my face to stop me from talking. "No, there's no reason, other than the fact that you are late to everything unless I'm here to drag you out of your own house."

I gather my bag with the pirate costume. "Okay, let's go then if you're so worried about being late." It's become a favorite at the hospital during the interviews. There's something about a fun costume that breathes life back into the dreariness of the hospital.

"Bye, Mamaw," I call toward the living room.

She lifts her hand up and waves to me without turning around in her chair. "Bye, honey."

I follow Birdie out the door. "We have to stop by the college still. I told Paloma I'd give her a ride."

"Double-booked yourself?" he says.

Before I can apologize, I notice Paloma sitting in the front seat of Birdie's Audie.

Birdie snickers to himself as he opens the car door. "You're lucky I'm a good friend." He plops into his seat. "To both of you!"

Paloma scoots her seat forward, providing me more legroom in the back.

She flips around. "Hey."

"Hey," I say.

"I have something to tell you," she says with a grin.

"Okay."

She and Birdie share a look, then she says, "But I don't know how to tell you."

I lean forward and kiss the tip of her nose. Then just loud enough so she can hear me, I say, "You just say it."

She folds her mouth in. Handing her phone to me she says, "Terra decided on a name for the baby."

"She had the baby?" I take her phone and inspect the picture of Terra looking down at her new baby with Lissy leaning over her shoulder. It makes my heart ache that Claude isn't here for this. But since Claude's been gone, Paloma has been spending a lot more time with them. *And so have I.*

Maybe a part of Claude can still be felt by the presence of his heart.

She nods. "Claude Jaxon Laurent."

I blink, shocked.

I'm stunned.
And thrilled.
But more than anything, I'm *honored*.

CHAPTER

TWENTY-EIGHT

Paloma

When I walk through the doors, an older gentleman is exiting. I hold the door open for him before entering the lobby at Pat's work.

Jax looks up from the front desk. "Hey," he says with a smile, then looks back to the computer. "Let me finish this real quick."

I slip my backpack strap off my shoulder. "Busy day?"

"Yeah, it was. But my dad's with the last client now." He closes the laptop and cuts his eyes to me. "When he's done, we can close up and get out of here."

He joins me on the couch.

I flop my chemistry book open on the coffee table in front of us. "Ready for some fun?"

He raises his eyebrows. "That looks *super* fun."

"College classes work out my brain more than it's ever worked out in my entire life."

"You don't work your brain out on a regular basis?"

I roll my eyes at him and pull my water bottle from my bag to take a sip.

Jax digs into his pocket. "Do you want to give your brain a rest and come over for dinner?"

I begin to close the lid on my water bottle, but he reaches for it. "Sure, what are you having?" I say, handing the bottle to him.

"Tex mex," he says before dropping his head back and tossing a handful of pills into his mouth then immediately forcing them down with the water.

I smile. "Sounds better than a brain exercise."

The corner of his mouth curls up into a grin as he places my water bottle on the coffee table. When he sits back against the couch, I nestle myself under his arm.

My head is resting right where I can hear the rhythmic sound of his beating heart.

"I still can't believe you have his heart," my voice is almost a whisper.

He looks down at me. "Me either."

I tip my chin up to meet his gaze. His eyes are shining equal parts happiness and sadness. I don't have to ask why, I know it's unexplainably bittersweet for him.

"Does it feel different?"

He blinks. "My heart?"

I nod.

"Not really." He searches the large front window facing the street—watching the standstill traffic. Then he laughs to himself. Not necessarily making a sound, but his shoulders gently bounce with his laughter as he grins.

"What?" I say.

He shakes his head.

"Just say it."

He adjusts himself so he can see my face better. "Sometimes I wonder if it's so much easier to love you because this heart loved you before I ever met you."

A part of me hopes that's true.

I wrap my arms around him and he does the same to me. "It really is a miracle you have his heart."

He gently strokes my arm with his thumb. "You keep saying that."

I let out a relaxed sigh, then say, "Maybe believing that good things are possible isn't such a terrible thing after all."

He kisses my temple, then with muffled laughter against the top of my head, he says, "I like this new Paloma."

I give him my most genuine and grateful smile.

I like this new Paloma too.

Resources

This story mentions some sensitive topics such as suicide, depression, and other mental illnesses. I don't write about these topics lightly. I don't write about these topics to glorify them in any way. But I write about the tough things in life because they are real. And I hope that if anything, this story brings awareness to the reality of mental illness as well as hope for those feeling stuck in their current circumstances.

For a depression self-screening visit
www.mind-diagnostics.org

If you or someone you know is having thoughts of suicide, please call or text the suicide prevention hotline at **988**.

And please, reach out to someone (a friend, cousin, sibling, grandparent, parent, teacher, boss, acquaintance) if you are having any thoughts of hopelessness. Reaching out is the hardest part. Help and healing come after the hardest part.

You're not alone.

Sometimes asking for help means *just saying it*.

More from the Author

This section is meant to be read after the last chapter. It includes spoilers.

They tell you to write what you know. It's supposed to help with the flow of the writing process. Although this book is fiction, it still captured a combination of events and situations that I've witnessed and encountered in my life and the lives of those that are close to me. Which made it equally easier to write as well as difficult and at times painful.

I chose Dallas as the setting because it's home to a lot of my extended family, as well as my sister and her sons. And it's the place I was visiting while my sisters and I were mourning our father's death. It's also the place where I came up with the storyline for this book. Dallas just seemed to fit.

My family has a history of estranged fathers. Like Paloma, I grew closest to my dad when I was older; before he passed away. Like Paloma, I felt my dad was taken too soon. It felt like I had just gotten to know him and there was more ahead for us. He was imperfect in many ways, but so is everyone in one sense or another. Despite his many imperfections, he was still my dad and the person that gave me life and the father in our home for the first ten years of my childhood. We had a lot in common in all of our weirdness and creativity—I do miss sharing those parts of my life with him.

When Paloma broke down after receiving the news about Claude, I felt it all with her. The confusion. The pain. The shock. The "never agains." *Death hurts.* And grief is strange. But I hope anyone else that has lost a loved one, especially when the circumstances of the relationship are difficult to understand, allows themselves space to mourn. Grieving is important. It hits us all in different ways. But it should be felt.

One of the hardest parts of losing my dad, was that I didn't get to share my first book with him. When I was twenty-two, I started writing a (terribly written) novel. I didn't finish. But I told him I had played around with writing, and he encouraged me to keep going. He said, "If you want to write a book, then write a book. You don't have anything stopping you from it." He was really good at encouraging me and celebrating my successes.

I miss that too.

There are true stories sprinkled throughout this book. Some came from my experiences from when my husband and I were foster parents. Others came from various women throughout my life.

One memory Paloma had of her mom running her car into her boss's car was a real event I experienced. Not with my mom. My mom is very gentle and patient. But I was with my brother and his friend. His friend took us out to get some food. On our way out of the parking lot, this guy's ex-wife rolls in. She was upset and started yelling. My brother's friend was trying to talk with her and get her to calm down, but she continued to escalate and before I knew what was happening, she put her car into drive and drove it into his jeep (with us in it) as hard as she could. We were fine. The friend's jeep wasn't.

Let's just say April is an all too familiar person to me.

With that said, just like Paloma, we don't have to cut people out of our lives that struggle with serious mood disorders like bipolar disorder. Paloma set boundaries for herself, but she still loved her mom and made an intentional decision to keep her mom in her life without allowing April to control her or manipulate her. Paloma died to all unrealistic ideas of what she imagined a perfect family was like. And accepted that we all live in a fallen world with imperfections. But she chose to make the most of it and to love her imperfect mother from a distance and in the healthiest way she possibly could.

I put the various aspects revolving around faith in this book because I wanted to portray how some people do have rigid beliefs and give God a bad rap with their behavior, like Levi's family. And I also wanted to show that while Jax and his family were far from perfect, they did a better job of loving people the way Jesus tells us to. And much like the way Paloma judged Jax's faith, I have been judged for loving Jesus before I'm even given the chance to know someone or show them who I am. In the same breath, I've been judged by believers too—but this isn't the place to get into that.

The town Mamaw is from is based heavily off of the tiny town, Pecan Gap, where my Mamaw and Papaw lived. Everything from the houses to the cracked sidewalks are real features from the town. I wanted to include a fictional Pecan Gap in my story because it's one of my favorite places I spent during my childhood. Just like the picture of the man praying over his food that Paloma saw in Mamaw's kitchen, my Mamaw and Papaw had a painting just like it too.

I debated on writing the parts about suicide. But ultimately, what I want to share in my stories are the tough parts of life that people don't always talk about. It's uncomfortable. It's raw. It's painful. No two situations are alike—I understand that. We've lost friends and family to suicide. We've had friends and family come close to committing suicide. It's not pretty. There's nothing glamorous about it. But it is very real, and it happens too often. I have a knot in my chest just thinking about the hurt suicide causes. My husband and I still carry holes in our hearts from the losses we've personally endured. Because suicide not only ends the life of an amazing human, but the heartache it causes after they are gone is unmeasurable and never ending.

With that said, I don't write about suicide lightly. If anything, I write about it because I hope that if someone is hurting they don't minimize their hurt. I hope that if someone sees those distancing symptoms of depression in themselves, that they reach out—*to anyone*. And I hope that if someone comes to you with even the slightest concerning statement, that you take them seriously and help them get help.

I also hope that the storylines in my book are able to provide tools for people. Like when Paloma was writing the story Lissy made up about the fish and the bee. This was a real story I listened to in one of the creative writing classes I teach. I thought I was helping students learn writing format and character development, but there's so many therapeutic aspects to writing I didn't realize. Sometimes writing can be an outlet, or form of communicating tough emotions, or a safe place to detangle your thoughts. And I've learned a lot about some of my students by allowing them to write fiction. Similar to the way Paloma experienced Lissy's heartache through her story. And my students have learned a lot about themselves by writing fiction too.

I do write as an outlet for myself. But I also write to encourage those that are struggling. I hope that anyone that identifies with my characters finds hope that keeps them moving forward, even when life seems impossible. If there is anything I've learned from my own life and my own darkness, is that there is an "other side" to the struggles in life. And also, that there is always someone rooting for you. There's always someone that wants to walk through life with you. It doesn't have to be a spouse or partner. It can be a friend, or sibling, or mentor. But life isn't meant to be lived alone. So don't give up the search for your person, and don't give up the search on yourself.

ACKNOWLEDGMENTS

First, I want to thank my daughters, Jailee and Amie, for their intrigue for my writing and constructive feedback, as well as the intense dinner conversations they have over my books and characters.

To my sons, Des and Evan, for making sure I'm living my real life and not hiding in a corner with my computer and imagination.

A big thanks to my mom for always being willing to step away from her life to jump into my raw unedited manuscripts. She's always encouraged my creative side and told me I was a writer before I knew I was. Thanks, mom, for being my biggest cheerleader! I wouldn't have made it this far without your support and enthusiasm for my writing.

Thank you to my wonderfully amazing husband. Without your help, patience, support, love and encouragement this whole *author* thing would be impossible. I love you, boo.

My sisters, all of you, thank you! I've never known life without you, and nothing is more special than our sisterhood. A special thanks to my big sisters Sarah, Amie, and Sandi for being the first to purchase my books and send me the best words of love and optimism—with whatever I'm doing in life.

Even though he's gone, I want to thank my dad for encouraging me to do the simple, creative, introverted things that I enjoy doing in life.

To my niece, Ava, thank you for being excited and sharing my words with others. You're amazing and I'm so proud of who you are.

Thank you to my sister-in-law, Malorie, who has enough excitement for everything I do to last a lifetime and supports me without question. Thanks for never losing your enthusiasm and joy for our friendship and sisterhood.

Thank you to all my friends and family that are too many to name and would fill up an entire book to name you all personally. By just being in my life, you are more than words to me, and I think of you all often when I'm writing.

Thank you. Yes, *you*, my readers. Thank you a million times over, and then a million more. Your thoughts, reviews, and insights humble me, as well as fuel me to keep writing.

And the biggest, most grand finale of thanks is to Jesus for the greatest gift of salvation. As well as the gift He's given me to write and share all the parts of me and my imagination with whoever is willing to open my books and turn the pages.

ABOUT THE AUTHOR

Aurora is the Author of *The Consequence of Audrey*. She has written for various blog platforms and teaches creative writing to students all over the globe. Most of the time you can find her curled up on the couch with her children listening to them read a book and helping them with their homework. Or outside with her ponies. She lives with her four children and wonderful husband in Wyoming on their miniature homestead she calls home. Learn more about Aurora at aurorastenulson.wixsite.com/website.

Made in the USA
Monee, IL
29 December 2022